*The Writing
on the Hearth*

THE WRITING ON THE HEARTH

CYNTHIA HARNETT

Drawings By Gareth Floyd

THE VIKING PRESS   NEW YORK

Cover painting by Trina Schart Hyman

FIRST AMERICAN EDITION

TEXT COPYRIGHT © 1971 BY CYNTHIA HARNETT
ILLUSTRATIONS COPYRIGHT © 1971 BY METHUEN
CHILDREN'S BOOKS LTD

ALL RIGHTS RESERVED
PUBLISHED IN 1973 BY THE VIKING PRESS, INC.
625 MADISON AVENUE, NEW YORK, N.Y. 10022
LIBRARY OF CONGRESS CATALOG CARD NUMBER: 72–91400

FIC
SBN 670–79119–9

PRINTED IN U.S.A.   1   2   3   4   5   77   76   75   74   73

Contents

THE RIVER THAME.

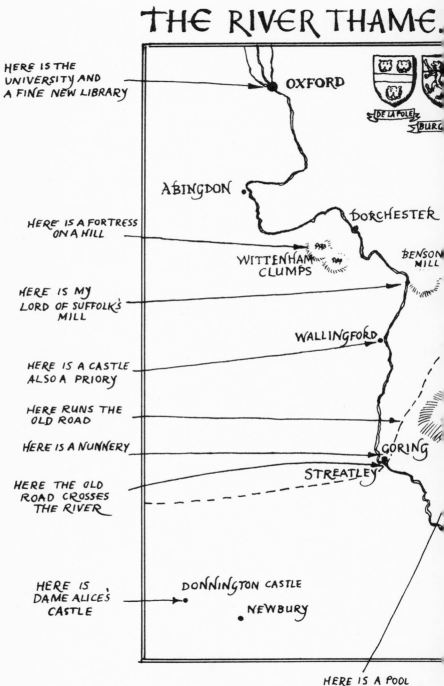

HERE IS THE
UNIVERSITY AND
A FINE NEW LIBRARY

OXFORD

DE LA POLE
BURG

ABINGDON

DORCHESTER

HERE IS A FORTRESS
ON A HILL

WITTENHAM
CLUMPS

BENSON
MILL

HERE IS MY
LORD OF SUFFOLK'S
MILL

WALLINGFORD

HERE IS A CASTLE
ALSO A PRIORY

HERE RUNS THE
OLD ROAD

HERE IS A NUNNERY

GORING

HERE THE OLD
ROAD CROSSES
THE RIVER

STREATLEY

HERE IS
DAME ALICE'S
CASTLE

DONNINGTON CASTLE
NEWBURY

HERE IS A POOL
WITH A DEAD TREE

nd the Chiltern Hills

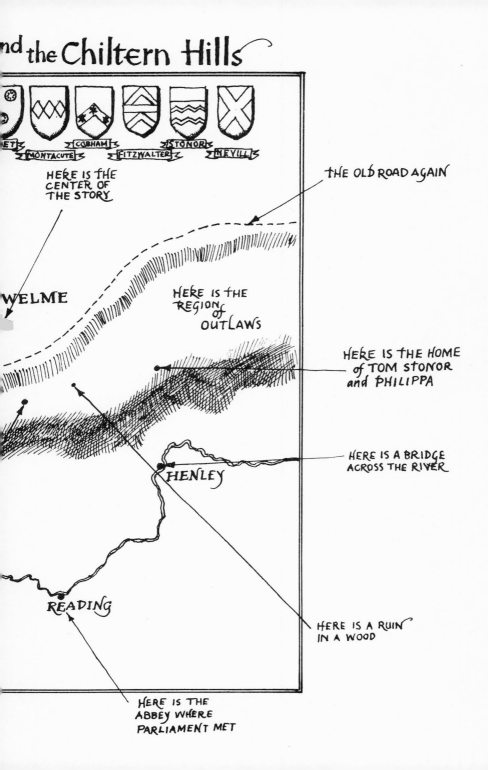

MONTACUTE   COBHAM   FITZWALTER   STONOR   NEVILL

THE OLD ROAD AGAIN

HERE IS THE CENTER OF THE STORY

WELME

HERE IS THE REGION of OUTLAWS

HERE IS THE HOME of TOM STONOR and PHILIPPA

HERE IS A BRIDGE ACROSS THE RIVER

HENLEY

READING

HERE IS A RUIN IN A WOOD

HERE IS THE ABBEY WHERE PARLIAMENT MET

The Palindrome

IT WAS not until he reached the top of the hill that Stephen noticed the storm clouds gathering over the Oxford plain. He had been climbing steadily through thick woods; now he emerged onto a bracken-covered slope and turned to look at the sky. The whole wide landscape lay under a threatening black pall. Obviously there was a storm brewing, but was it coming this way? Perhaps it would be better to wait before he ventured any farther from home.

From this stretch of the hillside the timber had been felled for the new buildings at Ewelme, his village, down in the valley, and the scrub was not yet tall enough to hide the view. He crossed the clearing and sat down with his back against a great beech tree. He was in no hurry. Parson Saynesbury, schoolmaster as well as rector of the church, had gone to Oxford on an errand for the Earl of Suffolk, William de la Pole, lord of the manor, leaving Stephen with a task of Latin translation which could be done later.

Stephen alone was accountable to Parson Saynesbury. The other pupils at the school were mere children and did their lessons with the parish clerk.

So, with the parson absent, today was a grand chance for a special outing. He'd left his sister, Lys, at the foot of the hill. She had begged to come with him, but he had firmly said no. The densely wooded Chilterns had a bad name among the people of the valley. They were said to be populated by outlaws, culprits fleeing from justice, and deserters from the French wars. To the village children they were strictly out of bounds and even the grownups kept well away.

Stephen, however, was not afraid. He lived quite near the hills and had often explored the woods without coming to any harm. Nevertheless he would never dream of bringing his sister.

All the same he had been sorry to see her turn back forlornly toward the lonely cottage where the two of them lived with their surly stepfather, Odo, the plowman. Their own father, soldier servant to the Earl of Suffolk, had been killed nearly ten years ago in France, after the siege of Orleans. He had died gloriously in a vain attempt to save his lord from being taken captive by that French witch, Jeanne d'Arc. His widow had married again to make a home for the two children. Now she also was dead. Stephen and Lys had no one but each other, and Lys did all the work of the cottage where they, the plowman, and his oxen shared the same thatched roof.

Stephen was better off than Lys. Because his father had given his life for my lord Suffolk, my lord had decreed that the boy should be taught by the parson to read and write. Now he had been allotted the first place in the newly opened grammar school, part of the new foundation called God's House built at Ewelme by my lord, William de la Pole, Earl of Suffolk, and his wife Alice. It was even whispered that if the boy did well at school he might be sent as a poor scholar to Oxford—a dazzling prospect, for Oxford, no more than a day's walk from Ewelme, was pictured by Stephen as being a place not far off from heaven, a wonderful city full of great lords and learned masters and clerks who grew to be wise and prosperous.

As well as the grammar school, the new God's House also included a cloister of little houses, a hos-

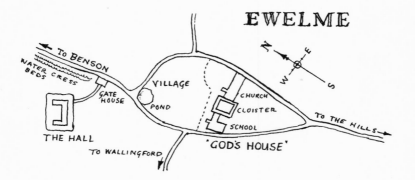

EWELME

pice, where thirteen aged men could end their days in peace, their only duty being to offer bedes, or prayers, in the church for the repose of the souls of my lord's parents, the de la Poles, and of my lady's, the Chaucers.

One of these bedesmen was Doggett, an old soldier, who had been a friend of Stephen's father and was now Stephen's friend. Doggett had fought at Agincourt twenty-four years ago in 1415 and had taken part in the triumphant march into London afterward in the train of Henry V. Doggett's stories of the war were never-ending. Stephen listened fascinated, though privately he had hated the thought of war ever since as a tiny boy clutching his mother's skirts he had heard an old comrade describe with gruesome detail exactly how his father had died.

Doggett had another interest which he shared with Stephen—a passion for heraldry. He could reel off by heart the coats of arms of all the lords and knights who had fought in France, and now, old and lame, he delighted in painting them in bright colors begged from the craftsmen who were decorating the inside of Ewelme church. But Doggett's brushes, made of hog's hair, were much too coarse for fine work. Parson Saynesbury said that the best brushes were made from the fur of squirrels or polecats, and it happened that Stephen knew exactly where he could get such fur, ready cleaned and cured. It was for that purpose that he had climbed the hill secretly today.

He had not sat long under the tree before he heard a distant growl of thunder. The sky was growing darker. Already Wittenham clumps, the twin tree-capped hills the other side of the river Thames, were shrouded with rain. Ought he to go home? It seemed a pity. If he made a dash for it he might reach the swineherd's cottage, which was his objective, before the storm actually broke.

He was just about to scramble to his feet when a stir among the bracken caught his eye. Something was moving across the slope a little way below him. He saw that it was a roedeer, a fine buck with a couple of does following it. Roedeer were growing scarce in the woods. Outlaws had accounted for too many.

The thunder rumbled again, nearer this time, and the three little deer bounded off toward a clump of bushes. But only two of them reached cover. The buck, struck almost mid-air, dropped with an arrow through its head.

Stephen gasped. Whoever had loosed that arrow must be hidden quite near at hand. There were stories told in the village about an archer, an outlaw, who never missed his mark. He was named, with bated breath, as Gilles the Bowman, and children were frightened into obedience by threats of being handed over to him. One day, up here in the woods, Stephen had actually come face to face with a tall gaunt man who had a longbow slung from his shoulder. The man had seen him too, but he looked friendly enough and certainly showed no signs of malice.

As he waited for the archer to come out and claim his quarry, he heard the note of a horn some way back in the woods. With it came the sound of men's voices and the baying of a hound. A hunting party: perhaps it was one of them who had shot the buck. But the voices were quite far away. It might be my lord of Suffolk a-hunting. He was steward of the Chilterns with rights of hawk and hound. Stephen wriggled farther into the shadow of the tree. If they were on their way back to Ewelme, they would pass along the bridle track from Swyncombe which lay halfway down the hill. It would never do to be caught on forbidden ground by my lord himself. The dead buck was invisible in the bracken. He wondered what had happened to Gilles. Probably, like himself, he was lying low.

Sure enough the party came into view. Stephen looked down on them as they moved along the track, three horsemen in front, each with a hawk on his wrist, half a score of followers on foot, and a couple of leashed hounds. My lord of Suffolk was at the head accompanied by two friends. Stephen knew both by sight: Sir Richard Drayton from the manor of Drayton by Dorchester, and his young stepson Thomas Stonor, a boy not much older than Stephen himself, who was frequently at Ewelme. Bearers carried the spoils of the hunt on poles across their shoulders. Stephen

14

chuckled silently as he noted that they had nothing but small game. The only likely roebuck lay dead in the bracken a short way down the hill.

Suddenly one of the hounds threw up its head, sniffed the air, and gave tongue. Its partner joined in. My lord of Suffolk reined his horse.

"A scent," he cried. "Templar has a scent. Unleash him. Quickly, fool. Let them range free."

His voice carried clearly. Stephen held his breath as the hounds plunged in among the bracken. They had wind of the roedeer. They were coming his way. Soon their sterns began to wave in ecstasy. Templar spoke again. There was no doubt about it. They had found the buck. The huntsmen struggled up the slope, followed by the three horsemen picking their way.

My lord of Suffolk leaned forward in his saddle staring down.

"Before heaven a buck," he cried. "Killed with a single shaft, and newly dead by the look."

A huntsman, crouched on the ground, raised his head.

" 'Tis blood-warm, my lord. It's been dead but a Paternoster while."

"Who killed it?" roared my lord of Suffolk. "Am I to be poached under my very nose? He can't have got far. Let the hounds seek him. By heaven if I catch him I'll string him from the gate of Wallingford Castle."

Stephen was almost sick with terror. He slithered cautiously down among last year's dead leaves. The hounds were ranging along the hillside, following the trail of the deer. He had crossed that track on the way up; how long before they picked up *his* scent? My lord of Suffolk's hounds were strong and savage. They might tear him to pieces, but in any case how was he to account for himself in full sight of the dead buck? My lord would think that he had shot it and thrown his bow away in the thicket. His heart pounded so loudly that it was like the hounds approaching. Every second he expected to feel their hot breath on his neck. He buried his face till he was nearly smothered, praying breathlessly, "Oh God! Oh God! Oh God!"

Then all at once with a deafening roar the storm broke right overhead. Thunder and lightning crackled together as though the heavens had split. To Stephen it was the jaws of Templar. The hailstones that flayed him, the branches that came crashing down were all part of the same horror. In a moment he would be dead. He stiffened, waiting for agony. It was the cascade of cold rain beating upon him that woke him to the fact that he was still alive. There were no angry voices, no savage hounds. The woods were just roaring with a gigantic thunderstorm.

It was some time before he dared to raise his head. Peering over the flattened fern he could see through a gray downpour the hunting party back on the bridle path in full retreat, the horsemen at a brisk trot, the others, with the hounds, helter-skelter behind. And they carried no buck.

He lay still for some moments, almost enjoying the storm. God had sent a miracle to save him. Then he scrambled to his feet. The thunder seemed farther away, but the rain was still lashing down. He must get to shelter. The swineherd's hovel, for which he was bound, was not so very far off.

The old woman who lived there was shunned by everybody. Though her husband, the swineherd, was long dead, she and her half-wit son still tended the pigs that roamed the beechwoods. She actually had a smattering of book learning, and it was whispered that she was a witch. Witchcraft was a terrible thing. It was nothing less than worshiping the devil instead of worshiping God, of deliberately serving evil instead of good. The devil himself made use of witches to do his work and the village people feared for their souls. If it were known that Stephen went there, he would be utterly condemned. The parson would certainly forbid it under pain of mortal sin, and he might even lose his place in the school.

But Stephen was fond of old Meg. It had begun when he had fallen out of a wild cherry tree, and she had picked him up and plastered him with herbs that took all the pain away. He did not believe for a moment that she was a witch. She was kind, one of the kindest people he had ever known, and surely nobody so kind could be evil. So, keeping it absolutely secret, he went quite often to see her.

His visit today was to get hair for Doggett's brushes. Wat, her tomfool son, was intelligent enough to snare wild creatures, skin them, and clean the pelts. These were taken by his mother to Wallingford market where they were bought by a furrier from Budge Row in London, who used them to make gowns for rich city merchants. Stephen had seen the furrier once, a tall spare man with a forked beard.

The storm was receding as he pushed through a tangle of undergrowth. Everything was beaten down, and it was quite difficult to find his way. He kept his eye open for a dead beech tree, white with age and riddled with woodpecker holes. It stood like a giant skeleton close to a woodland pool beside which lay old Meg's dwelling. He caught a glimpse of it at last and made his way straight to it, laying his hand upon it for a moment, as though it were an old friend.

The pool had spread with the storm almost into a lake. There was none of the usual reflection of the hovel that stood at the other side, very low on the ground only a few feet above the brink. Its one small window was shuttered, but he noted that a thin spiral of smoke rose from the hole in the thatched roof. Praise be to God, old Meg had a fire.

As he looked something else caught his eye. In the clearing at the back, beside a line of beehives on a bench, stood a rough shelter roofed with bracken, used for ailing pigs and for the drying of new pelts. Beneath this shelter a horse was tethered, not a common baggage horse but an animal well groomed, saddled, and with fine red leather trappings. Obviously someone was sheltering indoors. But who with a horse like that would be traveling through these wild trackless woods?

He made his way around the pool and rapped almost shyly on the closed door of the hovel. He had never seen it shut before. It stood open in all weathers.

There was a long pause. Then it was opened an inch or two, and old Meg peered out, wizened and unsmiling so that he scarcely recognized her. But as soon as she saw him her whole expression changed.

"Why, it's Stephen," she cried, "and by the look of it half-drowned. Come you in, young storm cock. Come and dry yourself."

She seized his wrist and dragged him inside, shutting the door behind him so that he stared into total darkness. He knew the place well enough with its earthen floor deep in litter that was never changed, its smoky hearth, and its rafters overhead from which bats hung in a festoon of cobwebs. But never before had he been shut in. There was a horrible foulness about it. He could see nothing, and a shiver crept slowly down his spine.

Old Meg still gripped his elbow. He felt her stir the embers with her toe. A faint glow tinged the darkness, and the whole place seemed suddenly to come alive. There were eyes everywhere, all watching him. A pair of yellow eyes stared up from below; green eyes peered down from above; across the hearth he faced a dim round moon with specks of light, like eyes, in the middle of it, and one brilliant orange spark twinkling underneath. Suddenly, a series of unearthly screeches broke out from a far corner. Panic seized Stephen. His teeth chattered, and he trembled from head to foot.

Old Meg tightened her hold. "Steady, boy—be not a milksop. 'Tis but the piglets in their bed. They were in terror of the hounds, poor babes, so I brought them in. Why, you're shivering! Wat—bring a faggot for a blaze."

Scuffling out of the darkness, the old woman's misshapen son threw sticks onto the fire. Flame shot up, and everything suddenly became clear. The yellow eyes belonged to the cat, the green ones to old Meg's tame owl perched on the kettle beam. Meg herself, a tiny figure with cheeks like wizened apples, stood stirring a hanging pot, while Wat murmured under his breath a sort of wordless humming like a great bumble bee—"*Dumma, dumma, dumma, dum—dumma dumma dumma dum.*"

Stephen glanced across the hearth and saw that the dim round moon had become the pale flabby face of a man, a stranger, with hair like faded straw and eyes like cold steel. Stephen's own eyes gave way before

them. Obviously this was the owner of the horse tethered outside. He looked a very fine gentleman. He
wore a gown the color of red wine, and twisted
around his head was a chaperon hood of red silk with
jagged points. His riding boots were of the softest
leather. The bright spark which had caught Stephen's
eye came from an ornament hung around his neck, a
device of triangles somehow linked together. It
looked as though it were made of copper.

"That's better, boy: you've got your color back,"
said old Meg cheerfully. "What frighted you? Was it
the storm?"

Stephen said indignantly that he wasn't afraid of
storms. Truth was he'd escaped by a hair's breadth
from being savaged by my lord's hounds. With some
satisfaction he told the whole story of the roebuck
and its discovery by Templar only a yard or two from
where he lay in hiding.

"Mercy on us," cried the old woman. "I'll warrant it
was Gilles who loosed that arrow. But what would
my lord have said if he had slain his best scholar in

the guise of poacher?" She turned to the stranger. "This boy, sir, is pupil at my lord's new grammar school at Ewelme."

"At the new God's House? I've heard of it," said the stranger gravely. "My lord would have said without doubt that he got no more than he deserved, being a fool to risk his good fortune. What induced you, young man, to play truant from your lessons? I had heard that the Chilterns were out of bounds to beardless boys, and my lord of Suffolk does not dispense his favors lightly."

Stephen said quite sharply that he was not a truant, and he had a purpose in the hills. He'd come to beg for some squirrel fur to make painting brushes for an old man who was lodged in one of the cells in God's House. It was the parson himself who had told him that for fine painting brushes squirrel hair was the best of all.

Old Meg joined in his defense. "Stephen is well placed, sir. He is son of my lord's late body servant. 'Tis said he may perchance be sent as scholar to Oxford at my lord's cost. You, sir, as master of arts yourself at Oxford, will know what that may mean."

Stephen's eyes opened wide. It was a great thing to be a master of arts. The only one he knew by sight was Master Simon Brayles, my lord's chaplain at the Hall. Even Parson Saynesbury himself held no degree as master; he was just plain Sir John Saynesbury.

He could not resist putting the question direct. "You *are* a master of arts at Oxford, sir?"

The stranger looked amused. When he smiled, his pale face was quite pleasant.

"Yes, boy, I am. If your curiosity still bites, my name is Roger Bolingbroke, and I was on my way back to Oxford when I lost myself in the woods and the storm caught me. I need to go to Wallingford, but how do I get there? Maybe when the rain ceases *you* could put me on the right path?"

Stephen agreed readily enough, though he wondered how a stranger, who had only arrived after the storm began, seemed so well known to old Meg. But the master from Oxford grew increasingly friendly as Meg ladled the broth into bowls. He had a mission, he said, to visit the miller of Wallingford—and for that matter all the millers up the river as far as Oxford. He was to arrange passage upstream for a precious cargo of books intended for the Duke of Gloucester's new library being built at Oxford. The books were priceless and were to travel in a special barge.

"Duke Humphrey—the Duke of Gloucester—and his wife, the Duchess Eleanor, are my most gracious patrons," he said. "So if you guide me, boy, you will be earning favor in high places."

While he mopped up his broth with a piece of hearth bread, Stephen stared at the stranger with growing respect. He'd heard from Doggett of Duke Humphrey of Gloucester and even remembered his coat of arms. Obviously Master Bolingbroke was a person of importance. It seemed odd to find him so much at home in old Meg's hovel. Then suddenly he remembered the object of his own mission. He plucked at old Meg's sleeve.

"Squirrel skins," he whispered. "Can I have some bits of squirrel skin before I go?"

Old Meg became strangely impatient. "Have what you will," she said. "Get you to Wat's bench and busy yourself there."

Feeling dismissed, Stephen made his way to a long trestle board standing against the far wall. It was littered with fragments of fur and rough tools for scraping the pelts. But more interesting still were sundry bits of dead wood, short knobbly spurs of oak or apple or cherry, which in Wat's imagination suggested figures, human or animal. It was his particular joy to whittle away until some shape appeared, like magic, from the gnarled wood. He stood now, droning as usual while he chipped out the figure of an old man in a hood and cloak—just a piece of applewood, yet it strangely resembled Doggett.

Squirrel skins forgotten, Stephen stood entranced, till a sudden breath of fresh air brought him back to life. Old Meg had lifted down the shutter, and she and Master Bolingbroke were both leaning out the open window. He imagined that they were looking to see if the rain had stopped. Then old Meg spoke. It was only a whisper but it carried on the draft that stirred right round the room.

"I've told you, Master, and I'll tell you again—I saw

death in the water. But now the surface is all spoiled. We'll see no more today."

Bolingbroke's answer was lost as the piglets, roused by the cold, began to squeal again. Old Meg turned, saw Stephen, and positively scowled.

"Is there nothing to your liking?" she snapped. "Wat, take him outside. The best pelts are under the roof. Let him pick at his leisure."

Stephen followed Wat out the door. It seemed that she wanted to be rid of him. An uneasy chill crept over him, like that first chill in the darkness. "Death in the water"—there was no mistaking what she had said. He followed Wat to that covered shelter where the horse was tethered. It was still there, waiting placidly. Stephen stroked the white star on its forehead while he looked for any tell-tale emblems on the harness. Wat still humming, fumbled among bunches of skins hanging from a beam. Stephen joined him but found the hairs too short and limp. These pelts had no tails. Maybe the parson had said squirrel *tails*. It was worth trying. He explained to Wat, who nodded vigorously and without warning vanished around the corner the way they had come. After a moment Stephen followed. The door of the hovel stood open, so he went in.

Old Meg and Bolingbroke were alone. They sat side by side, their backs toward him, bending over the hearth. Each held a stick like a wand, and Bolingbroke was drawing something in the embers. Both were so intent that they failed to notice Stephen, and he had time to see that the whole hearth was covered with patterns and devices of every shape: circles, stars, triangles.

At that moment Wat burst in at the door triumphantly waving a bunch of squirrel tails. Bolingbroke swung round to find Stephen just behind him.

"*Dies irae,*" he swore fiercely. With a wide sweep of his stick he scattered the ashes. Old Meg, breathing heavily, stepped back into the shadows. Stephen, though his heart was pounding, held his ground.

Bolingbroke was the first to recover. "You dumfounded me creeping up like that," he said lightly. "Tell me, in your grammar school are you taught to reckon?"

Taken aback, Stephen said that he could cast up a column of figures tolerably fast.

"Then see if you can reckon this."

With a stick he drew in the ashes three *C*s in a row, one after the other and, following them, three *X*s.

"Tell me what I am writing the moment that you wake to it," he said, and deliberately added another *C* at the beginning and, leaving a small space, another *X* at the end. "Now there are but two more letters needed. Can you tell me what they should be?"

Stephen looked for only a second. The line read CCCCXXX X. It was easy!

" 'Tis this year of grace in Latin characters," he cried. Carried away by excitement he grabbed the stick and drew an *M* at the beginning and an *I* in the space before the end. "MCCCCXXXIX," he read aloud. "One thousand four hundred and thirty nine." Then for good measure he added *"Anno xvii Henry vi"* (the seventeenth year of the reign of Henry VI), another way of writing the present date.

"You have quick wits. Mathematics should be no stumbling block when you come to Oxford."

But Stephen, stick in hand, was still staring at the hearth. One pattern in the ashes had not been swept away. It was a triangle, like the one that Bolingbroke wore around his neck. In the center were written the figures 1441.

"That will be the year after next," he cried triumphantly.

Bolingbroke's voice was cold and tense, as though he were holding himself back.

"The year after next? What nonsense. It is interesting because it is a palindrome. Know you what is meant by a palindrome? Something that reads the same from either end. Look you: 1441. You can write it back to front without change." Taking Stephen by the elbow he turned him away. "They are interesting, these patterns of digits. One can fill many an idle hour with them. But come now. If I am to do my work in Wallingford it is high time we were on our way."

His manner was once more easy and friendly, but Stephen felt that it was forced. He was sure that the palindrome in the ashes had survived by accident. It was something he was not meant to see.

"Put Me
on My Way"

*B*Y THE time they set off the rain had stopped,
though the trees still dripped heavily into the pool.
Master Bolingbroke, leading his horse, followed at
Stephen's heels as they squelched through the undergrowth. Since it would be impossible to take a horse
down the way that he had come up, Stephen decided
to make for the bridle path used by the hunting party.
It was a long way round, but it would be quicker in
the end.

He led the way in silence. The squirrel tails for
Doggett were safely in his satchel, but nevertheless
he was ill at ease. In spite of old Meg's warm welcome the whole atmosphere of the place had been
different today. And that strange business of the palindrome worried him. Was Bolingbroke really there
by chance? From the beginning he had doubted it.
And how came a master of arts to be mixed up with
old Meg? Against his will the stories about old Meg's
being a witch came flooding back. Of course he did

not believe them, but all the same it would be wiser not to go there any more.

As the bushes thinned and gave place to bracken, Bolingbroke called to Stephen to wait for him. There was room to walk side by side.

"There is no great haste," he said. " 'Twas only that I did not want to linger in that hovel. The old dame is kindly enough and strangely well versed in learning. But I would venture that it would not be thought a seemly place for my lord of Suffolk's scholar."

Stephen did not answer. The fine master's attitude did not ring true. He had been ready enough to accept old Meg's hospitality, but now it seemed he had changed his tune. Of course he was right about my lord. My lord would be furious if he learned of Stephen's visits to old Meg. Ever since the burning of Jeanne d'Arc, so Doggett said, any mention of witchcraft was like a red rag to a bull.

Bolingbroke began again, more cheerfully. "Where do you live, boy?" he inquired. "I know that your father is dead, but have you a mother, or brothers and sisters? Tell me about yourself."

Stephen answered a little stiffly that his mother was dead too. He and his sister lived with their stepfather who was a plowman. They had no other kin.

"That is sad for you," said Bolingbroke, "but seemingly my lord has his eye on you. Has he actually promised that you shall go to Oxford? If so you are truly favored."

Stephen said that he had never himself spoken to

my lord. But Parson Saynesbury had told him that if he were good and worked hard—

Bolingbroke interrupted. "Ah, there is the point: that you should be good and work hard—just as I have warned you. Now in your own interest listen to me. I confess I have been struck with you as a boy of quick wit and character, and I owe you much for guiding me. Suppose that my lord of Suffolk should not fulfill his promise and you need help in coming as a scholar to Oxford, call on *me*. I will find a place for you. I am principal of St. Andrew's Hall. I have many students in my care—some little older than you."

Stephen was completely taken aback. Not only master of arts but principal of St. Andrew's Hall and actually offering to befriend him if he should need it. He stole another glance at his companion, more curious than ever. His face now looked plump and good-tempered. He caught Stephen's eye and laughed.

"There's no need to look awestruck, boy; to be principal of a hall is an honor, but there are many such. One is appointed by the university to rule a hall where students live, and look to their well-being and their good conduct. In old days halls were no more than lodging houses often run by scoundrels for profit, where scholars starved and learned only wickedness. Now a principal has authority. I owe my fortune to my good lord Duke Humphrey and the Duchess Eleanor whose servant I am. Thus I can offer favor to you."

They had reached the steep slope that led down to the bridle path. There was no more talk until they and the horse stood safely at the bottom. Then Master Bolingbroke looked around him.

"Without you I should be lost again," he repeated. "Where does this path lead?" He pointed up into the hills. "To Ewelme?"

Stephen shook his head. Ewelme lay in open country, the other way, across the Old Road which ran for miles and miles, farther than he had ever been. The bridle path led to Swyncombe, a hamlet deep among the trees, with a little church and tumbledown cells where monks used to live before they were turned out, years ago.

Bolingbroke nodded. "French monks, I doubt not. There were many such, till Harry the fifth made war on France and sent them all packing. But tell me of your studies. Can you read Latin, and *speak* it? At Oxford everyone talks Latin; 'tis the rule, though I doubt if the Romans would recognize their mother tongue. What books do you read—Donatus? Cato? What lessons await you now, while you play what looks very much like truant?"

Accepting the word truant humbly this time, Stephen said that the task awaiting him was to translate one of *The Canterbury Tales* into Latin prose—far more difficult than putting Latin into English.

"But good practice, remember. I suppose you know that *The Canterbury Tales* were written by the grandsire of my lord of Suffolk's lady? Your Countess of Suffolk was by birth a Chaucer."

Stephen nodded eagerly. "Yes, sir, Dame Alice. Ewelme belongs to her. She was born and raised there. My lord holds it in her right. All in Ewelme claim her as *our* Dame Alice." He took a deep breath. "Sir, by your leave what does one do to become a master of arts? How long does it take?"

"How long? Seven years. If you want to know I'll tell you. There are seven arts and three philosophies. First the trivium, the three arts without which you can do nothing: logic, which teaches you to *think;* grammar, which teaches you to read and *understand what you read,* and rhetoric, which teaches you to put into words what you have thought and read. After the trivium comes the quadrivium, the other four arts: They are arithmetic, geometry, astronomy, and music. Add to all that the three philosophies, natural philosophy, moral philosophy, and metaphysics. Then, if you are found worthy, you may receive your M.A.'s gown."

"Does *every* master of arts go through all that?"

Master Bolingbroke laughed aloud. "Be not over-awed; you will have plenty of books to rely upon. Books are the most precious chattels in the world— more precious than gold, for all the wisdom of mankind is contained in books. Without them there could be no learning. Remember that every book depends upon the faithful labor of countless scribes, be they monks or tradesmen. That is why my mission is so vital."

"Mission?" repeated Stephen.

"Yes, I told you. My good lord Humphrey, Duke of Gloucester, is bent on forming a great library at Oxford. He has collected books from far and wide, and our late well-loved Harry the fifth left books for Oxford by his will, which have never reached there. There is a fine new building in the making, thanks to Duke Humphrey's purse, and books now in London or at Windsor or at Duke Humphrey's palace at Greenwich are to be carried to Oxford by river. My task is to visit all the millers to assure that the locks are opened and passage for the barge made safe."

"When will the books come?"

"I cannot tell exactly, but as soon as summer puts a stop to floods."

Stephen was trying hard to take this in.

"Is the Duke of Gloucester the king's brother?" he ventured.

"The king has no brother, more's the pity; no father, no mother, not even a sister, as you have, and he is not so very much older than you. Duke Humphrey is his uncle—the only one left of King Harry's brothers. There is of course the cardinal—Cardinal Beaufort, but he is an old man—a great-uncle to the king and only in half-blood at that; but he still seeks to dominate the realm to its undoing. But I must curb my tongue. Your Dame Alice is of kin to the cardinal, through the Chaucers. Her grandsire, Chaucer the poet, married a Flemish lady whose sister was wed to old John of Gaunt and was the cardinal's mother. From the marriages of those two sisters flow all the conflicts of today. When my lord of Suffolk took to wife your Dame Alice he became the cardinal's

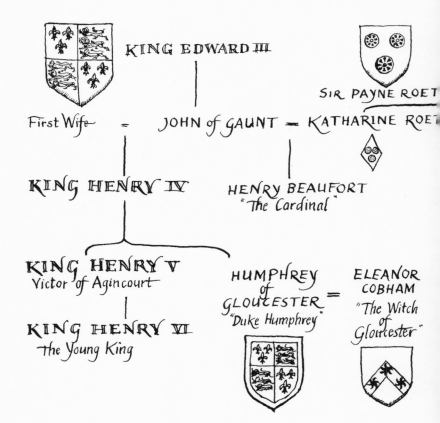

shadow, and so Duke Humphrey must needs look to the king."

"I saw Duke Humphrey in Wallingford once," said Stephen reflectively. "He was riding through the town at the head of a band of horsemen. He waved to the people and they all cheered him."

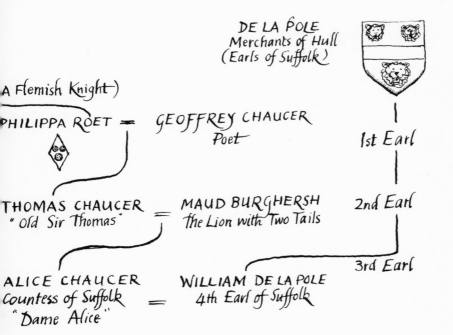

DE LA POLE
Merchants of Hull
(Earls of Suffolk)

A Flemish Knight

PHILIPPA ROET = GEOFFREY CHAUCER
Poet

1st Earl

THOMAS CHAUCER = MAUD BURGHERSH
"Old Sir Thomas"   The Lion with Two Tails

2nd Earl

3rd Earl

ALICE CHAUCER   WILLIAM DE LA POLE
Countess of Suffolk =   4th Earl of Suffolk
"Dame Alice"

"That may well be. He is exceeding popular. You may also see my most gracious lady, the Duchess Eleanor, for they lodge when they are traveling this way at the guesthouse of Wallingford Priory. The priory, doubtless you know, is a daughter house of St. Alban's Abbey where Duke Humphrey is *persona grata*. Of course since *your* lord, the Earl of Suffolk, is constable of Wallingford, I've heard that sometimes it comes to fisticuffs between the priory and the castle. I tell you oil and water mix more freely than the followers of Duke Humphrey with those of the cardinal and the Earl of Suffolk."

Suddenly he cut off short and pointed. "Look you!" he whispered urgently. "Look—on the hill. Men and dogs on their way up."

The bridle path which they were following ran, half-shaded with trees, along the bottom of the slope. Master Bolingbroke halted and backed the horse he was leading under an overhanging beech. Stephen's eyes followed the direction of the pointing finger.

"It's the huntsmen," he exclaimed. "Half a dozen of them. They've got Templar, my lord's best hound. I'll wager they're going to look for the buck."

"Then don't show yourself. You've escaped once. It would be a pity to be caught after all. Remember I've warned you against frequenting forbidden ground."

Stephen had not much fear of being caught now, and he was pretty sure that Master Bolingbroke was concerned mostly for himself, so closely did he press into the shadow. The huntsmen were using the very path that Stephen himself had used on the way up. He watched them carefully till they had all vanished over the skyline. Only then did he assure his companion that it was safe to emerge.

"That was a narrow escape"—Bolingbroke sighed with obvious relief—"escape for you I mean, of course. Have we much farther before we reach the highway?"

"We are almost at the Old Road," said Stephen. "Ewelme lies straight ahead, but you must keep left for Wallingford till the ways divide. Shall I come with you, sir, to make sure you take the right turning?"

"That is good of you, boy. I vow that I shall not forget it. I will repay you at Oxford; you may rely upon that. But in the meanwhile remember what I say. Have no more to do with that old dame by the pool. Will you be sure of that?"

Stephen said, "Yes, sir," without hesitation. He had been almost of that mind already. He would indeed be a fool to throw away dazzling prospects for so doubtful a character as old Meg. On reaching the Old Road, a muddy lane with high banks on either side, Bolingbroke mounted again, and Stephen padded along beside him, dodging the puddles, until they reached four crossroads leading north, south, east, and west.

"You go straight on for Wallingford," said Stephen, short of breath.

Bolingbroke reined in his horse and looked down at him.

"That is good," he said. "Now I think it is time to make a pact with each other. I give you my word that I will make no mention of having seen you at the old hag's dwelling, and you on your part will swear to hold your tongue about having seen me." He suddenly laughed, though it struck Stephen that the note did not wholly ring true. "It may seem strange that *I* should dread discovery. But I will admit to you that I am a vain man and cannot stomach humiliation. To be ridiculed for so losing myself would be more than I could bear. In your case it would be more serious still; so shall we agree to hold our tongues, the pair of us?"

Stephen said, "Yes, sir," without more ado. Bolingbroke seemed genuinely relieved.

"Good!" he said cheerfully. "And be it understood that if our meeting should ever come to light, I shall say what is the truth—that I missed my road in the storm and that you directed me. That is enough; and here is my hand on it."

He threw back his cloak to reach down to Stephen. Immediately Stephen noticed that the bright ornament which had shone so vividly in the firelight was no longer on view. It had been tucked away. But he raised himself on tiptoe to shake hands as required, and with a last cheerful wave the master from Oxford turned his horse and rode away toward Wallingford.

Stephen watched till he was out of sight. Then he

started back along the path to Ewelme. He felt definitely ill at ease. This insistence upon a pact had made it harder than ever to believe that Bolingbroke's visit to old Meg was pure accident. But after all it was none of his business and he had best forget it. He had firmly made up his own mind not to go to old Meg's any more. He was now far from sure that she was not a witch, and witchcraft was a deadly sin. Also in one thing Master Bolingbroke was right: it was stupid to risk my lord's anger. For now, more than ever, he wanted to be an Oxford scholar.

The storm had passed and the sun was shining brightly, making everything appear fresh and well washed. To his right the wooded Chilterns looked friendly, not sinister, with a veil of young green spread thinly over them. Wittenham Clumps on his left were near enough to be patted. Ewelme itself lay hidden in a hollow just ahead. As he reached the steep slope that led down to it he heard the sound of cheerful whistling. A boy was trudging up the hill toward him, a boy of about his own age, barelegged, with shaggy carroty hair and wearing a yoke across his shoulders from which dangled a pair of empty wooden buckets. It was Tom, the miller's boy. Stephen greeted him with a catcall, and Tom waved back.

"Where have you been?" he demanded. "I've been to the school to seek you, but old Ferry said you'd not been there all day."

"Old Ferry teaches the children," said Stephen loftily. "Parson is away so I can work at my own time. What are you doing here?"

"Master sent me with a catch of live carp for the fishponds. I was caught in the storm and got to the Hall as wet as a fish myself. Dame Alice bade me dry by the fire, and while I was there my lord came in, soaked and in a thundering rage because someone had poached a buck. Faith! you never saw such a rage. I felt safer in the storm."

Stephen quickly changed the subject. "What did you want with me that you went to the school?"

Tom grinned. "There's an old dog otter playing havoc with Master's fisheries just as the small fry are growing nicely. It's got a holt somewhere, with young, and Master's promised a penny for the old 'un or the bitch and a halfpenny each for the cubs." He lowered his voice. "*I've found the holt.* 'Tis in a runnel of the Ewelme brook. Now if we both took nets we could share the money. We might get tuppence each if we caught the lot. But I couldn't do the job alone."

Stephen's eyes brightened. This was good fun. "I'll come," he said. "What's the plan?"

They parted with an arrangement to meet an hour before dawn. Tom said the moon was so far on the wane that it rose only a couple of hours before the sun. That was why it was now or never. By the next moon the cubs would be too big.

Tom went off still whistling, and Stephen continued down the hill, glad to be back on familiar ground. On the left lay my lord of Suffolk's demesne, well wooded and stretching along the hillside as far as the eye could see, with the Hall itself and all its courts and outbuildings not much more than a bowshot distant. At the bottom the track ended in a lane which circled the village and on the right led off toward the hills. That was the way they would return with the buck; he peeped cautiously but so far there was nobody in sight.

On the opposite side of the lane stood the new God's House, its brick walls, rosy red, climbing the hill one above the other. At the bottom was the grammar school; farther up the hospice for old men with its thatched roofs and rows of chimneys; and finally the church tower, peeping over the top like a crown of creamy stone, gilded by the sun.

As Stephen looked at it his heart grew warm. This was *his* place. The very bricks belonged to him. As a small boy he'd been permitted to ride on one of the pack ponies to Crockers End, near Nettlebed, where brickmakers from Flanders had set up a kiln. He'd helped to load the baskets and then had tramped the whole five miles back to Ewelme like a real drover beside the pack horse train. He'd even laid a brick or two himself at the back of the schoolhouse, under the eye of the Flemish foreman who had come to teach the local laborers this newfangled trade. The old villagers called the bricks ugly and said that they wouldn't last; but *he* thought them beautiful with their red and blue and purple shades.

He entered the school porch, which was like a little

room with a bench on either side, a small window, and some steps leading up to the inner door. He stopped to listen before lifting the latch. All was silent. Good! The children had gone home.

The lofty schoolroom was swept and tidy, its bench well polished and the forms set neatly back against the wall. Even the desk of old Ferry, the parish clerk, was bare except for a covered inkwell, some quills, and a switch of birch twigs ominously handy. Twisting stairs led up to a tiny room over the porch, the master's sanctum, from which Parson Saynesbury could look down on the school. Stephen climbed the stairs and found, as he expected, a book left out for him on the parson's table—a copy of *The Canterbury Tales*. He carried it down with the greatest care and laid it on a bench, while from the aumbry, the little cupboard in the wall, he fetched a sheet of paper and a wax tablet with a bone stylo to practice with. Paper was precious because every sheet of it came from across the seas.

He began by writing the date neatly at the top of the page. He was proud of his handwriting, which had been carefully nurtured by Parson Saynesbury when he went for lessons to the parsonage, before the school existed.

Parson Saynesbury had left a marker for him in "The Nun's Priest's Tale," the one about Chanticleer and Pertelote, the little cock and hen. He knew it well. His mother had often told it to him and Lys as a bedtime story when they were small.

He had laboriously turned a dozen lines into Latin when the familiar story gripped him and the ink dried on his quill. Unable to resist he went on reading to the end and was just beginning "The Pardoner's Tale" when his attention was caught by a voice outside the school—a woman's voice: not the rolling gabble of the villagers, but a voice clear-cut and musical. He knew it at once. It was Dame Alice herself, my lady of Suffolk. Probably she was with her gentlewoman, or with young Mistress Jane, her stepdaughter and Mistress Jane's companion, Mistress Philippa, sister of that Tom Stonor whom he had seen with the hunting party. They had likely enough been to the church and were on their way back to the Hall. They would not be coming here.

Nevertheless he remained tense and motionless. Then he heard them enter the porch. The clear voice said. "Hold the little dogs, children. I shall not be more than a paternoster while." The door latch rattled as he bent studiously over his work.

"Ferry," said the voice. "Good Ferry, I need your help."

Red to the roots of his hair, Stephen sprang to his feet, bowing low to the slender figure silhouetted against the light. The sun fringed the edges of her mantle with gold and made a halo of the white coif on her head. Stephen could not find a word to say.

"Is that not Ferry? 'Tis dark in here. Know you where Ferry is, or Sir John Saynesbury for that matter?" She peered up the little stair.

Stephen said nervously that the clerk had gone home, and Sir John was in Oxford on my lord's business.

"Of course, of course," she said. "I should have remembered. Children, it is of no avail. And what shall I do for my copying? Master Brayles has business for my lord, and the clerk Barnabas writes like a sick spider." She turned and peered at Stephen.

"The light is dim," she said. "I am only just beginning to see. Who are you, good fellow? I seem to know your face."

He stammered out his name, and immediately she clapped her hands.

"Of course. Stephen, son of our good John Rudd, God rest him. You have grown so much that I scarce knew you. What are you doing here, all alone?" She stepped forward and leaned over the bench. "Why, this is 'The Nun's Priest's Tale' surely, done in Latin —but the book says otherwise: it is open at 'The Pardoner's Tale.' You have been reading on! I know it, you see. It was my grandsire that wrote it."

Recovering his courage Stephen said boldly that he remembered him well. Dame Alice laughed merrily.

"Indeed you do not. You may remember my father, Sir Thomas Chaucer, who is buried in the church. But it was *his* father, Geoffrey Chaucer, who made *The Canterbury Tales*. He died even before *I* was born. But no matter—you write a good hand."

She looked down at his work again. "Why should

not you do my copying? Look you: 'tis not a big matter." From beneath her cloak she produced a slim roll
tied with a silken string.

"There are but two or three pages, but the messenger to my castle at Donnington leaves early in the
morning, and I would that these lists should reach the
steward there without delay. Be not put out of coun-
tenance if it seems a weary task. Just copy every word
faithfully as it is written and bring it to me at the Hall
betimes. Can you do it? Of course you can. As I have
said, just copy faithfully." She fumbled with the silken
string. "A pest on this lace; it is knotted. Here, untie it
for yourself. Your fingers maybe are more nimble than
mine."

As he held open the door with the roll in his hand,
she smiled at him again.

"And when the good Parson returns, ask his pardon
that I have interrupted your work."

Two or
Three Pages

STEPHEN stood gazing after her as she walked away. He'd seen her often enough, but never before had she become real for him, a smile softening the lines of her thin grave face and her eyes bright with a merry twinkle. And *he* was to work for her! Blessing the clerk Barnabas who wrote like a sick spider, he fairly skipped back to the desk, untied the knotted lace, and spread the roll out flat. He saw at once that there were three sheets, not two. That did not matter; he had plenty of time. He put the precious book away, fetched more paper from the aumbry, and set to work on the first page.

It was addressed to the steward of Donnington Castle and it seemed to be just a long list of household stuff: "Item: a brass jug and basin, a brass chafing dish, two leather pots"; or "Item: a bed of feathers with two pairs of blankets, a pair of sheets, and hangings of striped serge"; or "Item: two turned chairs and four cushions." Clearly it was an inventory of things to be sent to Donnington when the family left Ewelme so that the Hall could be "sweetened." These periodical upheavals seemed to be a normal matter in great households. Stephen had often seen long lines of wagons and loaded baggage horses crossing Wallingford Bridge, all belonging to some great lord who was leaving one of his houses, foul from occupation, to live for a while in another.

He finished the page thankfully; it was dull work, and there were two more. But to his surprise the second page was not a list but a letter, a long letter, closely written, apparently in Dame Alice's own hand. He sighed. This would take longer to copy. He started immediately and shaped with great care the flourishes with which it began.

Right Honorable and Well-beloved Daughter

He stopped to wipe his quill and trim it carefully, reflecting that he did not know that Dame Alice had a daughter. Perhaps it was a daughter by her previous husband, the Earl of Salisbury, who had commanded the English armies in France and had been killed there, like Stephen's own father. The news of his death had caused a stir in Ewelme because Dame Alice was widowed by it. Two years later she married my lord of Suffolk, who had succeeded Salisbury as commander in chief. Doggett with strong ale in his cup had said that my lord of Suffolk must have been up in the morning early to win not only his overlord's command but his overlord's wife as well.

With the pen to his liking Stephen dipped it in the inkwell and started again. The letter went on.

I commend me unto you desiring heartily the welfare of my lord your husband and your sweet children. I write to you, daughter, begging your help in matters which are near to my heart. The first concerns our house in London. The ancient house in Lombard Street, built by my lord's forebears, is ill-conditioned for our present needs and my lord has cast his eye upon Pulteney's Inn, lying close to your own mansion, The Erber. I learn that this house has now become the property of your good cousin the Earl of Huntingdon through the death of his wife (may God rest her) but that he prefers to remain in his own mansion of Coldharbour because it has anchorage on the river. Therefore I write to beg you, Madam, for the love there is between us, that you will plead with your cousin, my lord of Huntingdon, to look kindly upon my good lord's desire to be possessed of Pulteney's Inn.

Stephen paused to rest his hand. All that was clear enough, but there was much more of it.

Now, daughter, there are other matters still deeper in my heart, but of the utmost secrecy. Doubtless you know of the meeting arranged by my lord Cardinal of Beaufort, which is to be held at Gravelines near Calais, with the purpose of ending the war with France, a cause for which my husband, my lord of Suffolk, would give his life. He believes that two things are needed to make peace: first that we should set free the French duke, Charles d'Orleans, who has been for twenty-five years prisoner in England, since Agincourt. He is well disposed toward the English and would act as emissary on our behalf. The second matter of even greater secrecy is my lord's conception of a marriage between our lord the king and some princess of France yet to be chosen. None is so fitted as the Duc d'Orleans to arrange such a marriage. But be mindful, daughter, that this is a secret 'twixt you and me. It might bode much ill to my lord if it became known too soon.

The stumbling block in the way of all these hopes is Duke Humphrey, who favors war with France and has no object but his own advancement and the vain glory of that bedeviled jade, Eleanor Cogham, his so-called wife. At one time my lord had custody of the French duke, both here and at Wingfield, and together they devised schemes to advance the cause of peace. But thanks to Duke Humphrey and his duchess, the prisoner was taken from us and given to her father, Sir Reginald Cobham, that Sir Reginald's purse might grow fat thereby.

It was beginning to dawn on Stephen that this was a very private letter. He laid down his pen and stared at the page. Did Dame Alice mean him to copy it? Could it possibly be there by mistake? He turned the pages over; the third, like the first, was a list. She had said *two or three* pages, and she had also told him to copy every word faithfully. It was not after all *his* business to question what she wrote. As he had gone so far he supposed that he had better finish. There was not very much more. Frowning and uneasy he began again.

Madam and dearest daughter, I hear on all sides that your husband, now Earl of Salisbury in your late father's stead, grows daily more powerful in the council of the king. Therefore I beg you, by the love between us when you were a child and my step-daughter, that you would persuade my lord your husband to further my husband's efforts in the cause of peace; first and foremost that the Duke Charles d'Orleans might return to my lord's custody and then that together they should go to the conference at Gravelines and stand up against Duke Humphrey's thirst for war.

Written at Ewelme on this fifth day of May *Anno* 17 *Henry VI* by your true and faithful

ALYSE SUFFOLK

He turned the sheet over. An address was written on the back, ready for folding.

To the most noble Countess of Salisbury
At the Erber by Dowgate in London
Be this delivered.

When he had copied the last word he read it right through again. He remembered the French duke well. He used to see him riding out with my lord of Suffolk and a train of gentlemen. With other village boys he had scrambled for the pence that "Monsynure" threw to them. But the most important decision now was what should he do? If the letter was there by mistake Dame Alice might be angry that he had read it, let alone copied it. On the other hand she had clearly said, "Copy every word faithfully," and for him to pick and choose might well be an impertinence. If *only* he knew what to do!

At that moment the church bell began to ring. It was time for vespers. Like a flash he decided. He would ask Doggett. Doggett was safe and had an answer for everything. With the other old bedesmen Doggett was obliged to attend vespers every day. The boys from the grammar school went only on feast days. Today was not a feast, so there would be time to copy the remainder of the list for Donnington while Doggett was in church, and take the whole lot to him, with the squirrel tails, after vespers.

He copied the third page without effort, carefully gathered them all together, and stowed them in his satchel. It was strange that until today he had scarcely heard of Duke Humphrey or the Duchess Eleanor or the cardinal, and now all of a sudden their names kept turning up. The striking thing was the contrast between Bolingbroke and Dame Alice. To Bolingbroke the Duchess Eleanor was "my most gracious lady," while to Dame Alice she was "that bedeviled jade."

He had time to return *The Canterbury Tales* to the parson's table before he picked up the satchel and climbed the steep path that led to the hospice and the church. Near the top he turned into a narrow brick passage, and emerged into the cloister where the old men dwelled. It was a cobbled courtyard open to the sky, with a well and a bucket in the middle and with a roofed walk on all four sides. From the cloister thirteen doors opened into thirteen little houses, the cells of the old bedesmen of God's House. Thirteen, the parson said, in honor of our Lord and His twelve apostles. Each cell had its living room and its own fireplace and chimney, with a loft upstairs. From the east walk a flight of steps led up to the church so that when the bell rang the old men could form up two by two and enter through the great west door without having to face wind or weather.

The cloister was deserted. Stephen listened at the foot of the steps. Vespers was still going on, so he turned back to Doggett's cell, the corner one, lifted the latch and went in.

Though the room was empty, a couple of logs smoldered on the hearth. He groped in the chimney corner for an old chipped and pitted broadsword to stir them to life. After vespers Doggett enjoyed the comfort of a fire.

The flame lit up the darker corners of the cell. In a special niche above the chimney was a wooden crucifix, a gift from Dame Alice to each old man. The place of honor above the truckle bed was given to a short French arrow, which Stephen knew had once pierced the chain mail of Doggett's thigh. Beside the arrow hung a pewter badge of St. Thomas of Canterbury, relic of a pilgrimage, while a peg in the corner supported an old stained leather jerkin, crowned by a cap of steel, bright with much polishing.

On a trestle table by the small window lay Doggett's painting gear: bits of paper or parchment

DE LA POLE   ROET   BURGHERSH

greedily hoarded, some jars full of colors begged from
the craftsmen working in the church, some sharpened
charcoal, and an old cooking pot which held his
brushes. Stephen looked critically at their stubbly
heads. The squirrel tails would make better ones than
that.

Apparently Doggett had been busy. The front of
the table was spread with sketches of different coats
of arms. Stephen knew them all. He was not Doggett's
disciple for nothing. There was one showing my lord's
arms, the lions' faces of the de la Poles, and another
the three wheels for Chaucer. Next to that was the
lion rampant with two tails, the arms of Burghersh
used by my lady because it was through her Burghersh mother that she had inherited Ewelme.

Next to that was the shield of Thomas Montacute,
Earl of Salisbury, Dame Alice's late husband—a fess
of sharp pointed lozenges which were supposed to
look like mountain peaks, *mons acutus*—a pun on the
name of Montacute, which Doggett liked to describe
as "canting heraldry." He wondered why Doggett

53

was so busy with all these family coats of arms. Then the *mons acutus* of the Earl of Salisbury reminded him of Dame Alice's letter. Would Doggett never come?

At that very moment he heard a shuffling of feet in the cloister, the door was flung open, and Doggett himself came stumping in, a grizzled little old man, bent almost double and dressed in a brown tabard with a red cross and a red hood, the livery of the bedesmen. At the sight of Stephen he grinned with pleasure.

"Hey, boy, where have you been all day? Here, help me out of this prayer harness. I was not born to be a monk."

Willingly enough Stephen dragged the habit over the old man's head, and Doggett emerged, tousled, in shirt and hose girded with a leather belt from which dangled a battered dagger sheath. In vain had Parson Saynesbury protested that a dagger was no fit wear for a bedesman. Doggett abandoned the blade but stubbornly continued to flaunt the empty sheath. Now he slipped on an ancient woolen gown, shook back his wiry hair, and looked at Stephen with eyes bright as a robin's under their shaggy brows.

"What have you been at? Playing truant? Have you heard the news?"

"What news?" Stephen asked impatiently. News was meat and drink to Doggett. He lived on it. One of his fellow bedesmen, old Nye, had a son, young Nye, who worked a barge on the river, and whenever young Nye visited his sire, Doggett appeared like magic round the cloister to gather any tidings that might have come upstream from London.

But this time it was local news.

"Why, my lord came back from hunting breathing fire and sword. A deer was poached under his very nose, and he's vowed to hang someone from the gate of Wallingford. All the village fears for its life."

Stephen could stand no more. "I know," he said. "I saw it."

"You *saw* it? Were you with the hunt?"

Stephen shook his head. "Parson was away, so I went to the hills on my own. I was lying hid close by."

"You young fool. My lord would have flayed you if he'd found you. Who *did* kill the buck?"

"I think it was the fellow they call Gilles, though I didn't see him. The buck fell just before the hunt came by and the hounds got wind of it. I tell you I thought I was finished, but the storm broke like hell let loose. My lord fled and I took shelter."

"Took shelter? Where?"

There was no help for it, and Doggett was safe enough. "I went to old Meg's—to get something for *you*."

"That old hag? Have you taken leave of your senses? She's a witch."

"Nay, she's a kind old soul; there's no harm in her."

"If she's a witch she's sworn to the devil; that's harm enough for any. You grin, do you? You'll grin the other side of your face one day."

Still grinning, Stephen dangled the squirrel tails. "I went for *these*. They are to make painting brushes. I won't go again."

Doggett stared for a moment before he put out his hand and took the tails. "*For me?*" he said strangely moved. "Who prompted you? If not the devil, then more likely my good angel. Did you know that Dame Alice was here but an hour since, bidding me go to the Hall and paint shields of arms on the walls of her new solar? What think you of *that* for an honor? I could scarce have managed with my old brushes."

The mention of Dame Alice made Stephen remember what he had really come for.

"Listen," he said. "I need your help. Dame Alice came also to the school. She left me copying to do."

"That's well," said Doggett absently. "Then we shall both be busy." He was running his finger up and down the fur to test the spring of the hair. Stephen grew desperate.

"*Listen*," he cried again. "I tell you I need your help. I'm in trouble."

Doggett looked up quickly. "In trouble? How? The witch?"

"No, the copying. Look you at this."

He untied the roll and spread out the sheets, explaining that Dame Alice had said they were for the steward of Donnington and all he had to do was to copy every word. But when she had gone he found two pages of lists for Donnington and a third page which was a long private letter to the Countess of Salisbury, her daughter in London.

"Her *step*daughter," Doggett corrected. "Daughter of Thomas Montacute, Earl of Salisbury, by his first wife; the title passed that way. Dame Alice was his second wife. I have to blazon the arms of Montacute on the wall."

"As you will," said Stephen impatiently, "but my problem is did she mean me to copy this letter? 'Tis a very private one and full of weighty matters. It was between the two lists for Donnington; could it be there by mistake? Look you at it and tell me what you think."

THE TWO ALICES

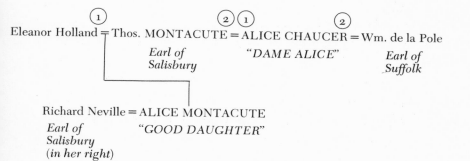

He held out the page. Doggett snapped at him, "Young fool! You know I am unlettered. But I've got ears. Read it out."

In spite of his sharpness it was plain that he was all agog. So, lowering his voice, Stephen read the whole letter through. Doggett exploded like a burst bladder.

"God and His holy Mother keep us! Is that all true or have you made it up? It shows the risk a man runs when he takes a wife! If that fell into the hands of Gloucester or the Cobham tribe, it could sink my lord like a stone, and not even his master the cardinal could save him."

This was even worse than Stephen had dreamed.

"Why?" he cried. "My lord does but seek to make peace."

"Yea, but to wrench the custody of the French duke from the Cobhams would make a bitter enemy of Gloucester. And if Gloucester knew of my lord's plan for the French marriage he could rouse the rabble with a vengeance. After all these years of war, ordinary folk abhor the French. Look how they reviled the king's French mother as a witch even here in Wallingford—and for that matter old Queen Joanna before her."

"But the letter," said Stephen desperately. "What must I do about the letter? Must I admit to having copied it, or shall I say I judged it private, which might be even worse?"

Doggett growled. "I see your trouble. You are in a cleft stick. Stay quite still now while I think."

He stood scowling, his jaw protuberant while he breathed through toothless gums the little tune that always accompanied deep thought. Stephen knew it well: it was the song of Agincourt, the anthem of that never-forgotten day when he had marched in triumph behind Harry V into London.

"I have it," cried the old man at last. "Now listen carefully and you need tell no lies. Can you lay hands on a page of your own writing—a page of lesson maybe?"

"There's the page I was writing when my lady appeared," said Stephen wonderingly.

"Good! Then here's a scheme for you. Roll your copy of the letter inside your own page and stow it in your satchel. Then roll all else together, Dame Alice's own pages with your copies of the lists; lay that on the top and get you to the Hall at once. If she has lost her letter she may well be in torment by now. Ask to see her in person, put the roll in her hands, and wait while she opens it. There's a good chance she'll not even think about a copy, and you'll have naught but praise. If she does ask then look in your satchel and find it caught in with your own work; plead sorrow for your carelessness and no harm done." He chuckled, obviously pleased with himself. "There's no sin in it. 'Tis what we at the wars would call mother wit. Now be off with you—the sooner the better."

Stephen, still uneasy, had scarcely reached the door when Doggett called him back.

"One thing I should have said—whatever comes

you must not keep that copy of the letter. If she does not have it bring it back here and burn it on the fire. That's a duty under God. Do you mark me?"

Stephen said yes obediently. He still lingered, loath to go. But Doggett had turned back to his table, still humming and fingering the squirrel tails. So, quietly, Stephen let himself out and went back to the school. It took no more than a minute to roll up his copy of the letter inside his page of "The Nun's Priest's Tale," as Doggett had suggested. On the impulse of the moment, he changed into his scholar's gown. It gave him confidence. Then he took up his satchel and with beating heart set out to find Dame Alice.

The Earl of Suffolk's Hall faced the village on the opposite hill. It had recently been enlarged and made modern, and the great house itself, with its long red roof and its chimney louver of carved stone, stood up above the jumble of old buildings that surrounded the outer court.

Thanks to his school gown, Stephen passed the gatehouse without question, and the men in the courtyard polishing harness scarcely looked at him. There was a moat around the Hall with a bridge leading to the big studded oak door that stood open, revealing a long passage with another door at the far end. He waited for a few moments hoping that somebody would appear. The view from here, of the school, God's House, and the church strung out in a chain up the hill, was new to him. But as time passed and no one came, he plucked up his courage and rapped with his fist on the door. An old man appeared wearing a doublet with my lord's badge. He looked dubious when Stephen asked for my lady. But he too noted the school gown and hearing that Stephen came by her order, said that she was up in her new solar and let him in. From the passage they went through an opening in the screens, and crossed the great hall to the bottom of a small flight of stairs. Here Stephen had to wait while the man went up to inquire. Then with beating heart he climbed the steps and pushed past a leather curtain into the room at the top. Its walls were of rough stone, undecorated, and though it had a fireplace with a small fire burning, it was bare of furniture except for a couple of joint stools and piles of bright cushions.

Dame Alice sat on a window seat with Mistress Jane and Mistress Philippa, sorting embroidery silks. As Stephen approached, two tiny dogs emerged from beneath her skirts and hurled themselves toward him, yapping savagely.

Dame Alice's voice called above the din, "Tansy! Belle! Be quiet, you noisy whelps. 'Tis but play, Stephen; they will not bite. Have you brought my copying? Truth, you have made speed. Give it to me. Children! Catch those little rascals; we cannot hear ourselves speak!"

Handing over the roll, Stephen thankfully dropped to the ground, his face hidden as he sought to catch the little dogs. He heard the crackle of pages and then, suddenly, a low cry.

"Jane, here's my letter—the one I thought I had lost. I never dreamed that it could be among the lists. Praise be to God! It might have gone to Donnington."

Stephen's heart beat fast. This was the critical moment. Would she ask if he had copied it? He continued to play with the wriggling Tansy till she called his name. Then he stood up. She was smiling. In her hands were only the Donnington lists. The letter was not in sight.

"Good boy! You have done these promptly and very well. And you had the sense to see that the third page did not belong. I shall find more work for you. Now go you to the buttery and bid the steward give you a mug of small ale."

Elated but at the same time secretly ashamed, Stephen thanked her and said that he would rather go straight home. He choked back an impulse to tell her that he *had* copied the letter, and to put the copy into her hands. But by now it was difficult to admit it, and he would be burning it anyway.

But as he prepared to bow himself out, he heard heavy footsteps crossing the hall below. They stormed up the stairs, the curtain was torn aside, and in burst William de la Pole, the Earl of Suffolk himself.

Stephen had never been so near to him before, and

though he had been brought up to think of him as his father's much-loved master, he realized all at once that this burly man with a grizzled beard had been the dreaded commander of the armies in France. His skin was red and leathery, and under bushy brows his eyes glinted with anger like touches of light on steel.

He strode across to his wife and stood squarely in front of her, his lower lip jutting truculently.

"Before heaven, madam, you have as graceless, poaching, murderous a set of scoundrels on these your lands as any I have met in the wars."

Dame Alice rose. "*My* lands, my lord? How say you *my* lands? You know well that all my lands are yours. What ails you, sir?" She laid two fingers on his hand. "Faith, but you are cold. You were soaked to the skin in the storm. A cup of mulled wine would warm you. Let it be brought while you tell me what the matter is."

She spoke as though to a hurt child, but he shook her off angrily.

"The matter? I'll tell you what's the matter. Templar is dead."

She was aghast. "Dead? *Templar?* My lord, how came it?"

"An arrow through his skull. There's some black-hearted outlaw hid in those woods who has the skill of the devil. Your father, madam, was too soft. Now that *I'm* steward of the Chilterns in his place, I'll hunt them like vermin. I'll raid the hills tomorrow, and if I catch this archer fellow I'll sling him from a gibbet over the walls of Wallingford."

"Tell me how it happened," she said soothingly.

"*You* nagged me," he retorted. "You bade me stay warm. So instead of going myself to see them carry in that dead roebuck, I sent William and his underlings with Templar. Templar ranged ahead, but as he reached the buck something nearby alerted him. He growled, then sprang and almost at once dropped back dead, an arrow through his skull. Our fools stood rooted, all except William who rushed forward. He thought he heard a child whimpering in the bushes— doubtless some outlaw's brat, which might well mean a whole band of outlaws hidden among the trees. So William bade them shoulder Templar and leave the buck behind. They needed no twice bidding. Crying 'sorcery' they all but fled down the hill."

"Sorcery? How sorcery?"

My lord shrugged. "Those clodhoppers look for sorcery at every turn. One actually declared that he *saw* the child that William heard. He called it a mooncald, a creature with a maid's head. All I know is that the arrow broke off and was lost, and so I am no wiser than before."

Grim-faced, he turned away to the window, where the two little girls were huddled together. Dame Alice, glancing back, caught sight of Stephen.

"Go you to the buttery," she ordered in a whisper. "Bid them to bring wine for my lord."

TWO OR THREE PAGES

My lord of Suffolk swung round. "I've told you I want no wine. Who is this boy? What's he doing here?"

"This is Stephen, son of your old John Rudd who died at Jargeau; do you remember? He has been copying some lists for me; copying very well. Jane, bring them here."

My lord looked Stephen up and down. He glanced at the writing and back again at Stephen.

"John Rudd's son?" he said gruffly. "Saints in heaven, how time flies. How long since your father died, God rest him? It must be nine years—after the Maid had raised the siege of Orleans, and we fought her again only to be captured—a bitter day." He took a turn across the room, then swung round to face Stephen. "Yes, John Rudd threw his life away to spare me. He was a faithful fellow. Are you like him?"

"Come to the window, Stephen," said Dame Alice in her soft voice. "I think you will see for yourself, sir."

My lord again ran his eyes over Stephen. This time they were friendly eyes.

"Yes, now I can see the likeness. He used to stand in my tent bearing my trappings much as you stand now, feet wide apart, belly sticking out." He laughed. The spell was broken. "And you write a good hand. Maybe we can make use of you. Begin now by going to the buttery, as my lady says. I'll have some wine after all."

Lys

*I*T WAS already dusk when Stephen left the Hall and set off for home. Odo's cottage, far up the Old Road, was a couple of miles away but less than half that distance over the shoulder of the down. He stepped out as though he were walking on air. Since this morning his prospects had changed completely. Then he had been just a schoolboy dodging lessons. Now the future had opened up. He stood well with my lord and also with Dame Alice, and Master Bolingbroke was ready, if needs be, to give him a place at Oxford!

He was longing to tell Lys about it. True there was much to conceal: old Meg and Bolingbroke and Dame Alice's letter were all secrets. But she would be thrilled about his copying Dame Alice's lists and still more about the meeting with my lord, who had said he was like his father.

The thought of the lists reminded him that his copy of the letter was still in his satchel. He could feel it rolled up with his own written page. He thrust in his hand, crumpled up the paper, and pushed it farther down. There had been no time to go back to Doggett, but it did not matter. Lys kept a good fire in the cottage. He could easily burn it there.

He topped the edge of the down and began to tread carefully down the steep side. It was growing darker every minute. The wooded Chilterns were black against the sky. Usually from here he could look down at the smoke curling up from the hole in the cottage roof, and often Lys left the top half of the door open for the firelight to guide him. But tonight there was no light at all! Perhaps Odo had come in cold and closed everything. He scrambled down a bank into the ruts and puddles of the Old Road. It was now so dark that he reached the cottage before he realized it. The scent of gilliflowers met him, and he sang out his usual signal to Lys, "Hi Hi Ho," like a huntsman's horn. The oxen in the byre heard it and lowed softly; otherwise all was silent. He felt his way to the door and lifted the latch.

Inside it was pitch dark; even the fire showed no light. He called Lys's name. Nobody answered. The place was empty.

He flung down his satchel, dropped on his knees, and blew the embers. As a spark glowed, he fumbled for a handful of dry kindling. The room was lit up. Surely Lys could not be ill: To make certain he climbed the ladder to her loft. Her pallet bed was neat and untouched. The old blue cloak that had been his mother's hung from a nail. At the foot of the bed stood an old chest that his mother had called her treasure house. In it she had hoarded a few possessions from her first marriage: a hood lined with fur, a kirtle too grand to be worn, and, hidden at the bottom, a silk purse containing some French gold pieces brought by his father from the war. They were to be a dowry for Lys.

On impulse he lifted the lid. A winter bedcover lay on the top, but to make sure he thrust his hand deep down till he touched the purse. Then, satisfied, he slid down the ladder and dropped onto the earthen floor.

This time he noticed the remains of a meal of bread and ale on the bench by the wall. So Odo had been in and gone out again. The lantern was missing from its peg. He might have gone to look for Lys. A slatternly family lived farther up the Old Road. Likely enough one of the gaggle of children was ill, and Lys, caught in the dark, had waited for her stepfather to fetch her.

Relieved at the thought, he went outside, leaving the door open. Sure enough, in the distance he saw the swinging light of a lantern. It must be Odo.

As the light approached he called out, "Hi Hi Ho!" There was no answer; he called again, but still no one replied. The lantern's flicker came steadily nearer till he could hear the squelch of his stepfather's sodden feet. He was alone.

"Where's Lys?" demanded Stephen quickly.

Odo's voice was surly. "How should I know? She went off a while since."

"Where to? To the cowherd's?"

Odo pushed past him into the cottage. "She's not there now any wise. Cock and pie, but I'm cold." He poked at the fire with his toe. "Fill the ale mugs quickly. I'll not catch my death for the tantrums of a stubborn wench."

"Tantrums? What's amiss?"

"Naught that I can see save that the silly maid doesn't know what's good for her. If you must have it, she flew off in mortal panic because I said it was high time she was wed."

"Wed?" Stephen could imagine Lys's startled face. "She's but a child. 'Tis too soon."

His stepfather, short, bow-legged, with shoulders rounded from the plow, looked up to him with a grin. "That's not for you to judge. 'Tis not too soon for some."

The blood mounted to Stephen's head. "In Heaven's name, what has been going on?"

Odo took a swill from the mug, choked, and spat. "Steady, young cock. Naught's happened save that I've found her a good husband."

Stephen caught his breath. "*You've* found—who have you found?"

"Rickman of the quarry; a fine match for any maid."

Rickman. Stephen knew him well; a huge flabby

man as old as Odo, with blackened teeth and arms
dangling like an ape's, who smelled worse than a
piggery. "No!" he cried. "You shan't wed her to a
great brute like that. She's no child of yours." Then
a thought struck him. "Where is she? He's not got her
now?"

Odo answered tolerantly enough. "Nay, nay. We'll
call the parson before we hand her over. But Rickman
bespoke her this morning. His mother's dead and
there's none to find for him, so I said he could have
her if he wanted. He came in with me for a meal and
she'd baked pasties. Maybe that finished him, for he
told her there and then that she was to be his wench
and said he'd wed her at the next moon. Faith! You'd
think she was a cloister brat. She just stood gaping;
then out of the door she went and I've not set eyes on
her since."

Stephen was shaking with rage. "She's not yours to
toss like a piece of hound's meat," he cried. "I'd have
you remember her father was my lord's man. I swear
I'll have my lord after you."

Odo got slowly to his feet, the ale mug poised
threateningly.

"Lord not my lord over me, you young whelp, or
I'll beat the life out of you. Who reared you both, pau-
per brats that you were? Your mother was good wife
enough to me, and I reckoned her worth the keep of
two stiff-necked bantlings. But now she's gone I've no
call to keep you. The wench shapes well, and I've

pledged her to an honest man who'll wed her, and that's good measure for a chit without a stitch to call her own. As for you, begone, before you bring the devil under my roof. Did you think I knew nothing of your traffic with that old hag up yonder? They call her witch and well she may be. Get you gone and good riddance. There's no place for you here. I'm taking a new wife."

He relit the lantern with a burning brand, seized a bucket, and stumped out to water the oxen, leaving the door open behind him.

Half-stunned by this new turn of events, Stephen took a staff from the corner and went out too. One thing was perfectly clear: he had to find Lys.

It was a dark night, but in the light that streamed from the cottage he could see the pale shapes of tree trunks and the glint of water in the ruts of the road. He prodded his way along, stopping every few paces to call "Hi Hi Ho." His voice echoed right up the valley, but the only answer was the hooting of owls. Suddenly the cottage door slammed, and every vestige of light vanished. It was pitch dark. Without a lantern he could not go on.

He remained still listening intently and trying to reason it all out. He had last seen Lys when he had left her at the foot of the hill, but she had been home since then. It was after dinner that Rickman had terrified her. When she ran away where would she have gone? Obviously she would have fled to the school to find him, but he had neither seen nor heard a sign of her.

Then a thought cold as ice made his heart stand still. In my lord's account of how Templar had died, those craven knaves had taken fright at *something* which they saw near the buck. They said it had a maid's head. Templar had sprung at it. William had heard a child's cry. He stood rooted to the ground as the horror gained on him. The story seemed to fit together. Lys had last seen him climbing. In her misery she had tried to follow him. The same path would have led her to the buck. By that time he had been on the bridle track with Bolingbroke. They had noticed the huntsmen going up the hill.

He turned and stumbled back toward the cottage, blundering into trees, slithering through muddy pools. It was Gilles the Bowman who had shot the hound: that much was certain. But who was Gilles? Where did he live? Only Gilles could tell him if Lys was alive or dead.

The first thing he needed was the lantern. Without it he couldn't move. The quarrel with Odo didn't matter now. When Odo heard his story, he would come with him and search the hill.

He reached the closed door and lifted the latch. Thank heaven Odo had not barred him out. Inside he was greeted by thunderous snores. His stepfather lay on the only bed with his mouth open. The sickly smell of mead hung on the air. He was dead drunk.

Stephen stared at him in dismay. His mother had always said that Odo had a secret store. The stuff was swift to act but took hours to wear off. There would be no help from him.

The lantern lay by the hearth. To his dismay the candle had burned out. Where did Lys keep them? He'd seen her making some only recently, brewing the mutton fat and hanging up the dipped rushes. He searched desperately but without success. Alone and with no light he could not hope to find his way up the hill. Then for the first time he remembered Tom from the mill. Tom had said there was a late moon. All he could do was to wait till it rose.

He propped the door open so that he could see out. Then he crossed to his own bracken bed and sat on it, his back against the wall. Whatever happened he must not sleep.

In the silence it struck him that he had not said a single prayer, which was crazy since only God could help. He began at once with the familiar ones, *Paters* and *Aves*—"Our Father" and "Hail Mary"—then the *Miserere*—"Have mercy upon me, oh God"—which was so apt that he said the first words over and over again. "Have mercy—Have mercy—" It swelled up from his heart as it dawned on him that all this was his fault. If he had not gone to old Meg's Lys would not have followed him. It was because he had defied all warnings that she might be lying there, hurt—in pain—even dead.

He knew now without a doubt that there was evil at work. Old Meg *was* a witch. Whatever he had thought before, he had become certain of it, almost from that first moment in the dark hovel when *something* had made his flesh creep. He had already made up his mind not to go there again; but now it was too late, the damage was done. Doggett's words came back to him. "A witch is sworn to the devil—" It was true. Witches were evil, and through him the evil had stretched out and seized Lys.

As he gazed at the square of velvet darkness outside the open door the horror seemed to grow. He tried to convince himself that the "child" near the buck was not Lys, though all the time he was certain that it was she. His head felt top-heavy; he could no longer think. But his pulses throbbed without ceasing —*dumma dumma dumma dum,* like Wat's humming. There were eyes everywhere. The rhythm quickened and became the thunder of hounds pounding towards him. He could hear Lys calling—far away—calling—calling.

He started up, suddenly wide awake. The doorway was filled with dim gray light and the air loud with the dawn chorus of birds. He was not dreaming. Someone *was* calling—it must be Tom. Cursing himself for having slept, he rushed outside.

At first he could see nobody. Then, as his eyes cleared, he could make out a tall figure standing at the foot of the hill where the woods began. With a thumping heart he recognized Gilles the Bowman. He tore through a watery ditch and up the bracken slope. The bowman's voice reached him, pitched low but reassuring.

"Steady, boy, don't kill yourself. Your sister's safe. I came because she said you'd be fearful for her."

"Where is she? Is she hurt?"

"No broken bones but torn about and sick from terror. I carried her up yonder"—he tossed his head back toward the hill. "It seems she tried to follow you—she had seen you go—and she had just reached the dead buck when the hound came bounding up the hill. She did the worst thing possible, screamed and ran away, which brought him after her. Then she tripped and fell among jagged brushwood. By God's grace it was at that moment that I came to carry away the buck—a miracle, no less. If I had delayed my going she would be dead. I sweated lest my bolt should strike the maid and not the hound, but I dared not hold back. The brute would have savaged her for sure."

"Where is she?" Stephen asked again.

"With old Meg. I carried her there. Old Meg will cure her quicker than any, but all the time she cries for you. She is in terror of something other than the hound—I know not what." His voice changed to a more cheerful tone. "Oh—I near forgot; she begs that you will bring her cloak and her shoon and any other clothing that hangs ready. All that she wore is torn to tatters. Go you now and fetch them. I will wait for you."

Stephen wasted no time. It was now broad day-

light, and he tiptoed through the cottage lest Odo
should wake up. The ladder creaked as he climbed it,
so he grabbed the blue cloak from its nail, seized a
pair of his mother's old shoes—which Lys wore
stuffed with hay—as well as a shift, an old kirtle, and
a smock all hanging on a line and carried them down
to his satchel, which lay where he had flung it near
the fire. He stuffed everything in except the cloak,
which he threw over his shoulder and made his escape, closing the door behind him.

The bowman led the way. Neither of them spoke.
Stephen was almost too dazed to think. It seemed as
though heaven were playing a game with him. He
had just made a solemn vow that he would never go
near old Meg again, and now here was Lys, through
his fault, delivered into her hands.

At the top of the hill the first pale rays of the sun
streamed through the trees. Gilles waited for Stephen
to catch up.

"I saw you in the wood yesterday just before the
storm," he remarked.

Stephen nodded. "I was there when you killed the
buck. 'Twas skill beyond belief. Did you see the
hunt? My lord all but caught me. He might have had
you too. I warn you he has vowed that you shall hang
for it."

The bowman laughed. "He's vowed that against all
outlaws. Most of them have moved farther away.
I'm like a cat: I have nine lives. But I grieve that I

had to kill his hound. It was a fine beast. Look you, the dead tree! We are nearly there."

The woodpecker tree was whiter than ever. Everything looked different in the morning light. The pool shone like a mirror of polished steel, reflecting the shaggy hovel on the other side. The door stood wide for the sunshine to stream in. At the sound of their voices Meg appeared, her old face wreathed in smiles.

"Hey, Stephen, the child is wailing for you." She wagged her head as though she were speaking of a baby. "Go you in and pet her. That is what she needs."

Lys lay on a deep bed of bracken, her head covered with damp green plasters and fusty bandages. All that he could see of her face was blue and swollen with bruises and much weeping. He dropped on his knees beside her, and she clung to him sobbing, repeating brokenly the whole long story that he already knew, beginning with the scene with Odo and the terrible Rickman. As he tried to soothe her, he struggled with the problem of what was to be done. Where could she go? They had no kinsfolk in the village; both their parents had come from my lord's Suffolk lands. If he took her to the parson for help, as other people did when they were in trouble, the whole story would come out and he would be ruined. For having dealings with a known witch and deliberately concealing it, he would certainly lose his place at the school, and all his new bright future would be gone for good.

On the other hand, with the memory of what he had learned yesterday, how could he leave her with old Meg? He felt so utterly helpless that it was almost a relief when old Meg thrust him aside. She carried a bowl and a wooden spoon, and taking his place she began to coax Lys, crooning over her, blowing on the broth to cool it, and feeding her drop by drop. Gradually Lys's tears dried; with her eyes on old Meg she took the food as, many years ago, Stephen had seen her take food from their mother's hand.

As he watched, Stephen grew more and more bewildered. This was Meg as he remembered her when he himself was hurt. Yesterday, with its dark shadows, had gone—But it *had* been true. It was not just his imaginings. Unconsciously he sighed so deeply that old Meg looked round.

"Tush, boy, be not downhearted. The maid is mending. A few hours more and you can take her home."

At that Lys burst into tears again.

"I won't go, I won't go," she cried, "He'll wed me to that man. I daren't go home. Brother, don't force me. I'll run away. I'll do anything, but I swear it, I won't go home."

Stephen suddenly lost patience. "That's all well enough," he cried, "but what will you do—roam the world in your shift? You're no fine lady to choose where you will wed. Run to the parson with your woes: he'll just bid you obey Odo, and Dame Alice

78

would do the same. Come home like a good maid. When Odo sees how you are set against it, he may give way to you. *I'll* be there. I'll look after you."

It was an empty brag. He knew it and so did Lys. She clung desperately to old Meg.

"Let me stay with you; no one will find me here. I'll cook and clean and do all your bidding if only you'll let me stay."

Stephen went suddenly cold. That mustn't happen. "You can't stay," he declared, at his wit's end for a reason. He looked down at Lys, now wrapped tenderly in old Meg's arms. "My lord is coming to search for outlaws. You'll put Meg in dire peril if you are found here. They'll take her for harboring a runaway."

Suddenly Gilles, who had stood silent by the door, spoke for the first time. "What would you say if the maid went as servant to the ladies at Goring?"

Stephen looked at him blankly. "The ladies?"

"Yes, the canonesses at Goring priory. The choir nuns are of noble birth. They are waited on by lay sisters, and the lay sisters by serving wenches. She would be well treated and none would seek her there."

Lys stopped crying. Stephen was incredulous.

"But would they take her?"

"I could arrange it. They know me well enough. I have the ear of the cellaress, the nun who caters for their food. The ladies are partial to venison, and when a buck is killed it is but an act of charity to take a portion to the nuns. And at this moment I *have* a buck. What say you? Shall I ask them?"

"Is Goring a great way off?"

"A half score of miles, no more; easy to reach but far enough to escape notice. She would be safe under the wing of Mother Church."

Stephen turned to Lys. "You heard, child. What say you? Would you go to the nuns?"

She nodded so vigorously that Gilles laughed.

"It seems that we have struck the mark. Bring out your salves and simples, Meg. Get the maid mended as soon as you can. I must carve up the buck before I go to Goring to beg my favor. And clear your pot out, old mother, for a fresh venison stew."

All Swept
and Clean

AFTER eating some bread and drinking a bowl of whey, Stephen set off down the hill hoping to reach Ewelme before the school bell rang. Though he was thankful to have found Lys safe, he knew that there was bound to be trouble ahead. He would be faced with endless questions, and he had not the least idea how to answer them.

To start with, when Lys did not return Odo would certainly go to Parson Saynesbury; the parson would immediately send for him, and what was he to say? If he could not produce a satisfactory answer, the parson would raise a hue and cry, and the whole village would turn out to search. Maids were not allowed to vanish in Parson Saynesbury's flock.

It did not help to remember that apparently Odo knew about old Meg. If he said again what he had said last night, they might go straight there and find Lys hidden. That would be disaster. What they might do to old Meg he dared not think, but Gilles would be taken for poaching the roebuck, and he himself would be utterly shamed. And it would all be for nothing, for Lys herself would be sent back to Odo and married to the quarryman. It was well known that the parson liked to get the maids of his parish wed at the first possible moment. He would certainly be on Odo's side.

Stephen shivered with sheer weariness, and paused, his back against a tree, thinking desperately. What he needed was some story to put them off till Lys was safely at Goring. Once she was in the nunnery, the parson would not be likely to bring her back. Of course there would be questions. He would be in as much peril as ever, but Lys, at least, would be safe.

Driven by despair, he began to invent a story. There was an old gossip of his mother's who lived near Abingdon. If he could make them believe that he had found Lys wandering and taken her there, it might be a day or two before anybody bothered about bringing her back. The parson was always busy, and Odo might well hesitate to face Lys in the presence of her mother's familiar friend.

He gave a deep sigh; it was a good story, well worth trying, and he stood a little while to get all the details perfect. Of course it was all a tissue of lies, but he *must* tell lies if he was to save Lys. The thought that followed made him turn cold. *This* was what came of dealing with the devil: the devil was the prince of lies.

That brought him straight back to the question of old Meg. Was she *really* sworn to the devil? If so, he was doing a terrible thing in leaving Lys with her. Lys might be lost, body and soul, through his fault. Then just as quickly as the thought had come, another took its place. He saw a picture in his mind of old Meg, her arm round Lys, feeding her with that warm smile of tenderness on her old face. Could anyone so loving be *evil?* Could anybody evil be compassionate? That was the problem. If Meg was of the devil, how came it that she was so kind, so gentle, so good?

His head swam with it. He felt suddenly grown-up. He was no longer a boy; he was a man, alone, and responsible for Lys. There was no one to help him. He must make up his own mind. He pulled himself together and continued down the hill.

The school bell was still ringing when he reached the village. But as he rounded the corner, a party of horsemen emerged from the gatehouse of the Hall, and he drew back into the shadow of a buttress. In front was my lord himself with the chaplain, Master Simon Brayles. For a moment his heart stood still. Was this to be the threatened raid into the hills? Then to his relief he noted that my lord was unarmed. He was dressed in dark clothes with an elaborate scalloped hood wound round his head and a riding cloak over his back. The four men-at-arms who followed had saddlebags and one led a loaded baggage horse. Obviously my lord was starting on a journey.

The bell had stopped by the time Stephen turned into the porch. His heart was beating noisily. Would the questions begin at once?

This morning it should have been Parson Saynesbury at the master's desk. He saw at a glance that it was old Ferry, the parish clerk: a gentle little man, bald except for a graying frill of feathery hair. What did this mean? Had the parson already been called out by Odo? Forcing himself to be calm, Stephen made his bow and murmured in Latin his act of contrition for being late. The clerk looked up with bright eyes.

"You've heard the news?" he said. "Parson has been summoned to the Hall. The Earl of Warwick has died in France, and my lord is riding to Westminster. Dame Alice is conferring with Parson about a requiem and a dirge as a mark of honor. And of course, as Master Brayles has gone with my lord, all the arranging falls as usual with *us*."

Stephen relaxed like a slackened bowstring. He was not sure who the Earl of Warwick might be, but if Parson Saynesbury's hands were so full he would have less time for Odo.

"Know you, has my stepfather been here?" It was a rash question but he could not resist it.

"Not that I've heard. Why?" The little man winked. "Have you been up to mischief?"

This was getting too near the mark. Stephen

grinned and retired with his Donatus to the quietest corner of the room. He was already bent over it when he heard the parson's cheerful voice booming its way toward the School. A moment later the door opened, and everyone stood up.

Parson Saynesbury had a smiling, rosy, apple face, a figure like a barrel, and a rolling gait that swung him briskly about his business. His hand was always poised to scatter blessings, but his shrewd eyes missed nothing. He swept through the schoolroom, waving the children back to work.

"Solemn requiem mass for the Earl of Warwick tomorrow," he called to Ferry. "My lady will be there. See that the children have clean faces." Then with astonishing agility he climbed the steep little stairs to his sanctum over the porch. Stephen heard the unmistakable creak of the stool as the parson set his weight upon it and remembered the copy of *The Canterbury Tales* under the parson's nose. It might serve as a reminder. He was right. Only a few minutes passed before he heard his name called.

"Where is your Latin from yesterday?" Parson Saynesbury inquired as Stephen stood before him. "And you did not present yourself to serve mass this morning. Were you ill, or did you laze abed?"

Thankful that the questions were no worse, Stephen answered the first part. He said quickly that Dame Alice had brought some copying, and he had laid everything aside to do it.

"Yes, I've heard about that. She told me how she found you turning her grandsire's good English into bad Latin." He paused for a rumbling chuckle. "Truth to tell you made your mark. If your Latin is bad your handwriting is considered excellent, and she graciously praised your manners. In fact you are in high favor."

Stephen, first hot then cold, murmured his thanks. He had expected so much trouble that to hear himself praised left him bewildered. For a moment he wondered if it would be wiser to own up now and tell the parson everything, before it all came out, as it was bound to do. But that would mean leaving Lys to her fate with the quarryman.

Parson Saynesbury settled the question by continuing. "My lord is pleased with you too. He sees the likeness to your father. They are both considering your future. When Ferry and I have finished trying to hammer some rudiments of learning into your thick skull, my lady would have you study with the chaplain, Master Brayles. Note that he is *Master* Brayles, a man of a university, as I am not. But you will have to wait. He has ridden to Westminster with my lord. Of course you know why?"

He waited for an answer and Stephen, his mind in a whirl, said, "Yes sir. The Duke of Gloucester has died."

The parson threw up his hands. "Heaven defend us. Are you a half-wit? Know you not Gloucester from

Warwick? The Earl of Warwick, the great Sir Richard
Beauchamp, was the noblest knight in England.
Henry the Fifth trusted him, and him only, with the
upbringing of his infant son, our lord the King now
reigning. 'Tis said he was a stern tutor, but the boy
loved him, and when his pupil came of age Warwick
of his own free will humbly took service again in
France though he was ripe of years. He died there,
may God rest him. There are few like him though
some would fancy to wear his shoes."

Stephen suddenly caught his breath. He seemed to
hear Meg's voice as he had heard it yesterday. "*I tell
you, master—I saw death in the water.*" The parson
glancing at him misread his response. "Yea, boy, the
world is like that. I'll warrant that others besides my
lord are racing to Westminster. Ambition can stir
even the noblest. The apostles themselves were not
free of it. You remember James and John who begged
to sit on the right hand and on the left?"

Stephen said "Yes, sir," and then begging to take
The Canterbury Tales again, he managed to get himself dismissed. Back at his bench he stared into space.
Another thought had come to him. He *had* written
nearly a page of Latin yesterday, but he had used it
to roll up the copy of Dame Alice's letter. He had intended to burn that letter on the cottage fire, but the
worry about Lys had put it completely out of his
head. Surely it must still be in his satchel. He glanced
across the schoolroom to the peg where, from force of

habit, he had hung it when he came in. The satchel was there sure enough but it drooped emptily. He wanted to get up and look forthwith, but with all eyes on him he did not dare. His face might give him away. So he bent over his work, silently praying "Oh God, let it be there. Mary and all the saints, *pray* that it may be there."

Deluged with one trouble after another, he forced himself to wait quietly till the bell sounded for the midday break. Only then did he stroll across with a casual air and fumble in the satchel. Except for a handful of crumbs and his old hood, it held nothing at all.

As the children all hurried away to the buttery, he stood rooted to the spot. The roll could have fallen out when he flung down the satchel and kneeled to rekindle the fire last night; the floor was so deep in rushes that anything could be lost there. Or possibly he had carried it to old Meg's with Lys's clothes; possible but not likely, for somebody would have noticed it, himself or Lys or Meg or Gilles, or even the half-wit Wat. There had been bright sunshine this morning whereas last night at Odo's it was pitch dark.

In the meantime he was hungry. He followed the children to the buttery and accepted the "pittance" of bread and broth provided daily for the scholars. That finished, he considered where he would go to avoid being questioned before school began again. It was a miracle that Odo had not appeared already; he might arrive at any time. Often in the middle of the day Stephen went to see Doggett, but now he must avoid Doggett until he could say truthfully that he had burned Dame Alice's letter.

The most promising place was the church. It was empty except for a couple of old women telling their beads, who took no notice of him. So he settled behind a pillar where he could see anybody coming. He crossed himself devoutly and tried to say a prayer, though he almost feared to pray, seeing that he was planning to tell a pack of lies. But he had so much to ask: that Lys might go to Goring before anyone should question where she was; that Dame Alice's letter might be at Odo's cottage; and that his guardian angel would find him somewhere to live. It had just begun to dawn on him that he himself was homeless. He could not go back to Odo's without giving Lys away, and to sleep at old Meg's would only sink him deeper into the mire.

He was almost relieved when he heard the bell ring for afternoon school. Kneeling by himself in the church, it was almost impossible to escape the thought that everything that had happened had been his fault. It had all started with his visit to old Meg.

The light outside was dazzling after the dark church. The first thing he saw was a solitary figure climbing the steep path toward him. At first he thought it was Odo, and his heart missed a beat. But soon he recognized Tom laboring up the hill with a sack of flour from the mill slung over his back. The relief was so great that Stephen cried, "Hi! I'll give you a hand with that."

Tom let the sack slide to the ground and wiped his sweaty brow. "We got the otter," he cried triumphantly. "Master came himself but he gave me a groat just the same. What happened to you? You slept late?"

"In a sense," said Stephen. "I'm sorry. If you'd been going tonight I could have bedded at the mill and been on the spot. I'd have been glad of it." He decided to be frank. "Truth to tell there's trouble with my stepfather and I've nowhere to sleep."

"You can sleep at the mill if you want to," said Tom hospitably. "Master would be glad enough. One of the lockmen has a sick wife, and we could do with an extra hand toward night. Doubtless you'd get your supper for your pains."

If this was the answer to his short prayer, his guardian angel was certainly giving good measure. Stephen joyfully helped to carry the heavy sack to the buttery before he ran down the path to the school. Old Ferry saw him come but took no notice of him. Obviously there was still no trouble from Odo. He settled down at his bench suddenly realizing that he was very tired. It was hot. He'd slept little last night. The parson's bees droned outside. The children droned inside. Stephen's chin dropped on his chest.

He was roused by the noise of the children tidying

the room and glanced guiltily at the desk. Had old Ferry noticed him? But the clerk wasn't there. The light streamed in from an open door. He looked around. Old Ferry stood in the porch talking earnestly with Odo.

For a moment Stephen was dazed. Then his wits returned to him. If Odo was here, the way was open to get Dame Alice's letter. Whatever trouble he had to face afterward, he would feel safer when that copy was on Doggett's fire.

A tiny door led from the schoolroom to the yard. He plunged through it, scattering the children, and, well out of sight from the porch, he made for the hill and the short cut to Odo's cottage.

He arrived to find the door barred from within. That was unusual, but it did not trouble him. He went around to the byre at the back where the oxen knew him and did not even pause in their munching. One of the wattle screens that shut off the byre from the cottage was loose. He prised it open and pushed through.

Inside he stood rooted to the spot. The whole place had been swept clean. Even in his mother's day he had never seen it cleaner. The inches-deep litter of old rushes was gone; hardly a handful of ashes remained on the hearth, and the caldron, newly scoured, lay on its side to dry. There was an acrid smell which meant that the refuse had been thrown upon the fire before the hearth was cleared. Appalled, he poked about among the thin scattering of new rushes, but the earth floor underneath was as bare as a plate. If the roll of paper had been there, it must have been burned with everything else.

Some woman had been here—presumably Odo's intended wife.

On a sudden impulse he climbed to the loft. There was no change here. He himself had taken the cloak and shifts from the clothesline. Then it occurred to him to look in the coffer. The winter bedcover lay flat at the bottom; everything else had gone. Odo had seized all Lys's treasures.

Stephen's fury had almost reached boiling point when one of the oxen lowed softly. The others joined in. It was a gentle friendly sound, and he knew what it meant. Odo was coming. Without hesitation Stephen leaped down the ladder, pushed through the hurdle, and darted into the nearest thicket.

He heard Odo's voice crooning to his beasts. He would find at once that someone had broken in, but that did not matter. This part of the wood was home ground to Stephen; he knew every inch of it, and he put a good mile between himself and the cottage before he stopped to draw breath.

He had convinced himself completely that the letter had been burned with the old rushes. Either at night when he threw the satchel down or in the morning when he seized it again, the roll had fallen out. Somebody had gathered it up and cast it on the fire. Whether it was Odo or Odo's wench did not matter at all; neither of them could read and neither would care a jot for a paper of his, mixed up with the rubbish. It was as safely burned as if he had burned it himself. As for his mother's treasure, for the moment he could do nothing.

But what Odo had said to old Ferry was a different question. He must certainly have reported that Lys was missing. The two of them would have gone to the parson. Even now a search party might be setting out. It was odd that Odo had come home. Perhaps he had come to fetch his lantern. Perhaps—

Suddenly overwhelmed with weariness, Stephen leaned against a tree. He could think no more. The only course for him was to keep out of the way. Luckily no one would suspect that he was sleeping at the mill. He would give the village a very wide berth.

Jak the Miller

Stephen set off at once, making a beeline across open country toward the river. At first it was all downhill, but presently the land flattened into water meadows, lush with spring grass and shaded mauve with dancing lady's smock. Angry peewits circled overhead as he crossed their nesting ground, but he took no notice. There was no Lys to welcome a capful of plover's eggs.

It was nearly two miles to the mill from Odo's cottage. He had been there once before, seeking Tom, but had left in a hurry and never returned. Red Jak the miller, one of my lord's old warriors, was a huge man with a rough tongue, a fiery red beard, and one dark bristling eyebrow; the other had been cut away in battle, leaving an eyeless socket and scars that were horrible to see. In the village they said he was half-crazed, a dangerous fellow. But he was loyal to my lord—an enemy to my lord's enemies—and Tom called him a good master if one learned to turn his wrath.

Stephen had met him only once, when, trespassing along the riverbank in search of swan's quills for Doggett, Red Jak had come raging after him, suspecting a raid upon his fish kiddles, the enclosures where he raised young stock for fishponds and small fry for pig food and manure. This one encounter was enough, and Stephen had ventured there no more.

Today however was different. Red Jak's reputation was all to the good. Nobody from the village ever approached the mill. Stephen would be safe there from prying eyes.

All the same his heart quickened as he drew near to the screen of trees sheltering the island on which the mill stood. There were several islands divided by separate branches of the river, all half lost in a tangle of reeds and willows. The sound of rushing water grew steadily louder, and here and there he caught a glimpse of tumbling white foam.

The miller himself was alone on the near bank tossing great sacks of meal into a barge as though they were mere loaves of bread. Stephen slowed down. Obviously the miller was unaware of him until the sloping sun threw Stephen's shadow onto the grass. Then, with a startled grunt, Red Jak swung around.

"Who's this?" he demanded, looking Stephen up and down. "Saints in heaven, surely you're not the extra hand that Tom bespoke? I said a *strong* fellow, not a whipster in a clerk's gown. What good are you? Have you ever raised a flash from the lock with the stream behind it? It's like a bucking horse." He stopped and bellowed through his hands, "Tom— Tom!"

He roared so fiercely that moorhens beneath the bank fled screeching across the water.

Tom came bounding sure-footed across a plank bridge. "You said get *somebody*, master," he declared unabashed. "If Stephen and I work together, we'll equal one strong man."

"More like one tadpole," the miller growled. "If he drowns I'll not answer for it. Still, I suppose he's better than none. At least he can look out for barges. Take him and rid him of that holy gear. I've had enough of clerks for one day. And mark you, my fine scholar, your learning will not save your skin if you let down my head of water."

Wishing he had never come, Stephen followed Tom across the bouncing plank that crossed the swirling torrent from the millrace. On the other side stood the granary, a large shed built of tarred wood.

"You can doff your clothes here," Tom encouraged him. "Just gird your shirt as I do. You'll need no more. Your toes will grip better than your shoon on wet planks."

"What's a head of water?" Stephen inquired anxiously. "He said he'd beat me if I let it down."

"Take no heed. He's in savage mood thanks to some fat lordly clerk who came to order special passage for a barge of books to pass upstream to Oxford. To order, mark you—order the toughest miller on the river. To make matters worse, the fellow spoke in the name of Duke Humphrey, which is like waving a red flag at a bull—I know not why; some grudge begotten in the wars, I think. But mark you my words, there'll be trouble in plenty when that barge does appear."

Stephen drank this in. He was certain about the identity of the "fat lordly clerk," but it seemed wiser to say nothing.

"You've not told me what's a head of water," he repeated.

"It's just the water flowing into the millstream to keep the mill wheel turning. If the lock is open too long the upper river drains away, and time is lost till the head of water builds up again. There's always trouble between millers and barge masters because both need the water for their trade. I've known heads broken over it. Hurry up now. Aren't you ready? If a barge should come when no watch is set, we'll both get a beating."

With his shirt girded round his loins Stephen followed Tom out onto the narrow island on which the millhouse and the granary were built. The noisy mill-race lay behind them. Ahead was another thunder of water from the weir built right across the river where the stream plunged over the clifflike edge in a flurry of foam.

" 'Tis one of the deepest falls on the river," shouted Tom, as though he were proud of it. " 'Tis a real peril for a barge to face the rapids."

"Why have a weir at all?" Stephen shouted back. "Can't the river look after itself?"

Tom shook his head vigorously. "You must hold up the water level or it would soon run to shallows and be of no use for shipping. You're standing on the lock now. Hold on tight and look over the edge."

Stephen found that he was clinging to the handrail of a long, rickety bridge poised on the crest of the cascading water. He could feel the pressure beneath him as he looked from the level of the upper river onto the eddying pools several feet below.

"How do you open it?" he gasped.

"That's the rub! Deep in the water is a wall of paddles, called flashes, which fit into sockets. These upright shafts are the handles, and you have to pull up several to open a gap. The water rushes through, and as soon as the two levels are nearly one, the upgoing craft is dragged up and downward ones shoot the rapids. Lay your hand on a shaft to know what it feels like— Nay! For pity's sake don't raise it on our own, or we lose that head of water with a vengeance."

Stephen was thankful to let go. Red Jak had spoken truly when he said "a bucking horse."

"You see now how it is," grinned Tom. "But don't worry. Your job is but to watch for barges coming up or down. They'll pull into the bank and hail you. All you have to do is to fetch *us*. I'm off to help the miller at the fish kiddles. There was a pike about this morning. There'll be havoc if it gets in among the small fry."

The footbridge bounced up and down as he pushed past Stephen and made off toward the mill.

Left to himself Stephen stood clutching the rail and staring downstream. In spite of the weir it seemed wonderfully quiet after all the turmoil of the day. A pair of mallards skimmed in a silver line across the surface of the water. Overhead, swallows and swifts hawked for flies. Up in those hills, which looked so far away, Lys was for the present safe in old Meg's keeping. Odo's cottage was more distant still. Even Ewelme itself was hidden from sight. Nobody knew where he was: for the moment he was at peace.

So much had happened in one day that it seemed impossible to believe that it was barely twenty-four hours since he had walked home eager to tell Lys all his good news. A stranger had offered him a place at Oxford; Dame Alice had trusted him with her copying; and my lord had seen in him the likeness to his father and instantly shown signs of favor. And then suddenly everything changed. Odo had become an enemy. Lys was lying at old Meg's, and he feared what might happen if she were found there. And to make matters worse he had lost the fatal copy of Dame Alice's letter—for, though he told himself that Odo had burned it, deep within him there lurked a nagging doubt.

He tried deliberately to forget that in the morning he would have to face problems again. Odo's meeting with old Ferry could only mean that Lys's absence was now public property. Ferry would have told the parson and the parson would demand the truth— He rested his head upon his arms and yawned. He was utterly weary. Come what may, he could not think any more.

A voice from the island brought him back to life. It was the miller's wife, a neat little woman with gray hair tucked under a spotless coif. She smiled as she beckoned. He stepped cautiously off the bridge and went to her.

"You're Stephen Rudd?" she said. "Faith, how the years do fly. I saw you last clinging to your mother's gown, God rest her. Come you now and eat. There's a trout for you and barley bread if your stomach wills."

Stephen's stomach was certainly willing. He followed her past the granary to where the millhouse stood overlooking the quiet corner of the millstream. On the bank lit by the golden evening sun sat Red Jak himself, straddling a tree trunk and nibbling a broiled fish impaled on a wooden skewer. He grunted pleasantly enough at Stephen while his wife vanished indoors and reappeared with more fish on a trencher of dark bread, followed by Tom bearing a jug of ale and a basket of little barley loaves.

"Here you are, boy," she said cheerfully. "Get you to work; you must be hungry."

Stephen needed no persuasion; little did she know how hungry. He propped himself against a pollard willow and holding a trout by head and tail picked the backbone clean. As he licked the last vestige of juice from his fingers, he looked up to see Red Jak, the scarred side of his face in shadow, actually grinning at him.

"Take a swill of ale to wash it down," he invited. "I had not grasped till now that you are John Rudd's son. He fought beside me at Orleans. How fare you with that clodhopper of your mother's now she's gone? 'Twas sad that she had needs wed a great boor like that."

Stephen seized his chance. He had left Odo, he said, and was seeking a place to live where he could work his keep after school hours.

"You can sup and bed here till you find better," said the miller promptly, "though we're unlettered folk to mingle with booklearners. Tell me, an' you're at God's House, how fares that old bludgeoner, Doggett? His mother-wit has got him a soft dwelling."

Stephen said that Doggett was in good heart. He was to paint shields of arms on the walls of Dame Alice's solar.

Red Jak chuckled. "He's coveted a herald's tabard all his days. I mind me that after Agincourt, when he was already seasoned and I but a hobidyhoy, we joined some Kentish men turning over a monstrous pile of French dead. It was Doggett who spotted the lilies of France on a surcoat among all the blood and havoc and read the blazoning—none other than the Duke of Orleans. But one of the Kentish men, a squire named Waller, saw that the corpse still breathed and dragged the duke out, to his glory, where the glory should really have been Doggett's."

"Was that the French duke that was prisoner here at Ewelme?"

"None other. 'Twas strange that he and Doggett who saved him should both have taken their place in the king's triumphant return to London. Poor young man, I'll wager that he would rather have been left for dead, if he had known how long he was to lack his freedom."

The miller's wife broke in. "Talking of grand folk, husband, who was that fine lord who angered you this forenoon—the one in dark red, leading a horse? I heard you raise your voice to him."

"Lord?" said the miller scornfully. "He was no lord; just some bragging clerk claiming Duke Humphrey's authority to send a great barge of books up over the weir without so much as a by your leave. I told him that Duke Humphrey did not own the river Thames, and I'd douse him and his books as readily as I'd douse any that stole my head of water."

His wife shook her head at him. "Much good all that will do you. The one you want to douse is the witch of Gloucester, his so-called duchess. 'Tis she who has been his ruin. He was a fine young prince when his brother Harry the Fifth had him wed to a true princess. But when King Harry died this she-devil, Eleanor Cobham, cast her spells over him, parted him from his true wife, and turned him into a vainglorious braggart."

"True enough," growled the miller. "I'll swear that these books are but more vainglory. It would do my heart good to let the river take the lot." He tossed his fishbones angrily to an eager cat and stretched his great arms wearily. But his keen little wife pricked up her ears.

"Hark! There's a shout upriver. Tom, go you and look. Maybe there's a barge waiting."

While her husband grumbled that he'd not open for any after sunset, Tom ran off and came back breathless to say that it was a barge to go down without delay, adding nervously that it was for the Duke of Gloucester, who had ridden in haste to Westminster, leaving his gear to follow.

Red Jak jumped angrily to his feet. "That coxcomb again? Am I a serf to cringe before him? First his gear and next his books—at any moment, regardless of my head of water. Before heaven, one day I'll teach him a lesson—"

"*One* day but not *now*," said the goodwife calmly. "Let's be done with it while there's light to see." As he strode away, she held the two boys back. "Get you to the lock and be ready," she whispered. "He'll let it through *this* time but God assuage us at the next."

With a knowing grin Tom led the way. Stephen, following, thought of my lord of Suffolk also riding to Westminster, both, it seemed, intent upon a pair of empty shoes.

Soon Red Jak appeared grunting orders that only Tom could understand. But, copying Tom, Stephen boldly gripped a paddle shaft, the miller's great fists gripped below his, and to his astonishment the paddle slipped out smoothly, was laid aside, and three others followed it. The water of the upper river burst forth in a torrent; the barge like a dark shadow floated faster and faster toward the edge of the weir till it plunged swiftly downward in a cataract of spray. Stephen held his breath until the barge had slackened speed beyond the rapids of the lower river. It was so exciting that only when he reached a deep bed of chaff in the loft above the granary did he realize that he ached in every limb.

Tom, no stranger to aching muscles, slept at once, but Stephen, weary to death, lay on his back wide awake. His mind tossed from one problem to another. First of all what was he to say to the parson in the morning, for without doubt Ferry would have handed on Odo's news? Would they have found Lys at old Meg's? Would they think she was already besmirched with witchcraft? What was the truth about these accursed witches who lurked in every corner? There was this new one, the witch of Gloucester, whom he had never heard of before. There was the French witch, Jeanne d'Arc, who had a hand in killing his father. There was the other French witch, the young king's mother, Queen Katharine, widow of Harry the Fifth. She had lodged at Wallingford Castle; he'd seen her often when he was small, and now people said that she had been a witch. And there was *an-*

other queen, an old one, Queen Joanna of Navarre. He didn't know who she was, save that she'd been a friend of old Sir Thomas Chaucer and given him lands which belonged to Dame Alice now. Doggett had told him all this because she had a rare coat of arms, like a great spider; Doggett had drawn it. It *was* like a spider. Perhaps the spider was a witch— Suddenly he realized that Tom was shaking him.

"What is it?" he gasped. "I was dreaming."

"*Dreaming*, did you say?" growled Tom. "You've been roaring the place down. What ails you?"

"I was dreaming about witches," said Stephen wearily. " 'Twas a vile dream. Is it true, think you? Is the world full of witches?"

Tom dived back to his bed. " 'Twas talking about the witch of Gloucester set you off," he observed sagely. "As for witches, the paternoster says 'deliver us from evil' and we pray that all the time, so I suppose it's true. I've heard of one witch near Abingdon who makes cows go dry. My grandam says there's a witch up in the woods who stares into the water to

COBHAM   NAVARRE

see signs; but she does brew potions that do people good, so she can't be *all* evil. My grandam says that her salve for curing corns is like none other. She got some from her once in Wallingford market."

He yawned noisily, and soon his heavy breathing proved that he slept. Stephen lay quiet, no longer tossing and turning. As he too drifted off for the second time, Tom's words remained with him: "*She stares into water to see signs.*"

"It Is Burned"

IN SPITE of bad dreams Stephen woke early and, grateful for the invitation to return in the evening, left the mill before the sun was up.

Even at this hour Red Jak and Tom were busy with the lock. There were already two barges waiting to go upstream and three others, heavily laden with stone for the king's new college at Eton, ready to go down. The miller was in high spirits. He could clear all five, two up and three down, at a single lifting of the paddles and pocket five separate payments with only one loss of his head of water. Stephen trudged up the hill growing more sick at heart with every step. In spite of all the near-miracles which had turned up to save him, he was well aware that he had devised no story which would stand up to the parson's questioning.

But the greatest miracle was yet to come. He arrived with plenty of time to prepare for the solemn requiem for the Earl of Warwick. When the altar was set and the candles all lighted, Dame Alice appeared with members of her household. The bedesmen formed their procession, the ceremonies were carried through without a hitch, and at the end of it all he met the parson face to face in the sacristy. The parson smiled at him—and said nothing at all.

Stephen made his way slowly toward the schoolhouse, his knees shaking as though he had already been questioned and condemned. Unable to bear it any longer, he turned into the school and sat down at his bench. He was early. The place was empty except for old Ferry. With his own eyes he had seen Ferry deep in talk with Odo. Now it was *bound* to come.

Sure enough the clerk left his desk and came across to him. "I've had you in mind ever since I saw your stepfather last night. Tell me, how will you fare when he weds again?"

Stephen gaped at him. "*Weds,*" he repeated.

"Surely you know? He came to give notice so that Parson might call the bans." He tutted with annoyance and slapped his leg. "Forsooth now, my head is like a sieve. I've just been with the parson and I've not yet told him— What of the young woman? She's from Brightwell Salome, it seems. Is she comely?"

Stephen held his voice steady. "I've not seen her. Did Odo make mention of me—or my sister?"

"Not a word. That's why I wondered how you would fare. I would have sought you out yesternight but I was sent to the Hall with messages. Shall you leave home?"

"I've left already. I lodge at the mill. Red Jak has given me place. He used to know my father." The words were hardly out before he wished them back. The next question would be, "Where then is your sister?" But it did not come.

Old Ferry nodded. "At the mill? That's a good notion, if you can abide Red Jak's bullheadedness. I suppose your sister will wait on the new wife till she too gets a husband? If the bride is from Brightwell seemingly the wedding will be there—just a porch wedding I'll be bound. If *she* has no more piety than *he* has, they're not likely to beg a nuptial mass. I venture we'll see little of them here. Come now, we must stay our tongues. Parson is with my lady, ordering matters, and I must keep the children busy."

Stephen leaned over his bench, scarcely able to take it in. At one stroke his nightmare had been broken. Odo had said nothing at all except about his own marriage. Maybe he was ashamed of his treatment of Lys, or more likely he had helped himself to Lys's treasure, knowing full well that Stephen could not mention it without giving himself and Lys away. Now the one thing necessary was for Lys to go to Goring. With miracles plentiful he shut his eyes and prayed so intensely that he felt that he was *ordering* God. Of course there *would* be questions about Lys, sooner or later. But if they were later and he could just say that she was a serving wench at the nunnery, all would be well.

At midday he decided to visit Doggett. Perhaps as

he had been saved from questions about Lys, he might also escape questions about the letter.

Doggett, chilly with age, sat on a stool by the hearth, supping bread and broth. He raised one bushy eyebrow, nodded, and spooned up all that was left in the bowl. Then smacking his lips he handed over bowl and spoon and pointed to the pot.

"Help yourself," he said. "Though you're a worthless knave, I suppose you'll not say nay." He watched cunningly till Stephen's mouth was full and then demanded, "Why have you not come to tell me what befell with my lady's letter? What said she? Was it there by mischance?"

Stephen, breathless with hot soup, nodded and gasped out, "Yea. She was overjoyed to see it."

"I'll warrant she was," Doggett chuckled. "Did she ask if you had copied it?"

"Nay. Seemingly it did not enter her head."

"Then what did you do with it? I told you to bring it back here for burning."

"It is burned," said Stephen without hesitation. "I was so late that I went straight home. My lord had come in lit up with wrath. You know that Templar was shot dead?"

"None could live here and not know that. What said my lord? The village whispers sorcery."

Stephen suddenly decided to tell him the whole story about Lys being struck down by Templar while running away from Odo, about Gilles killing the hound to save her and carrying her to old Meg, to be nursed and kept safe from Odo and the quarryman.

Doggett sat frowning heavily. "I'll keep your secret," he said, "but I like it not. An old witch is no nurse for a young maid. You may have saved her from a luckless wedlock only to hand her to the devil."

"Old Meg is no servant of the devil, that I'll swear. You should see her with Lys: she's as gentle as a mother. And Gilles is going to find safe lodging for the child with the holy nuns at Goring."

Doggett still shook his head. "Then bid him be quick about it, and if she goes do you go with her to put her safely in their hands. I trust not these outlaws."

At that moment the school bell rang, but as Stephen made for the door the old man called him back.

"Now that your copy of that letter is burned," he said, "see that you never refer to it again. If Dame Alice realized that you had copied it she would suffer the pains of purgatory, even though the copy is safely burned. And if any is to suffer, better you than she. So lie about it if you must." He sighed. "In any case I would be thankful to know that the letter itself has safely reached her daughter Salisbury. In the wrong hands it could be deadly as a viper."

Stephen returned to school with his conscience faintly pricking him. Had he made it clear to Doggett that he had not *watched* the letter burn? Though of course there was no possible doubt about it; nothing could have escaped the heavy hand of Odo's new wife.

But the first thing was to go to Lys. How was she? What was to become of her? Had the archer managed to find a place for her with the ladies, and if so how soon could she go?

As soon as afternoon school was over, he slipped away toward the hills. The undergrowth was still flattened where the buck had been killed, but the sun shone and the woods were dappled with light. It seemed no time before he caught a glimpse of the silvery woodpecker tree. Cautiously he called out "Hi Hi Ho," his special signal with Lys. To his delight she called back to him clearly and strongly, not so very far away, and as he rounded the edge of the pool he saw her actually running to meet him. Except for a bruise and a few scratches, she looked the picture of health.

"What has she done to you?" he exclaimed holding her at arms' length. " 'Tis but two days since you were near to death."

"She is wonderful," cried Lys. "Never was anyone so good. She plastered me with salves and tended me without ceasing. Then she dipped me three times in the pool and laid me in the sun to dry. 'Twas like a miracle. But listen; I've not told you the best—I am going to the nunnery. The ladies have said they will have me. I'm to work in the kitchen. 'Tis Gilles who has done that. He came in last night and said he would take me on Sunday."

Stephen remembered Doggett. "I will come with you," he said quickly. "I am your brother. I must see where you are lodged."

"Well spoken," said old Meg from behind them. She stood in the doorway, her hand stretched out to Lys. "Are you pleased with our handiwork? The maid has been a good maid and done all that she was bidden. She slept like a babe last night and rose fresh this morning. You have heard her story, I can see. Now come you and tell us yours."

With all the strains and miseries gone from him, Stephen sat down in the sun, his back against the wall. This was the peace which he had so often come here to seek. He told them about lodging at the mill and that Odo, soon to be wed, had not mentioned either Lys or himself. He had stolen Lys's dowry, but surely it was wiser to keep silent until she was safely in the nunnery.

Lys clasped her hands. "I need no dowry," she cried. "I am to be a kitchen wench."

"And a good one too," old Meg broke in. "All the morning I could not stay her. She has swept the floor clean with rake and broom, and Wat has carried all the muck away. The Ladies should be glad of such a work-hungry maid. Look you for yourself.."

He glanced obediently over his shoulder and saw to his surprise that all the dirt had vanished. Gone were the heavy festoons of cobwebs, the droppings under the owl's perch, the bones among the sodden rushes on the floor. As the sunlight poured in, it reminded him of the spring clean at Odo's cottage. A thought came to him.

"When you were sweeping," he said, "did you perchance come upon some papers, rolled tightly together? 'Tis a Latin lesson that I have lost. 'Tis possible I dropped it here when I brought your shift and shoon."

She shook her head. "I swept carefully. The floor was quite bare when I spread fresh bracken. Was it a big roll? And will you be in trouble for it?"

"It is really no great matter," he said quickly; it seemed wiser to make little of it. " 'Tis certain that I left it at Odo's and it went upon *his* fire." To amuse them he described the changes already wrought by Odo's future wife. Then arranging that he would meet Lys and Gilles on Sunday morning after the parish mass, at the point where the Old Road divided, he cheerfully took his leave. There could be no mistaking the spot. It was where he had parted from Master Bolingbroke.

He set off at a brisk pace, not by the woodpecker tree but by a steeper path which would lead more directly to Benson Mill. As he turned to look back at Lys and old Meg from the far side of the pool, he felt a wave of thankfulness. His prayers had been answered in good measure. There were only two more days to Sunday, and after that he would be able to say truthfully that his sister was serving wench to the canonesses at Goring priory.

The woods were quite different on this side of the hills. There was little undergrowth. Tall beech trees rose from a carpet of bronze and gold. Here and there were deep pits where leaves collected and fluttered crisply when the wind blew.

Before he had gone far a foul smell assailed him. Was it a dead deer, he wondered? Out of sheer curiosity he stepped aside to look. One glance was enough. The smell came from a small pit half full of dirty rubbish. Obviously this was Wat's shambles where he threw the remains of the animals he had skinned. Stephen was turning away in disgust when something white caught his eye sticking out of a pile of newly discarded litter. Holding his breath, he plunged down into the pit and plucked it out. It was a torn piece of paper covered with his own handwriting. As he stared at it he saw that it was *not* Dame Alice's letter; but it *was* the corner of the Latin lesson in which the letter had been rolled.

Frantically he turned the pile over and over with a stick but could find no more; so he scrambled back to the surface to get fresh air and reason it out. Lys had been so sure that she had swept carefully, and yet this— He continued slowly down the hill worrying at the problem as a dog worries at a bone. By the time he reached the bottom, he had worked out an expla-

nation that seemed to fit. When he had flung the
satchel down beside Odo's hearth, the roll must have
dropped out with one corner torn away. That corner
had remained in the satchel, caught up with Lys's shift
and shoon. This fitted perfectly; nothing else was possible.

By the time he reached the riverbank he had convinced himself. Only one disturbing thought remained. Unlike Odo, old Meg could read and write.

The river looked peaceful in the evening light.
Midges rose in clouds. It would be fine tomorrow.
Would it last till Sunday? He walked fast. It was a
pity that the stream curved; it made the distance
greater. But it gave him a clear view of the mill and
the weir. Something was going on. The foam was very
white, as though the upper river overflowed. Several
barges were moored below the lock, and soon he
could hear angry voices as, apparently, their masters
argued with Red Jak because he would not let them
through.

Suddenly he saw Tom running toward him.

"Come on," Tom cried. "You are missing everything."

A thought struck Stephen. "Is it the barge of
books?"

"Books forsooth! 'Tis the Duchess Eleanor herself,
coming from Oxford in a golden barge, while these
fellows are waiting to go up. She's sent messengers
ahead to claim royal rights. Red Jak and the water-

men are in a fury. He's built up a great head of water and swears he'll see her sink or swim like any other witch. Come on. We'll need all hands."

The two of them took to their heels, Stephen pausing only to toss his gown aside before he bounced expertly across the plank. Red Jak, with a couple of watermen dragged into service, stood on the lock bridge staring upstream. The barge was late, he ranted; it had stuck at Long Wittenham; the miller there was a blockhead; he could not handle his weir. Well—he grinned, his scarred face all distorted—if it foundered *here* Wittenham could take the blame.

Suddenly Tom cried "Hoy!" A gilded prow appeared round a bend upstream, followed by gilded blades flashing through the water. Even from so far Stephen spotted the fluttering pennon—a chained white swan, the badge of the Duke of Gloucester. As the barge swept into full view the sun lit up the colors of rich fabrics and the gay clothes of the passengers. One, a woman in bright green and silver with a coif of dazzling white, sat higher than the others. Stephen knew at once that this must be the Duchess Eleanor, "the witch of Gloucester," Master Bolingbroke's "most gracious lady." He watched her intently while the barge drew into the side to await the opening of the lock.

Then Red Jak roared an order, and, with the watermen, threw his great strength onto the shafts, opening not only one or two paddles but the full width of the lock.

With a roar the upper river broke loose and was borne down over the edge in a great foaming torrent. Surely nothing could survive in it? Stephen, poised on the bridge, felt that he too must be swept away, but someone grabbed him, and he found himself head downward clinging to the rail. As he hung there, the barge shot through just beneath him, oars shipped and passengers huddled together screaming, their mouths open but their voices lost.

For one instance the witch of Gloucester herself stared up at him and he stared back. Her coppery hair streamed from her coif, her face was chalky white, and her green eyes, wild with terror, actually met his own.

In a moment it was over, and the barge was riding safely on the lower river. The oarsmen slipped their golden blades back into the rowlocks. Stephen gazed after it, suddenly aware that in that mad turmoil he had caught an impression of a stout man in red. Now from a distance he saw that he was right. Close to the duchess among her companions was Master Bolingbroke.

All night long Stephen dreamed of rushing water and woke to find himself facing a whole day with Red Jak. It was Saturday. Schools were closed on Saturdays so that children could help their parents in the fields. Until now he had always worked with Odo, scaring birds, scouring plow shares, mucking out the byre, or painfully learning to plow a furrow. Now that he was free of Odo, it was his plain duty to earn his keep at the mill.

But today the river was quiet except for small boats carrying people back and forth to market at Wallingford, and Red Jak was in a genial mood, gossiping with neighbors as they lifted the little craft bodily overland or letting them through in shoals, a score or so at each lifting of the lock. Stephen was sent with Tom to clean out the fish kiddles, a messy job, for the sludge of fish scales had to be carefully set aside for the peddlers who bought them to be made into beads for rosaries.

When Red Jak was well out of the way Stephen straightened his back and spoke his thoughts aloud.

"What would have befallen Red Jak if the duchess had really perished yesterday?" he inquired.

Tom grunted. "Ask another. 'Tis his way to strike first and think afterwards."

"Then if he could risk Duke Humphrey's duchess, what will happen to Duke Humphrey's books?"

"Why set such store on books?" said Tom lightly. "What good are they? That fat clerk was on the barge last night. Did you notice him? I'll wager that Red Jak did; 'twill sharpen his temper marvelously."

"All the wisdom of the world is written in books," said Stephen solemnly. "They are more precious than gold. Somehow we must save that barge."

"You can try if you've a mind to, but *I'll* not risk my

skin. Stay, though—I tell you what I'll do. If I hear that they are coming and you are not about, I'll do my best to let you know. 'Twill be for you to save them—if you can."

The Kitchen Wench

*F*OR STEPHEN as scholar of the grammar school, Sunday was hardly a day of rest. First there was matins, sung with candles and ceremony, not merely recited by the parson and the bedesmen as on ordinary days. Early as it was, all the parish came, those from afar making a day of it, tethering their nags at the churchyard wall, sharing food with their kinsfolk or eating their own till it was time for the parish mass. This too was as grand as everyone could make it, with a procession, a sermon, and full-throated singing. It was Stephen's business to light the many candles stuck on prickets all along the rood beam, on the candle wheel hanging from the roof, and of course the tall ones on the altar. In addition he had to carry the holy water when Parson Saynesbury went round dousing the devil out of his flock; and to hold the wide basket of blessed bread at the end of mass, for the people each to take a fragment as a token of the brotherly love which should bind them together.

But after the parish mass he was free till vespers, which in summer was combined with compline, the late evening service, leaving the people just enough time to trudge home peacefully before dark. The parson spent the time visiting the old and sick while the congregation enjoyed their leisure gossiping, shooting at the butts, or playing games on the green. Stephen reckoned that, if only Lys and Gilles did not keep him waiting, he could get to Goring and back in good time.

He hurried up the rise out of the village and soon, to his great relief, saw them waiting far off at the appointed spot. Gilles had brought a small shaggy pony to carry Lys if she grew tired. Seven miles was a long way for a maid who had been ill. But for the present, he said, he would walk ahead so that brother and sister could talk freely. It might well be long before they could do it again.

Left alone with Lys, Stephen was tongue-tied. It came to him suddenly that she was really going. Since their mother's death there had been just the two of them. Now he would have nobody. He stole a glance at her as she tripped along beside him. Though he had prayed so earnestly that the ladies would take her, he would have been better pleased if she had looked a little sad.

But the sun shone from a cloudless sky, and Lys was in high spirits. She chattered merrily about how old Meg had patched her cloak and how Wat had made her mother's old shoes fit her by mending the soles and lining them with soft rabbit skin. Grasping his elbow she stuck out a foot for him to see.

He nodded absently. There was something else on his mind.

"Listen," he said irritably. "That Latin lesson that I lost—are you salvation sure that I did not drop it at old Meg's? I found a corner of it in the rubbish pit, among the dead rushes."

She looked at him blankly. "Then I know not how it got there. I told you 'twas I who swept the floor. I could not have missed it."

He was still uneasy. "Could old Meg have picked it up? She can read and write, you know."

"I *know* she can read and write—and cast up figures too. I watched her with the merchant who came yesterday."

"Merchant? What merchant?"

"I suppose he's the one who buys the furry pelts. Does he come from London? He's clad like a lord."

"What's he like?" Stephen demanded, suddenly wide awake. "Is he a big man, tall, with a thick neck?"

"That's it. He was dressed all in red, with something gold on a chain, and they were counting together. But I couldn't see much. Old Meg sent me out to gather dry wood for kindling, and when I came back he'd gone."

Stephen's heart was throbbing in his throat. He had

no doubt at all that the merchant was Bolingbroke. Suppose, just suppose, that the copy of Dame Alice's letter *had* reached old Meg's—He went quite dizzy as he remembered what Doggett had said about the consequences of that letter going astray. Lys, however, did not notice the change in him. She skipped along beside him chattering happily, until quite suddenly and without warning she turned and faced him with a question.

"Brother, what would you say if I became a nun at Goring?"

Maddened with her prattling he snapped back at her.

"*You! A nun?* You've lost your wits. The nuns at Goring are canonesses—ladies highly born. You are going there as a kitchen wench. You'll earn yourself a beating if you are so bold in your ideas."

But Lys remained serene. "But I *shall* be a nun," she said firmly. "Old Meg saw it in the water, and she called me to see for myself. She was staring into the pool, as she does every day. She bade me lean over till I saw my own face. *Me*, with a white wimple and a white veil. Do the nuns at Goring wear white veils?"

His fury grew. Old Meg, witchcraft, Bolingbroke, Dame Alice's letter—it was all evil, and he and Lys were caught up in it. He rounded on her.

"You dreamed it," he cried. "Either you dreamed it or you are bewitched."

"I didn't dream it. It was day and the sun was shining and I've been so happy since. Oh brother, don't look so angry. It can't be wrong if God means me to be a nun."

"God doesn't show things in water; it's the devil that does that. Old Meg is a witch: everyone knows it. God forgive me for leaving you there. Did you say your prayers?" He seized her by the wrist. "*Can* you say them? Say them now. Say the Our Father."

She began to cry. "Of course I said them. I said them every night and every morning."

"Well, say the Our Father. Now, at once. Let me hear you. Come on—Our Father—"

He gripped her more tightly than ever—shaken as much as she was. Terrified, she struggled with it through her tears: "Our Father who art in heaven, hallowed be—be—be— " Her voice rose shrilly. "I can't. I—I can't remember—"

He dropped her arm roughly. It was true then. She *was* bewitched. The devil had her. To say the Our Father was the test; everyone knew that. Lys stood sobbing helplessly while he stood like a statue, unable to find any words himself. Suddenly he heard Gilles's voice.

"What's amiss? Is the maid hurt? Child, weep not so. What's come to you?"

Lys flung herself upon him in a torrent of tears.

"She's bewitched," said Stephen grimly. "Old Meg has bewitched her. She made her see things in the pool. I bade her say the Our Father, and she can't remember it. Can't remember the Our Father! That's sure proof that she's bewitched."

"You'd not remember if you were stricken like this," said Gilles, his arm round Lys. "Quiet, child, quiet. Break not your heart. Your brother is afraid for your soul because he loves you. 'Tis he who needs the comforting. Stop crying now and humor him. If he wants an Our Father then say it. Come, just to put his mind at rest."

Tremulously Lys began again. This time between sobs and gulps she got to the end. The archer looked at Stephen.

"Make yourself easy," he said. "There's no devil here, only a frightened maid. You are not yet wise enough to tell good from evil. I will tell you how, though as you will recognize, it is not *my* wisdom. *'By their fruits you shall know them.'* That's the test. *'Does a man grow grapes from thorns, or figs from thistles?'* Three days ago this child was all but broken." He lifted Lys gently on to the pony's back. "See her now. Without doubt you see *good* fruit."

Supporting Lys with one hand he led the way. Stephen followed at a distance. What Gilles had said was true. Lys's cure and the promise of her future were both thanks to old Meg. But on the other hand there was not only the gazing into the pool to be accounted for: there was also the writing on the hearth. It was now perfectly clear that Bolingbroke's visit on that stormy day was no accident. Lys had revealed that he was there yesterday.

Immediately his mind went back to Dame Alice's letter. Was it possible that old Meg herself had picked it up and handed it to Bolingbroke? The mere thought of it made his blood run cold. No amount of talking could make good out of that. If it had really happened the devil was in it, and he himself had been the devil's tool.

Left to walk by himself, the way seemed endless. The old road now clear of trees wandered up and down across undulating country, just a track baked hard and fringed with grass and wild flowers. A mile or more away a shimmering mist marked the course of the river. Beyond it another ridge of blue hills ap-

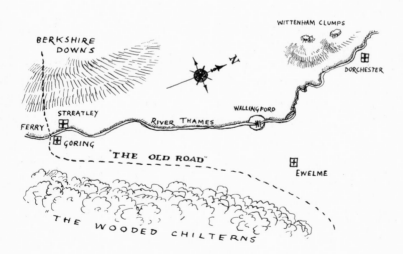

proached to meet the Chilterns, like two clenched
fists with only a crack between them to let the water
through. He knew that Goring lay in that gap. But
the sun blazed down, he had a splitting headache,
and, right or wrong, he wished that he had not
scolded Lys just as he was going to leave her. To his
utter relief he saw that Gilles, with Lys on the pony,
was waiting for him in the shadow of a tree.

"Listen!" cried Gilles. "There lies the object of our
journey. If you cannot see it yet, you can hear it: the
bells of Goring priory."

Noting that Lys was once more happy, Stephen
halted obediently. The chime was short: only three
notes and one of them was cracked. But the sound
floated clearly on the still air.

"There's the river just below," said Gilles cheerfully. "The nunnery stands close beside it."

"Do we have to cross?" asked Stephen, thankful to
be on good terms again.

Gilles shook his head. "Nay, the other side is Streatley, so called, they say, because the Street—the Old
Road—crosses by ford or ferry and climbs that great
hill beyond. Goring lies on this bank."

The nunnery, with its square church tower, its high
boundary wall, and its gatehouse, stood between the
village and the river. Gilles rapped upon an iron-
studded door, and as it opened Lys silently gripped
Stephen's hand.

The doorkeeper, a fat old woman, greeted Gilles merrily.

"Ah, here you are," she said. "Is this the wench you were to bring? She looks likely enough, though a touch more flesh on her bones would do no harm. Come you inside and tether the pony. The ladies are in choir, but Dame Cellaress left word that I should take you to the kitchen. She will not be long."

Gilles thrust the halter into Stephen's hand as they stepped into a cobbled courtyard surrounded by a range of low buildings, much like the outer court of any great house. The old woman pointed to a patch of shade where Stephen could tether the pony and then vanished with Gilles and Lys through a farther door. Nearby stood a well with a bucket attached. Stephen took it upon himself to draw up some water and tip it into a horse trough, cupping his hands to quench his own thirst at the same time. Soon Gilles appeared and beckoned.

Bidding him speak up clearly when he was spoken to, the archer led the way into a large kitchen. Along one wall ran a fireplace furnished with numerous hooks and spits and caldrons. At a table, obviously made from the trunk of a split tree bleached by constant scrubbing, sat a nun, large and plump, wearing a white habit and a black veil. Whispering that this was the lady cellaress, Gilles bade him kneel.

The cellaress looked at him, at Lys who stood beside her, and finally at Gilles.

"So this is the wench's sole kinsman, eh? He is young to be so heavily charged. Tell me, boy, is it true that both your parents are dead and that you alone are accountable for this maid, and further that you wish to leave her here in this house of the canonesses of St. Austin to do such tasks as we may bid her, and to be subject in all things to our obedience? Think well before you answer."

Stephen glanced at Lys. Her eyes, clear and shining, were fixed upon him. She at any rate was in no doubt. So he said, "Yes, madam," boldly and rose to write his name on a piece of parchment where the cellaress indicated. Smiling at the pair of them, she then tore the parchment down the middle in a deliberately jagged line and handed one half to Stephen.

"This is the maid's indenture," she said. "It commits her to serve us for one year. If after that she wishes to leave, bring that back, and we will fit the two halves together to destroy the contract. That completes our business. Now you shall eat before you go, and it shall be your sister's first task to wait on you." She turned to beam at the archer. "There is a pasty which you must taste, good Gilles: it owes its meat to you."

She clapped her hands and a scurrying little band of kitchen wenches, each wearing a wimple and an enveloping white apron, appeared from nowhere carrying bread, cheese, a jug of ale, and finally half an enormous venison pasty. So many wenches all at once embarrassed Stephen. He stared right past them and discovered that they had left a door half-open through which he could see into the cloister.

It did not look much larger than the little cloister of God's House at Ewelme, though the arcade was of dazzling white stone instead of dark timber. There was a similar square plot in the middle and a similar pattern of sunlight and shade. Suddenly the sound of chanting drifted along the vaulted roof, as though the church door had just been opened. The chanting soon stopped, but in its place came a soft rhythmic padding of feet as two by two the canonesses, eyes cast down, passed through the cloister on their way back from choir. The cellaress made a sign to one of the kitchen wenches who quickly closed the door, but not before Stephen had noticed that all the novices heading the procession wore white veils.

Lys was still serenely happy when the time came to leave her. It was Stephen who found it difficult to say good-by. A week ago he had both a sister and a home, even though the home was a place of little comfort. Now Lys had gone and he had no home at all—though he told himself that he was fortunate to be welcome at the mill.

The afternoon sun blazed down, and Gilles suggested that they should return another way. He knew a path through the woods which left the Old Road just above Goring. It was narrow and they would have to go single file, but at least they would be in shade.

Halfway up the hill they turned off. It was steep but beautifully cool. Gilles, leading the pony, went ahead, his long legs climbing easily. Stephen had all he could do to keep up, and after a while he slackened his pace. So long as he could see Gilles between the trees, there was no fear of getting lost. Indeed, though concealed from the road, the path was perfectly clear. He wondered whether it had been made by outlaws in the days when so many lived hidden in the woods. He began to notice landmarks, such as a group of tall oaks among the beeches, chalk pits half-full of water, sharp hills down and up again, and occasionally distant glimpses of the familiar Wittenham Clumps.

But however easy it was to follow, the way seemed to go on forever. He grew more and more weary. It was a lifetime since he had left the mill. As his body flagged his mind refused to stay still. It darted about like bats in the twilight, never giving him a moment's peace. From Lys to Odo, from Odo to Ferry, from Ferry to Doggett, from Doggett to Dame Alice's letter, from there to Bolingbroke, from Bolingbroke to Old Meg and the writing on the hearth and the pool —and so back to Lys again, until he could go no further and sat down on the ground with his back against a tree.

Before long he heard Gilles calling him, but his voice would not carry, and soon the archer came back to look for him.

"Why, boy, you are completely spent," he said. "I should have remembered that you had already lived a long day before we started. Now get you up on the pony. It will at least take the weight from your feet."

Feeling almost ashamed, Stephen felt himself hoisted up as Lys had been hoisted in the morning. With Gilles at his head the pony plodded on and on until they reached a steep bank thick with undergrowth which seemed vaguely familiar. Stephen looked anxiously around.

"Where are we going?" he inquired. "*Not* to old Meg's tonight?"

Gilles grinned at him. "Nay, not to old Meg's tonight," he repeated. "You may measure my trust when I say that I'm taking you to *my* lodging. I promise you, few know it."

Gazing down the slope Stephen suddenly realized where he was. Below him was a huddle of broken walls overhung with bushes and tangled with ivy. It was the ruins of the monks' dwelling at Swyncombe. He had never been so near to it before. Now, as the pony picked its way down, he could see that one corner was roughly thatched. On the flat ground outside the open door was a flint hearth, a pile of ashes, and a cooking pot.

"Now you have me at your mercy," said Gilles lightly. "Come in and rest you on the bed while I fetch a draft of water from the well."

Stephen looked around the little cell. In all the

time he had known the woods, he had never suspected its existence. It was a poorer place even than
old Meg's. The roof covered only part, and sunlight
flooded through broken walls. But it was white-
washed. The earth was swept clean, and it held nothing but a neat bed of bracken, with a worn sheepskin
as covering, and a wooden stool. Above the bed hung
a small cross with the figure of Christ crucified. He
recognized the gnarled and twisted wood from which
it was made. Obviously it was Wat's handiwork.

The bracken bed was deep and springy. The only
sounds were bird songs and the rustle of leaves. Suddenly he felt safe. When Gilles returned with a
pitcher of water, he looked up at him.

"Must I go back?" he said. "Can't I stay here with
you?"

"You are tired out," said Gilles gently. "Because
your sister has gone, and your home has gone, you
feel that you have naught left. But believe it your
courage has not gone. Life lies ahead for your own
making. Now drink some water and rest back awhile.
There is plenty of time before vespers."

But, walking again, Stephen discovered a blistered
heel and reached Ewelme with only a minute to spare
before Parson Saynesbury was ready to enter the
church. He saw the parson look at him keenly, but it
was not until he was trying to slip away after vespers
and compline that he heard his name called. One
glance at the parson's face and his knees again almost
refused to carry him.

"Stephen, where is your sister?" Parson Saynesbury's voice was stern. "I have this day seen your stepfather. He says that you have snatched her from his charge and are keeping her hid. Tell me at once what you have done with her."

With an extra effort Stephen managed to keep his voice steady.

"She is at Goring, sir—with the nuns—as kitchen wench."

"The canonesses?" The parson was obviously astonished. "Is that true? How came it? Who took her there? Ask me not to believe the ladies accepted an unknown chit unsponsored from a gangling schoolboy."

Suddenly inspired, Stephen dived into his gown and brought out the jagged parchment that the cellaress had given him. Parson Saynesbury examined it closely.

"This is a true indenture of service. But still you have not told me how you came by it. Are *you* known to the ladies of Goring? Come now, why so covert about it?"

Stephen thought quickly. At all cost he must keep old Meg out of it. "There is a fellow, sir, who comes from somewhere nigh to Swyncombe; he serves their larder—"

To his surprise the parson ceased to frown.

"Serves their larder, eh? *Now* I see daylight. You mean the fellow they call Gilles the Bowman. Folk whisper about him because he is an outlaw, though he is not by that token a sinner, and 'tis no part of my priestly duties to hunt outlaws. So I'll not inquire further, though remember, Stephen, the hills are no playground for you. Not all who dwell there are so virtuous. But God be thanked, the child is in good hands. And you—old Ferry tells me you lodge at the mill? That's well enough. Someday we may do better for you."

He raised his hand in blessing, and Stephen started on his final trudge with his mind at last at rest. Lys was settled. The parson knew about it. For the present there was nothing he could do about Dame Alice's letter, except pray unceasingly that it had in truth been burned and had not passed into the hands of Bolingbroke. As for old Meg, she had been good to Lys and he was thankful to her. But she *was* a witch, and, he resolved, he would not go that way again.

He slept all night without waking, and the next morning he was late for school. He told himself that Parson Saynesbury would make allowances, and old Ferry's punishments were not worth worrying about.

The children were reciting their lessons when he arrived, and he went to old Ferry's desk to say his *mea culpa*. The clerk looked at him with surprise.

"Stephen? I thought you were at the Hall. Dame Alice sent word this morning that she must see you immediately."

The Hall

STEPHEN's legs would hardly carry him. He knew without a shadow of doubt exactly why he had been sent for. It was the letter. Bolingbroke had wasted no time, and the trouble that Doggett foretold had already reached Dame Alice. How she could have connected it with him he did not stop to think. What would happen next? Would it be disaster for her and for my lord? What could he do? What should he say? He felt at this moment that he would gladly die if dying would wipe out his part in it.

The gatekeeper told him that Dame Alice was in her arbor. He pointed at an archway cut in a tall hedge. Sick with foreboding, Stephen found his way.

Beyond the hedge lay a garden arranged in neat square beds and quartered with paved paths. As she had been when he last saw her in her solar, Dame Alice was sitting with Mistress Jane, sorting embroidery silks. As before, the two little dogs rushed at him barking. This time he ignored them. He went straight forward and stood before her with bent head.

Her voice was as gentle as ever. "Stephen, you

have come promptly. I did not mean that you should drop your work. Never mind, we will get straight to business. Jane, look you to Belle. She is chewing the blue silk."

This did not sound like anger. Stephen ventured a quick glance. Dame Alice looked serene and untroubled. He watched her fingers, small and slender, steadily rewinding a skein.

"I had word with Parson Saynesbury this morning," she began. "He told me of your stepfather's marriage, which leaves you without a home. Thank God your sister is so well placed, but how is it with you?"

Nonplussed, he murmured something about Red Jak and the mill. She smiled.

"Red Jak is hardly the best master for you. My lord and I had already resolved to further you for your father's sake. My lord was struck by your likeness to him, and it was our intention that you should live here, serve us as a household clerk and study under our chaplain, Master Simon Brayles. Master Simon has gone to London with my lord so all was left in abeyance till his return. But now that you have no home I have decided that you shall come at once."

Stephen could not find a word to say. How could he possibly live here at the Hall, specially favored, knowing what he had done? Every day he would be on tenterhooks waiting for the blow to fall. What must he do? Say no like a churl to her bounty? Confess the truth? Or just accept, and live as a traitor under her roof?

She looked up and saw his face.

"Why so dumfounded, boy? I thought Parson Saynesbury had spoken of this long since. The only new thing is that you should come now, before Master Simon returns. There is plenty for you to do. Bylton the steward has no one but the boy Barnabas to write the household rolls." She twinkled at him. "Barnabas is a good fellow, and willing, but you may remember I would not even leave my lists for him to copy."

Stephen's heart pounded. This was his chance. He had only to say, "Madam, you remember the letter that was with those lists. . .?" But his mouth went dry; the words would not come.

Without waiting she continued. "Till Master Simon returns you can take your Latin grammar to the parson—" She looked at him with a twinkle. "Or maybe you can continue your latinizing of *The Canterbury Tales*. And one thing more: old Doggett is painting the walls of my solar; I would have you give him any help he needs. He is an old man to be mounting ladders. But go you now to the steward. He is expecting you, and I will send word to the miller that you have got a new lodging."

With this maze of instructions he left her, thankful to escape. He knew his way to the buttery where he would find the steward, but for the moment he paused, out of sight of both house and garden, to get his wits back.

To live at the Hall was an idea so wonderful that he could hardly take it in. But just now, coupled with his terror that Bolingbroke had the letter, it was as though the devil was on his track.

What could he do? Doggett had warned him that Dame Alice would suffer the pains of purgatory if she knew that the letter had been read, let alone copied. Doggett himself believed that it was burned and had never so much as heard of Bolingbroke. To tell either of them the truth would be impossible. He could almost hear Doggett's voice: "If any is to suffer it had best be you." That settled it. He must go on and bear the suspense alone. He pulled himself together. He had orders to report to the steward and after that to join Doggett in the solar. That was the rub. Would Doggett ask any further questions or would he have forgotten the whole business in the excitement of his work?

He found Will Bylton the steward in the kitchen court supervising the dismembering of a dead pig. When the joints were trimmed to his liking and safely laid in brine, he gave his attention to Stephen and looked him up and down much as he had looked at the pig. He'd heard well of him, he said. The parson said he was obedient and my lady declared that he wrote a good hand. That was something to thank heaven for. Barnabas, the other clerk, could not add two and two, and the household rolls when *he* wrote them might just as well be the litany of the saints.

Stephen dutifully laughed, and the steward, gratified, launched upon a catalogue of instructions. Stephen would share Barnabas's bed in the closet outside the chaplain's room. He must go to the tailor, in the loft above the harness room, who would fit him out with my lord's livery, and with fresh small clothes too, though he might retain his scholar's gown. His main duty, save what my lady ordered, would be to keep the accounts and write out afresh the lists that Barnabas had played the fool with. Then there was Doggett in the solar; he was another under my lady's special care. Maybe Stephen had better go there forthwith. Did he know the way?

Stephen said yes, and set off through the screens passage into the deserted hall.

He had barely reached the little stairs leading to the solar when a loud sneeze behind him made him swing round. In the shadow of the screen sat a boy at a bench strewn with pens and paper. As one sneeze followed another, the boy buried his face in his hands while the inkhorn, delicately poised, discharged its contents in a thin black stream.

Stephen sprang to the rescue, snatching up the papers before they were all engulfed, while the boy, still snuffling, dabbed at the ink with his sleeve, wiping his fingers on the front of his gown.

He looked up at Stephen with watery eyes.

"I swear that inkhorn is bewitched," he said. "It spills if I do but breathe. I'm Barnabas. I suppose that you are Stephen. My lady said that you were coming and that you could write like a true scrivener. Do you use a quill? I can do well enough with a hard point on a wax tablet, but no pen will obey me."

Stephen laid the papers back on a clean part of the bench. One glance warned him that if he did not take care, he would have all this confusion thrust upon him.

"I'm told to go to Doggett," he said. "Look, there's ink on your cuff. Wipe it well or you'll have it everywhere."

He hurried back to the stairs and reached the leather curtain before he remembered that he had dreaded meeting Doggett. He pushed it aside and stood open-mouthed at what he saw.

The principal wall was coated with wet plaster on which was drawn a flowing pattern like the branches of a tree. From the branches hung shields, some of them still in outline, others aleady glowing with bright color. He recognized the Burghersh lion with two tails, the three lions' faces of the de la Poles, and some sharp points which must be the beginning of Montacute. In the middle of the room stood Doggett, his grizzled hair on end, his face spattered with paint, his old eyes bright as a terrier's.

"So you've come," he cried. "I thought you had left me in the lurch."

"I've taken Lys to the nunnery," said Stephen. "She is safely enrolled as a serving wench."

"Good," said Doggett absently. "Now, what think you of *this?*"

Stephen almost sighed with relief. Clearly Doggett was interested in nothing but his art. "It's *wonderful*," he cried. "Tell me how is it done?"

Doggett swallowed the bait.

"The mason lays the wet plaster—only as much as I can finish in the day. From the ladder he draws the branches and the blank shields. I'm in charge of the coats of arms. That is *my* responsibility. They are to show my lord's forebears and my lady's. See! I've done de la Pole and Burghersh already. *You* are to attempt the two empty shields above: Stafford and Roet. She'll not trust me on a ladder, forsooth—as though I were a dotard."

"Stafford and Roet," repeated Stephen. "Do I know them?"

"If you've got eyes you do; they're both in the church window. Stafford—*or, a chevron gules*—for my lord's mother. Roet is *three wheels, two and one,* again *or* and *gules*. That is canting heraldry, a pun on roue, the French for wheel."

"Surely the three wheels are Chaucer," said Ste-

STAFFORD

phen, glad to lead him on. "They stand for Chaucer on old Sir Thomas's tomb."

Doggett began to chuckle. "That's the joke of it. Old Sir Thomas used the three wheels as though they were his *father's* coat, whereas in truth they were his *mother's*. She was Philippa Roet, daughter of a Flemish knight. The crux is that *her* sister was wed, tardily enough, to old John of Gaunt and thus Dame Alice is cousin to the Beauforts—think on it, kinswoman to the cardinal. 'Tis Roet which is the link with the blood royal, so to this day 'tis used for Chaucer."

"Then what is the Chaucer coat?"

Doggett laid his finger on the side of his nose. " 'Tis my belief there is none," he said with bated breath. "Old Sir Thomas's father, Geoffrey Chaucer, was a vintner's son. Though he made a name for himself, 'tis my belief he'd naught but a merchant's mark."

He nodded knowingly and Stephen nodded back. Chaucer or Roet, wheels or a merchant's mark, it mattered little. His purpose was to keep Doggett from the subject of the letter.

But Doggett, once started, was ready to go on. "Mark you, the de la Poles themselves were but merchants who came from Hull and fed the royal purse," he continued under his breath. " 'Tis the same story everywhere. Chaucer, Beaufort, de la Pole—all great names now, but where were any of them, I'd like to know, when my grandsire strung his bow at Crecy?"

"Within a
Bordure Argent"

LIFE AT the Hall was so different from anything Stephen had ever known that he might have been in a foreign land. He slept for the first time in his life on a real bedstead in the closet outside the chaplain's door. The bed which he shared with Barnabas was furnished with plump sacks of hay, shaken daily, and coverlets of shaggy gray wool. They ate in the buttery where mugs of small beer and chunks of crusty bread, with cheese or bacon or pieces of dried fish, were set out for the clerks, who were not expected to mix with the kitchen staff.

The midday meal, comfortably belly filling, was eaten by all ranks of the household in the great hall, presided over by Dame Alice, who sat at the high table with the two young mistresses and with her gentlewoman, Mistress Eleanor Thorn, a dignified lady nicknamed by Will Bylton, whose wit spared none, The Thorn in the Flesh.

Stephen, as the only reliable clerk available, was

seized by the steward each morning and sent scurrying from one job to another, armed with wax tablets
on which to make notes of every household detail, indoors and out. There were weigh bills to be checked
for the bushels of grist sent to the mill and the sacks
of flour which came back in their place; notes from
the stables about which horses the farrier had shod;
from the farm about how many cows had calved and
how many score of poultry had had their necks
wrung. All this had to be checked by the bailiff and
then entered on the household rolls—long strips of
parchment, rolled up tightly and stowed away, apparently forever, in an old coffer under the buttery shelf.
When this was finished there were Barnabas's blotted
records to be recopied—a puzzle in themselves, for
they were all mixed up and out of order, varying from
an important charge like refurbishing my lord's armor
in the latest fashion to a mere trifle regarding the
number of candles burned in a single night or the
pence paid to a barber from Wallingford summoned
to bleed the laundress when she fell down in a fit.

In itself all this copying was dull, but it suited Stephen nicely. He had no wish to meet people from the
village and answer awkward questions, and was still
more pleased to avoid any chance encounter with
Bolingbroke if that master from Oxford should happen still to be in the neighborhood. The only time
that it was necessary to leave the demesne was in the
early morning, when he and Barnabas escorted the la-

dies to church, carrying prayer books and cushions since, with Master Brayles absent, there was no mass in the chapel.

Two or three weeks passed without anything to disturb the peace. The household rolls were almost up to date, and Stephen began to wonder what he should do next if Master Brayles did not return soon to order him back to lessons. But so far there was no sign of my lord or his chaplain. Then suddenly the weather broke. The sunshine of early May changed to a chilly downpour more like February. The stream in the village where the watercress grew became a torrent, across which no one ventured except Doggett, who arrived clad in borrowed buskins tied on with string and a great hooded cloak devoured by moth, which had survived since the campaign of Agincourt. He was the hero of the hour, and Dame Alice decided that the time was ripe for Mistress Jane and Mistress Philippa to take lessons in heraldry. Every gentlewoman should be familiar with the rules of coat armor, and here was a fine chance for them to learn. Doggett was in his element and Stephen found himself called upon to illustrate the difference between a chief, a fess, a bend, a chevron, and the rest of the nine ordinaries.

But one morning Doggett arrived more bright-eyed than ever. When the lesson was over and the pupils had been shepherded away by The Thorn, he beckoned to Stephen, laying his finger to his lips.

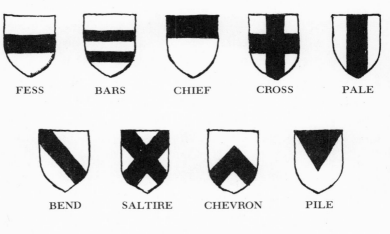

FESS   BARS   CHIEF   CROSS   PALE

BEND   SALTIRE   CHEVRON   PILE

THE NINE ORDINARIES

"How does my lady like the news?" he whispered eagerly.

"News? What news?" Stephen asked, taken aback.

"News of my lord, of course. Is it not known here? Young Nye came in yestereve. He'd brought a tun of wine by barge for the prior of Wallingford and came to visit his sire at God's House. He says the city is full of rumors, but this one he vouches for. The conference to make peace with France is to be held quite soon, near Calais. The cardinal will lead it, with the French duke to act as go-between. My lord was to go with them because it was *his* idea, so everybody said. But, suddenly, he is out of it; he is to be left behind. Duke Humphrey is triumphant. What has happened? Tell me that. Is it all true? Has my lord heard of it?"

Stephen shook his head. Deep within him he felt a sudden quiver of fear, but he checked it, assuring himself that even in Bolingbroke's hands the letter could not have caused so much damage *yet*. Ill news travels apace. Dame Alice would have been the first to hear of it, and Dame Alice so far was cheerful and serene.

She was still cheerful when, a few days later, she sent for him. As the solar was unfinished, he found her in a small anteroom leading to the Great Chamber—my lord's own room, the grandest in the house, with a splendid curtained bed which he yielded to important guests. The anteroom was small and dark, and the ladies with the two little mistresses were all clustered around the one small window with their needlework.

As Stephen made his obedience, Dame Alice pointed to a desk set with writing things, a lighted candle sconce, and a pile of dusty parchment rolls.

"I have a task for you," she said smiling. "All those documents concern the business of the manor of Ewelme. In my father's day they were kept faultlessly, but since he died they have been neglected. They do not need to be copied but just inscribed on the outside with the subject and the date of each one. Do you understand? I am sure that it is not beyond your powers."

Stephen glowed and set to work at once by the window, against a background of women's voices.

These documents were obviously business of high importance, such as agreements to lease parts of the manor land, agreements about the number of acres that a tenant must plow, how much stock must be fattened for the Michaelmas slaughter and salted down for the winter, about fines to be levied on a tenant when his son went to work outside the manor or his daughter married a "foreigner," or about leave granted to cut "great timber" for the object of repairing the tenant's house.

He had been busy for some while when Dame Alice called him. "The clouds show no sign of lifting," she said. "Maybe it would help to pass the time pleasantly if you should read to us while we work."

He gasped. "*Read?* Aloud?"

She smiled at him. "Yea, read aloud. I've heard you read the lesson in church. And there was a day when I found you reading *The Canterbury Tales*. So what shall it be?" She led him to an aumbry in the wall which held more books than he had ever seen in his life. "Shall we improve our Latin, children? Here is Cicero's *De Senectute*." She smiled as cries of protest came from the window seat. "Then how about *Troylus and Cressid?* Nay, that is unsuited for young maids. Ah, *Gawayne and the Green Knight*—that should be a good choice. Come then, Stephen. Begin you without delay."

Stephen started hesitantly, but as he became absorbed in the story he gradually lost his nervousness.

Except for those rare glimpses of *The Canterbury Tales* he had never read a romance before, and he began to look forward to wet days. The only person to disapprove was Doggett, who treated the whole matter with contempt, observing tartly that unless my lord or the chaplain came soon the boy would end up as a mere squire of dames.

One morning while the rain was pouring down, Bylton came hurrying through the hall, carrying a letter with a great dangling seal.

"A letter from Wingfield, my lady," he declared. "Morton, who brought it, had my lord's orders to deliver it into your hands, but he is so bespattered with mud that he trusted it to me."

Stephen saw the blood drain from Dame Alice's face. "From *Wingfield?* Has my lord left London so suddenly? How comes this?" Then calming her voice she instructed the steward to see that Morton the messenger was given mulled ale and dry raiment at once. Only when he had gone did she turn away to the window and unfold her letter.

The very air itself was tense. Even Mistress Jane and Mistress Philippa were quiet as mice. Stephen stayed, book in hand, afraid to move. At last The Thorn could restrain herself no longer.

"I trust the news is to your liking, madam?"

Dame Alice turned around, her face still white and grave.

"There is something amiss, Thorny, though my lord

is cautious in putting pen to paper. But I can read between the lines. The main fact is that he has been left
out of the party for Gravelines by Calais—the party to
make terms for peace. If you remember he was the
prime mover in the matter. 'Twas wholly his idea to
allow the French duke to be our spokesman; after
twenty-five years of captivity in England he could
speak better than any for both sides. It began in my
lord's house in Lombard Street while Monseigneur
was *our* prisoner and the envoy from Burgundy
supped there. The scheme was approved by the cardinal who gave my lord full credit for it. When he
rode off to London for my lord of Warwick's requiem,
he rode in good heart, despite the sad occasion. The
peace conference was to start shortly. He was to be
the cardinal's right hand, with his good friend the
French duke as emissary. They would bring home
peace. And now all is changed. The cardinal and the
French duke have actually embarked. Duke Humphrey remains at Westminster with the king. And my
lord has speedily retired to Wingfield. That alone
shows the way the wind blows."

"Maybe he seeks diversion in some sport, madam?"

Dame Alice smiled wanly. "Sport would not hold
him back from *here*. The reason is all too plain to me.
Wingfield is a *castle*, not an unarmed manor house. It
has stone walls and a moat; if needs be he could
defend it. Moreover he will not bring strife here, to
Ewelme, *my* home. I know his mind too well. Nay,

my good Thorn, we must be patient. Pray you with me to God our Savior and His blessed Mother. If the sky clears my lord will come here for the twelfth of June. I rest my hopes on that."

Stephen, forgotten, stole away miserably, more afraid than ever that this sudden trouble came from the letter in Bolingbroke's hands. He tried to remember what was in the letter—something about a French marriage, but all that he was clear about was Doggett's warning of the harm that could come to my lord if that letter reached his enemies.

He tiptoed up to the solar, full of dread. But as chance would have it Doggett had just put the final touches to the walls of the solar and could think of nothing else.

"Everybody says it is a great work," he declared, stumping about well satisfied. "I thank you for your help, boy—the little that you have done. I would that my lord were here to see it while it is fresh. But I suppose we must wait for the twelfth of June."

Stephen pricked up his ears. This is what Dame Alice had said. "Why the twelfth of June?"

Doggett turned on him. "Shame on you!" he cried. "Do you not pray for your father as a son should? It is his *obit*, the day he died. 'Twas on the twelfth of June, ten years ago this year, that my lord suffered his great defeat at Jargeau. Your father died in vain. My lord was forced to yield to a young French squire, whom he first knighted with his own sword to satisfy the laws of chivalry, and thus was prisoner to the Maid. To cap it, his own brother took his place as hostage and died a prisoner. My lord had his body brought back to Ewelme—it lies in the church beneath the floor; and every year on that inglorious day he withdraws here to remember those who stood with him. And *you* ask *me*, 'What is the twelfth of June?' "

With so much food for thought Stephen settled down as best he could to await what happened next. Everything was now quiet. The news had crept out that my lord was at Wingfield, not in London or France, and all the manor from Dame Alice downward awaited the accustomed visit in June.

Much of Stephen's time was spent in the now finished solar where the closet for the gentlewomen opened from it by one door and the ewery, furnished with jugs and basins and towels for bathing, opened from another. The big curtained bed stood in the middle of the room, but there was still plenty of room to see Doggett's walls, and the children never tired of asking for stories about the people and the families whose shields were painted in such bright colors. Dame Alice's desk and her precious books were brought upstairs. The room was light instead of dark, and the wide window seats were gay with cushions.

On the rare fine days, Stephen and Barnabas were sent out for exercise, kicking a ball about in the park, following the falconer as he trained a young hawk, or practicing archery at the butts. Strangely enough,

Barnabas, so hopeless with a pen, proved to be handy with a bow—good enough to keep Stephen on his mettle.

Returning one evening with their bows and quivers, they were met at the door by Bylton the steward.

"The boy from the mill has been after you," he said to Stephen. "He was in a fine fret but he wouldn't say why. If you hurry you may catch him."

Stephen took to his heels. Once over the hill he saw Tom ahead and yelled. Tom heard him and cupped his hands.

"The books," he shouted. "Duke Humphrey's books —they're coming. I swore I'd let you know."

Stephen reached him, breathless. "When?" he gasped.

"Before sunset—any moment now. A waterman from Wallingford brought word. Red Jak took it quietly till he'd gone; then he burst forth fire and brimstone. I've never seen him quite so mad. The moon is near the full. Even the goodwife is afraid."

"But what can he do? He dursn't sink it."

Tom snorted. "Dursn't? There's nothing he dursn't when he's as crazed as this. Unless that barge is safely through the lock tonight, by dawn it will lie in a fathom of mud. He knows all the currents and how to use them."

Stephen gasped. All those splendid books! Something must be done. "Come on," he cried. "We must get help. Come on, hurry."

He started back up the hill, with Tom at his heels protesting that Red Jak would kill him. Taking no notice, Stephen led the way straight through the screens passage without pause and into the great hall. A maid-servant cried out at Tom's girded shirt and mud-caked legs, but Stephen did not slacken speed till halfway through the hall he skated to a standstill with Tom on top of him.

At the high table sat Dame Alice herself while Bylton and Mistress Thorn spread out tapestries for her inspection. The steward spun around angrily.

"What's all this noise? This is no bear garden. Down now on your knees and ask my lady's pardon."

Stephen took no notice. " 'Tis the books, madam," he cried, directly to Dame Alice. "The barge of books for Oxford. They are nearing the mill, and Tom says Red Jak has sworn to sink them!"

She stared at him. "Books—what books? You cannot mean Duke Humphrey's books and King Harry's books from Windsor? I know the miller is reputed mad, but surely not so mad as that?"

"He bears a grudge against Duke Humphrey. He all but drowned the Duchess at the lock. I saw it with mine own eyes." Stephen was still breathlesss.

"That story is everywhere," Bylton broke in. "It seems there's truth in it."

"But how can he sink a great barge? It must have men in charge of it." She turned to Tom. "What will he do, boy? Speak up, we will protect you."

Tom's voice was steady. " 'Tis simple, madam, if he has the mind. He'll run the stream low so that they must lie by till morning. Then while they sleep he'll build his head of water to bursting point. Then last of all the millrace will open—it will seem by the devil's chance. The barge will swing out midstream. It is heavy. In that surge it will sink like a stone. The crew will save themselves, but the books will be lost in mud."

"Great heavens, this is truly devil's madness! Bylton, we must send help from Wallingford. But"—she looked again at Tom—"in the meanwhile what's the remedy? How can we stop him till the help comes?"

"There's but one way, madam. The barge must get through before dark and be safely on the upper water."

She nodded. "Then we must use guile as well as force. First, Bylton, send an order to Wallingford. Stay, though, I needs must sign it. Fetch pen and ink. Now you, boy, get you back to the mill at once so that he may not suspect. Do all you can to keep him calm. And, Stephen, you must use your wits and play him like a fish till help arrives. I'll write a letter as from my lord which you may carry as authority. Quickly with that pen and paper."

She sat deep in thought until the quills, the ink-horn, the sheets of paper, and the sand were set down before her. Then in her own flowing handwriting she dashed off a note to the captain of Wallingford Castle. As Bylton carried it to the messenger, she started again, writing more slowly and carefully. At the end she shook sand on it and while it dried actually read it aloud.

"You shall know what I have written," she said to Stephen, "so that you can make the best use of it. I have contrived to leave out the name of Gloucester, referring only to the books left to Oxford by King Henry the Fifth which shamefully have never been delivered. By good fortune there are some of them in this consignment—so I am told. Now listen, boy, and then begone."

The letter ran:

> To Jak the miller at Benson Mill—*I greet you good Jak and would forewarn you of a great barge soon to pass from Windsor upstream to Oxford. This barge carries a load of precious books including many the gift of our late liege lord King Harry the Fifth, whom God assuage, under his will and testament. It is a matter of honor for all who loyally served King Harry, as did my lord of Suffolk, and as you did good Jak under my lord's banner, to carry out this charge with all speed and good will, that this precious load may travel with safety past this our Benson mill.*
>
> *Signed by me in my good lord's intent.*
>
> Alyse Suffolk

With his heart thumping Stephen raced down the hill. As Dame Alice had put the letter into his hands, she had lowered her voice to say, as though it were a secret between them, "Think what it could mean if Gloucester's books should perish at *our* mill." It needed no more to make his mission a crusade. The thought came to him that Bolingbroke might be there, but he pushed even that aside. That was a matter bigger than anything.

Near the mill Tom was waiting under a tree.

"The barge is just in sight," he pointed to a line of silver far downstream. "Take heed! Red Jak is ripe for anything."

Stephen nodded and tiptoed cautiously, noting as he went that Red Jak had not tampered with the water level, so that the barge was not yet cut off from the upper river. It was not too late for him to change his mind.

But on the island stood Red Jak, as though in readiness, savagely sharpening a heavy stake. The scars on his face stood out as Stephen had never seen them before, great bloated weals of purple and white. At the sight of Stephen his scowl deepened.

"What do *you* want?" he growled. "I've had enough of pestering clerks. Get you gone."

A swift glance over his shoulder showed Stephen that the silver streak had widened and now stretched from bank to bank. The faint outline of the barge crept up behind it. There was no time to spare.

"I've come with a letter from Dame Alice," he said. "It speaks as from my lord of Suffolk to his trusty comrade at arms. Look you and see."

The miller peered with his one eye. "Suffolk," he snorted. "Another fighting man turned coxcomb. No word now but '*Miller, open, I would go up*' or '*Miller, open, I would go down,*' losing my head of water for their pleasure. None stayed the river of blood at Orleans for *books* to go by.

The purple spread till his whole face was suffused and the scars shone like silk. Stephen was appalled. He longed to turn tail but the silver line of ripple crept ever closer.

"Hear what the letter says," he urged. " 'Tis for my lord's honor—the lord you served in battle." He held it out, exerting all his will to keep his hand steady. Rumbling in his throat like an angry dog, Red Jak snatched the paper, glanced at it, and gave it back.

"Read it out," he growled. "Mine eye is stuffed with spume."

The barge was approaching fast—a huge craft low in the water with a great painted sailcloth stretched over its cargo. Stephen mastered his voice enough to read with a deceptive calm. "So you see," he announced at the end, "these are King Harry's books— Harry the Fifth."

Red Jak's one eye stared at the barge. "That fat bedizened braggart said that they were Humphrey of Gloucester's books."

At any other moment Stephen would have laughed aloud. "Bedizened braggart" fitted Bolingbroke perfectly. But the barge was now only a few yards away, and the master was trumpeting through his hands.

THE KING   GLOUCESTER

Suddenly Stephen noticed the stretched sailcloth: on it was painted the royal arms of England. The sight of those arms actually gave him courage to grip the miller by the wrist.

"Look!" he cried. "The lilies and leopards! The king's own blazoning; the same as on his banner at Agincourt. *Now* do you believe me?"

The triumph in his voice carried conviction, but the words were hardly out of his mouth before his blood ran cold. The arms of England were surrounded by a broad white border. Doggett would have known it at once. "*Within a bordure argent quarterly. . . .*" The white border differenced the arms of Duke Humphrey from the arms of the king. Both carried the royal lilies and leopards, but for the king himself there was no border.

But Red Jak was no Doggett. He stood stock-still, intent upon the painted cover. Then dramatically he drew himself up straight, squaring his shoulders.

"Lay to," he shouted, raising his arm. "That load needs special care. Hold fast with your poles while we work speedily to get you through."

161

Neither poles nor horses were enough to heave that great weight. A tackle of chains and winches tethered to the mill quay was produced. Stephen threw all his strength into it with the rest. At the end everyone was dripping with sweat, but the barge floated safely on the upper river.

Stephen slipped away unobserved and started wearily uphill. On the first ridge he paused for breath and looked back. By now it was nearly dark, but he could pick out a group of shadowy figures approaching along the far bank. One remaining ray of light gleamed upon steel. He laughed aloud with triumph. It was the guard from Wallingford.

The Hall was all in darkness. Bylton opened the door by the light of the lantern in the screens passage and Stephen told him briefly that all was well. The barge had gone through—without the help of Wallingford.

"Well done, boy; well done in truth. The ladies have gone bedward, but I was to send you to the solar as soon as you came in."

Stephen fumbled his way across the dim hall and up the narrow stairs. There was a light inside the drawn leather curtain. He tapped on the lintel and, hearing a murmur which he took for an answer, pushed his way in.

The solar was lit by candles on a candlestand. The curtains of the bed were drawn on three sides except on the near side where the sheets were neatly folded back. Dame Alice in a furry bed gown was kneeling at a *prie-dieu* with Mistress Thorn at one side and the two young mistresses at the other. They were murmuring prayers, so he kneeled down too until they crossed themselves and Dame Alice rose to her feet.

"Tell me," she said quickly, "has it gone well?"

"Yes, madam, praise be to God." As the ladies clustered round him he told his story. When he came to the part about the sailcloth with the royal arms Dame Alice clapped her hands delightedly.

"Children, see what comes of old Doggett's training! But, Stephen, you look worn out. Get you to bed now. But first tell Bylton from me to give you a cup of wine—the good wine from mine own table."

"I Like
Not That Fellow"

*L*ULLED by the "good wine," Stephen slept like a log and woke too late for his duty of attending Dame Alice to mass. But she only smiled when he asked pardon and said that he had earned his rest. In any case she had decided that, as a reward, he should have a nag from the stable and go to Goring to see his sister. Stephen glowed with gratitude. Already he had been bombarded with questions on all sides, and questions were still something that he would rather avoid. One thing could all too easily lead to another.

The "nag" turned out to be a sturdy donkey, and he reached Goring in half the time it had taken on foot. The porteress at the gate remembered him; so did Dame Cellaress, who commended Lys as a good hard-working wench and said that he might walk with her in the orchard. The orchard bordered the riverbank, and it was sunny down there.

He did not have to wait long before Lys came, looking grown-up in a long kirtle of gray homespun,

with an unbleached apron and a white cap that concealed her hair. She was shy but obviously overjoyed
to see him. They sat on the bole of a tree, both
tongue-tied, watching the ferryman punt not only
people but horses and light carts across, where, as
Gilles had told them, the Old Road crossed the river.

It was news to Lys that Stephen was now serving
Dame Alice at the Hall, and soon she began to ply
him with questions about how he fared, what was his
work, and what would his future be? With every answer she grew more delighted.

"You see," she cried, "it is as I knew it would be.
Old Meg saw it in the pool—I would be here at the
nunnery and you would be a clerk at Oxford."

"I a clerk at Oxford? You did not tell me that."

"I durst not," she said. "You were so angry about
me that I dare not tell you what she said of *you*."

"I was not *angry*," he said quickly. "I feared for you
because you were in peril of being caught by witchcraft, and witchcraft is evil."

She shook her head vigorously. "Old Meg is not
evil. Naught will make me believe that. Why,
brother, she was so *good* to me. None but our mother
had ever been so good."

"She deals in magic," said Stephen stubbornly.
"I've tried hard to believe otherwise but there's no
gainsaying it. Magic is the devil's art; any will tell you
that."

"Any can say what they will. Old Meg does no

harm to them, that they should wag their tongues at her. Mark you what I say, brother. She is true friend to you as well as me."

Stephen felt oddly shaken. Till now it had always been he who laid down the law and Lys who obeyed. He decided that it was time to change the subject.

"With your new finery I see you still have your old shoon," he said lightly.

She stuck out a foot and waggled it. "Poor Wat made them so strong the Dame Cellaress let me keep them. She said it would be wanton to throw such good shoon away before I had outgrown them. Look, see how good they are."

He nodded absently. He wanted to ask her about Gilles, but just at that moment another wench came scurrying through the orchard with a message from Dame Cellaress saying that Lys had lost enough time for one day. If her brother came again it should be on a Sunday. Lys obeyed instantly, and Stephen made his own way back to the courtyard where the donkey was tethered, thankful that he did not encounter any canonesses on the way. The old woman at the gate asked him if he had eaten dinner, and when he said no gave him a large lump of bread and cheese which he munched as he tramped up the hill. He looked for a moment at the path through the woods, the way that Gilles had led him last time. He was sure he could find his way but on second thought decided against it. It was not too hot on the Old Road today, and he did not really want to encounter either old Meg or Gilles.

He enjoyed the saunter back to Ewelme, well content with Lys, with himself, and with the whole world. It was high afternoon when he reached the Hall and led the donkey back to the stableyard. A strange horse was tethered in the shade. He stared at it suddenly aghast. He knew that horse only too well —a white star on its forehead and trappings of crimson leather.

Trying to convince himself that he was wrong, he tiptoed round to the buttery door where he was met by Barnabas.

"I was to watch for you," said Barnabas. "You are to go to my lady at once in the solar. She has a visitor."

"Who is it?" Though he knew the answer he could not resist asking.

"A master from Oxford. Hurry! He's been there a great while."

With the feeling that he was going to the scaffold, Stephen crossed the hall. At the foot of the solar stairs he paused to collect his wits. He had never dreamed that Bolingbroke and Dame Alice might come face to face. What had happened? Why was Bolingbroke there? Was it to confront her with her letter? Had he told her how he had come by it? Had there been some terrible scene between them? Bolingbroke was close-knit with the Duchess Eleanor, and in the letter

Dame Alice had called the duchess a bedeviled jade.

But there were no angry voices. As he pushed past the leather curtain and went in, he saw Dame Alice and Bolingbroke standing by the desk examining a pile of books, while Mistress Thorn sat by the window with her embroidery.

A friendly scene was the last thing he had expected. He shuffled with his feet and Dame Alice looked up.

"Ah, here's the boy. This, sir, is Stephen. 'Tis he who has earned your thanks for the safe passage of the books."

Bolingbroke turned. His pale eyes met Stephen's and held them with the same intensity as on that day by old Meg's fireside.

"So," he said very deliberately, "*this* is Stephen. It strikes me that I have seen him before. Was it not you, boy, who showed me the way to Wallingford when I was lost in that storm?"

Stephen, red to the roots of his hair, mumbled and looked at the floor. This was the explanation that Bolingbroke had decided upon when he had made the pact between them about the place of their first meeting. At the time it had seemed simple enough. Stephen's only concern had been to preserve the secret of his visits to old Meg, and Bolingbroke's had been the same. But now everything was different. It had turned out that Bolingbroke was hand in glove with my lord's enemies, and through Stephen's fault he had got hold of my lady's letter. Yet here he was feigning friendship and actually in my lady's presence covertly reminding Stephen of an understanding between them which Stephen dared not deny.

Dame Alice looked from one to the other, as though she sensed trouble, but she merely said, "That dreadful storm in the spring? Well do I remember it. My lord lost his best hound, and later we heard of the Earl of Warwick's death, God rest him. My lord went to London and he has not returned home yet."

Bolingbroke smiled, as though he had been waiting his chance. "My lord of Suffolk, I understand, has been busy assuring that the Duke of Orleans should go to Calais for the conference on peace, although unhappily he cannot go himself." There was no mistaking the gibe, but he continued pleasantly enough. "They say that the two of them were notably fine friends when Monseigneur le duc was prisoner here at Ewelme, talking and versifying together. Your pretty countryside is good for poetry-making—Will my lord find Pulteney's Inn equally inspiring for his talents?"

She stared at him, off her guard for the moment. Stephen almost gasped out loud, suspecting that this talk about the Duke of Orleans and Pulteney's Inn came straight out of the letter.

"Pulteney's Inn?" she cried. "How came you to hear of Pulteney's Inn?"

He smiled gently. "Madam, any movement of yours and my lord's cannot be hid for long—just as it will soon be known that you are generously giving books for the new library. I shall inform the masters of convocation as soon as I get back."

Stephen could see that Dame Alice was disturbed, but she responded graciously enough when, with elaborate courtesy, he took his leave. Bylton was summoned to serve him with wine in the hall, and before long the clatter of his horse's hooves died away. Mistress Thorn peeped from the window.

"I like not that fellow," she said. "Think you he *really* came to render thanks for the safe passage of the books?"

"I should doubt it," said Dame Alice gravely. "I trust him no more than you do. Maybe he came to spy if my lord was here. He seemed to possess more knowledge than I like. How came he by it?" She turned back into the room and her eye fell on Ste-. phen. "You are still here, boy? Tell me, were you allowed to see your sister? It is as well that you went today, for I have news for you. Master Brayles comes home tomorrow. From now on your time will be full, for I would have you take over the duties of chaplain's clerk. Barnabas drives Master Simon to despair. He is a good boy; but our Lord God makes saints according to His own pattern and not always to our convenience. Here is a task for you at once. I will give you the key of the great standard and you can straightway unpack the chapel gear. Barnabas can help. He watched Master Simon put it all away."

Carefully clutching a large gilded key, Stephen left the solar. The "great standard" must be that enormous ironbound chest which stood at the top of the steps that led from the great hall to the chapel. It was used to carry the vestments and altar furnishings when the household moved from one mansion to another.

Barnabas was hovering, obviously in expectation of being called. At the first mention of what they had to do, he grabbed the key from Stephen, and dropping on his knees, managed to turn it in the lock. Stephen bent over to help, but Barnabas would have none of it. Using all his strength he raised the massive lid, the hinges creaking under the weight. Clearly it was too heavy for him, but before Stephen could get a grip upon it there was a great crash and Barnabas, his fingers trapped, kneeled there screaming with pain.

His cries raised the household. Bylton came running with a crowd behind him; Dame Alice and Mistress Thorn hurried from the solar. By the time they arrived, Stephen had lifted the weight enough to free the hand, a hideous mess of blood and pulp. Barnabas, half-fainting, was carried to Dame Alice's ewery where stood bowls and jugs of water. Mistress Thorn took charge, and presently Barnabas emerged white as a sheet, his left hand wrapped in bulky swathes of linen. Downstairs in the buttery Bylton railed at him as a clumsy half-wit unfit to be trusted with the simplest task. Barnabas was promptly sick and dragged himself off to bed. When Stephen joined him later he could hear muffled sobbing.

"Does it hurt very much?" he asked gently.

Barnabas emerged from beneath the bedclothes, his face swollen with crying.

"It's not *that*," he whimpered. "It is that Bylton is right. I'm no good. I'm clumsy and stupid and everything I touch goes wrong. But it's not my fault." His voice rose shrilly. "I'm not just an ordinary fool. There's a curse on me. I'm bewitched!"

"Bewitched!" said Stephen sharply. "What are you saying? How bewitched?"

"My mother told me. I've been bewitched from birth. When she was carrying me she had a morbid pox and someone bade her go to the old witch—the one who lives up there, beside the pool. The old troll bade her do something, I know not what, and when she wouldn't she laid a curse on her and on her unborn child. That's why I was born a half-wit!"

Stephen was suddenly hot with anger. "Stop talking like a dolt. *Why* should she lay a curse on you? You're a half-wit because you've swallowed all this flummery. Old Meg would never lay a curse on anyone, let alone upon a babe. She's *kind,* I tell you, the kindest person I've ever known. Stop blaming her for your tomfoolery. If you were born thus 'tis not *her* fault."

He broke off as Barnabas stared at him, openmouthed. It seemed that the words had struck home, for he stopped crying. Climbing into bed Stephen lay motionless, astonished at himself. He had actually spoken up for old Meg. What was more he had not troubled to conceal that he knew her. What had come

over him? Had he gained courage from facing Red
Jak? Was it thanks to Dame Alice's praise? Or could
it possibly be due to Lys?

Master Simon Brayles arrived the next morning riding a well-groomed mule and followed by a servant
on a baggage horse. He was a tall spare man with a
long face, graying hair, and a quiet voice. Stephen
had seen him often enough but had kept out of his
way, for the chaplain at the hall was not merry, like
the parson, and all the village stood in awe of him.

On his arrival he was taken straight to Dame Alice
and did not appear again till dinner, when he said
grace from the high table, and then sat listening cour-
teously to Dame Alice throughout the meal. Stephen,
cutting Barnabas's meat at the clerk's bench, was able
to stare from afar, till suddenly the chaplain glanced
round and met his gaze fully, as though he had been
aware of it all the time. Stephen dropped his eyes in
embarrassment. He had already learned one lesson.
Master Simon Brayles might be gentle in his ways but
there would be no hoodwinking him.

When dinner was over and the ladies had gone, the
priest beckoned. Stephen went forward obediently
and dropped on one knee to receive a blessing, noting
that Master Brayles's sign of the cross was small and
unobtrusive, not like Parson Saynesbury's, a gesture
that embraced the whole world. He looked up and
caught a twinkling eye.

"I've been hearing of your exploits at the mill. You

should it seems be a herald's clerk, but my lady
would have me make a scholar of you. Have you any
turn for scholarship? Sir John Saynesbury once told
me that you had plenty of good will, but abominable
Latin— But that for the present must wait. Our first
task is to disembowel the great standard. I hear 'tis already sadly stained with the blood of martyrs. Come
now, fetch me the key and bid Barnabas keep a safe
distance."

Suddenly cheerful, Stephen hurried off. It seemed
as though a fresh breeze had blown through the hall.

Unpacking the great standard occupied the rest of
the day and transformed the bare empty room known
as the chapel into a treasure house of glowing color.
The packing had been done, it seemed, for the pro-
jected move to Donnington that had been interrupted
by my lord's sudden departure for London. Now for
some reason, which Master Brayles did not explain,
the household would remain at Ewelme for some time
further, and so the chapel must be furbished again.
Stephen did not need explanation. From one source
or another he had only too good an idea of what lay
behind the quiet retirement to a country manor. The
Duke of Gloucester's banner was flying high, and it
was wisdom for my lord of Suffolk to bide where its
shadow would not fall. He helped to unfold and hang
two fine tapestries from Arras, one depicting the life
of St. Anne and the other the Last Judgment, where a
border of horned devils snatched away souls for Hell.

All these preparations must surely mean that my lord would come soon.

But for the moment there was nothing to show that Doggett might be right. There was a mass in the chapel every morning, but otherwise the household settled back into its old routine.

Only for Stephen did the coming of Master Brayles turn life upside down. For the first time he learned what work meant. He was still obliged to help Barnabas with the household rolls and still wrote, in a hand which improved every day, such letters as Dame Alice required of him. But with the chaplain goading him, these things took only a short time. There was no more leisurely reading aloud; instead there were long hours poring over Latin grammar. The old dog-eared dead pages of Donatus came to life.

"You *could* go to Oxford as a schoolboy, if my lady wished it," remarked Master Simon. "They have grammar schools for children younger than you. But it would be a stain on Ewelme to send its first scholar so ill equipped. It matters vastly that you should be well grounded. A scholar should be hammered out as an armorer tempers steel so when he comes to the seven arts and the three philosophies his blade is sharp enough to cut his way through to his master-ship."

Seven arts and three philosophies. He had heard that before, from Bolingbroke. "Seven arts, sir? Does one have to learn *seven* arts?"

"Seven arts in all: the trivium and the quadrivium. But, mark you, you do not *learn* an art; you learn *by* it. The object of the arts is to train your mind, like the steel blade we spoke of. The trivium, for instance covers three arts; logic, grammar, and rhetoric. By logic you learn to think clearly, to examine an idea and come to a conclusion. For instance, water is wet, your hand is wet: therefore it is likely that your hand has been in water. *That* is logic. Grammar is the art of understanding what has already been thought or spoken or written down, whereby you may learn from the ideas of others. And rhetoric is the art of saying or expressing your own ideas, of saying or writing what you mean. Logic, grammar, and rhetoric—those are the basic three, without which you are as lost in a wilderness of thought as you would be in those woods up there."

They were seated on a bench by the open casement of the chaplain's closet, and Stephen's eye traveled unconsciously to the line of the wooded Chilterns, but he was too engrossed to spare thought for where he had heard this before.

"What are the other four, sir—the quad—quad—?"

"The quadrivium? They are arts too: geometry, arithmetic, astronomy, and music, but we will confine ourselves to the trivium for a start. The first step is to read Latin as freely as you read English. All wise books are written in Latin, and at Oxford all lectures are in Latin too. In fact scholars are bid speak nothing else. So come now, back to Donatus and so on to Cato. That is the way you will open the door to your future."

Stephen picked up his book again, suddenly wide awake. For the first time he began to *care* about learning. Even in church he noticed the Latin words as having a meaning of their own: *"Dominus vobiscum,"* instead of being just a gabble, meant "The Lord be with you" and was answered by *"Et cum Spiritu tuo"*—"And with thy spirit." It made sense. And when it came round to his turn, as a clerk, to read the epistle in Latin he pronounced it as carefully as though he were reading Cato to Master Simon.

The days passed quickly, and then quite suddenly my lord of Suffolk came home.

"A Fortress
on a Hill"

*F*OR DAYS there had been a bustle going on, a scent
of new rushes in the hall and the fragrant brightness
of beeswax everywhere. But absorbed in his new interest, Stephen had paid no attention. He was actually in bed and asleep when he woke in a panic,
convinced that the house must be on fire. There were
loud voices outside, and the place was lit up by the
blaze of flaring torches. He had just begun to tug at
Barnabas when Master Simon emerged, fully dressed,
from his closet.

"Fire?" he exclaimed, as he passed by. " 'Tis no fire.
'Tis my lord arrived. My lady did not expect him till
the morrow. Get you back to bed. There's no call for
young clerks at this hour."

Stephen dropped back on to the bed. Barnabas
rolled over and asked sleepily what was afoot.

" 'Tis my lord, ridden through the night. We're not
needed. Go to sleep again." Then a thought struck
him. Doggett had said "About June 12." What day is
it?" he demanded.

To his surprise Barnabas answered promptly. " 'Tis
my feast day—at least it will be my feast on the morrow."

"Your feast?"

"St. Barnabas, of course: June 11. My lord always
comes for my feast. I wonder if he does it of a purpose. Maybe Dame Alice tells him."

Though it was dark Stephen held back a grin. Barnabas was but a simpleton. 'Twas like him to imagine
that my lord and my lady ordered their lives by his
feast day. Doggett had supplied the real reason. And
that, when he came to think of it, had to do with *his*
father. Reminded of his duty, he crossed himself and
said a quick prayer for his father's peace before he
went back to sleep.

Although he was aware of my lord's presence
kneeling at ·his stall in the chapel for the morning
mass, Stephen's first encounter with him was in the
screens passage, as, tablet in hand, he went to the
solar on my lady's orders to take down some letters.
My lord was just emerging from the hall, and though
Stephen flattened himself against the wall, there was
no escape. My lord looked him up and down.

"You here?" he exclaimed. "I had forgot about you.
By heaven, you grow more like your father every
day." He snapped his fingers under Stephen's chin.
"Hold up your head and you'll do."

He swung round and walked out of the door with a
slight limp. Stephen pulled himself together and continued on his way to the solar. My lady's face was
bright.

"Come, boy. There are two letters to be written and I've little time to spare. My lord is waiting to make his survey of the manor."

Stephen propped himself against the desk and began at once. The first letter was to a merchant in London about certain fine furnishings for Pulteney's Inn, my lord's new house in the City which he had just purchased from the Earl of Huntingdon. Stephen wrote steadily but took her news in all the same. So my lady *had* succeeded in her letter to her daughter of Salisbury, and there was no longer any secret about it.

The second letter was more interesting still. It was addressed to the chancellor of Oxford University, and it made formal offer of a gift of books, which she would dispatch shortly by the hand of her chaplain, Master Simon Brayles. After she had signed both letters with her usual deliberate flourish, she left him to fold them and seal the ribbons with her personal seal, a favor which, she told him with a smile, she would bestow on very few.

The letters finished and handed to Bylton, Stephen returned to his work. Master Brayles was not there, and for the first time since Stephen's interest had been awakened he was in no mood for books. His mind wandered to my lord, to his father, and the likeness that my lord saw. He stood up deliberately, his feet well apart, his belly stuck out, and his head high, resolved to hold himself that way if it would earn my lord's approval.

It seemed to be a success, for when he approached the high table with Barnabas after dinner to offer the bowl and towel for finger-washing, my lord noticed him for the second time.

"Can you sit a horse, boy?" he demanded.

Stephen hesitated. He'd perched on a farm horse often enough, but when it came to riding he'd never straddled anything larger than a donkey. Nervously he said that he could mount a baggage horse.

My lord chuckled. "We'll have that old brown mare that's broken-winded. *She'll* not throw you. I've a mind for you to ride with me tomorrow."

Stephen withdrew, divided between gladness and dread. He had no idea what would be required of him, who else was of the party, where they would go, how he would acquit himself. But he did know that as this was St. Barnabas's day, June 11, tomorrow was June 12, the day of Jargeau, the day his father died. That surely must be why my lord had ordered him.

He slept restlessly and served mass, noticing that Master Simon was saying a requiem, the mass for the faithful departed. As he was clearing the chapel Barnabas came running and told him to hurry. There were cheese and ale for him in the buttery. My lord would be ready soon.

He gulped his food and rushed to the courtyard to find no one there but a groom holding two horses, my lord of Suffolk's charger and the little old brown mare. Was no one else coming? At that moment my lord appeared and without ado swung himself up into his saddle, calling to the groom to put the boy up. Before Stephen had time to feel any fear, he found himself pacing soberly down toward the gatehouse at a safe distance behind my lord.

Outside the gatehouse they turned away from the village, beside the stream where the watercress grew. Stephen knew it as the way to Benson, Dorchester, or to faraway and unknown Oxford. Where were they going? he wondered. But even that question faded compared with the amazing truth. He was riding alone with my lord of Suffolk.

They skirted Benson village and plodded on with the Thames on their left, its course marked by a line of willows, where men were pollarding the young growth for baskets and hurdles. Ahead of them across the river rose the familiar twin hills Wittenham Clumps, each with its heavy crown of trees. There were wooded slopes at the foot of them, and presently a track led off in that direction. Stephen suddenly remembered a ford, the Shelling ford, where the bed was gravelly and the water shallow. Was that what they were making for? Unexpectedly they reached the water's edge. My lord's great horse splashed noisily across, and the mare followed, carefully picking her way.

Suffolk waited for him on the further bank.

"You do well enough," he said. "You have no reason to be afraid. Know you why I have brought you out today?"

Just for one moment Stephen hesitated. Then, blessing Doggett, he said. "Yea, my lord. It is my father's *mind*."

Suffolk nodded. "Good. You have been well raised. 'Tis ten years this day since Jargeau, and I would remember *all* who perished there, may God assuage them." He turned and pointed to the first of the two Clumps ahead. "We are going to climb that hill. There is an old fortress on the top, so old that none knows who made it. Nothing remains but mounds of earth instead of moats and ramparts, and the Thames below looks like a winding brook compared with the mighty Loire, where my wars were fought. But it is an old battleground; men have died there and it fits the day." He shook his rein and moved gently ahead. "Come on, now. We will ride as far as may be, then tie up and trust our feet for the rest."

Stephen followed as though in a dream. It was hard to believe that this man with his memories was really the dread Earl of Suffolk. Presently the path grew steeper and the scrub closed in. Suffolk dismounted and himself saw to the tethering of the horses. Then he nodded toward the hill.

"Go you ahead," he said. "My pace is slower than yours. Wait for me at the top."

Seeing that my lord was lame and preferred to take his time, Stephen obeyed. The slope was short and steep. Here and there he used both hands and feet. Then quite unexpectedly the bushes ceased and he emerged onto a plateau, a wide table top from which grew a great circle of beech trees, most of them monsters with sweeping sheltering boughs. It was like a watchtower, with the country spreading away on all sides into endless distance, except where the second hill blocked out the sky with its crown of trees. As my lord did not appear, Stephen circled the top, staring at the view. The river twisted like a silver ribbon, now in full view, now lost again. Almost underneath, as it seemed, the white stones and red roof of the abbey at Dorchester shone out in the sun. Could Dorchester *really* be so near? His eye followed the horizon to the line of the Chilterns, picking out in imagination the place where he had rested before the storm and seen *these* hills against the sky. Gradually he worked around the edge, seeing country that he had never seen before. Then he heard Suffolk's voice behind him.

"Well, boy, have you found the ramparts yet? Look at them on the side away from the river. These old men knew that assault would be fiercest from the plain where the land is open. See you, the great ditch with only one entrance way?"

They strolled together right around the top, and then my lord sat down on the mound of the ditch, nodding to Stephen to sit beside him. "In a fashion this place reminds me of a castle I once owned in Normandy," he said, "a castle on a mound. Bricquebec was its name. Henry the Fifth bestowed it on me. The country around it was like this. I could have lived happily at Bricquebec."

"Do you own it still, my lord?"

Suffolk shook his head. "It went as part of my ransom when I was captured."

Stephen ventured another question. "Was Jargeau at all like this, my lord?"

"Not in the least. Jargeau is a walled town on the river Loire. We were besieged there, with the French attacking by assault—a contrast to the siege of Orleans where the shoe was on the other foot. At Orleans *we* were the besiegers with a garrison of starving French locked up inside. Orleans is a great city, the buckle that holds together the body of France. If we had won Orleans, the whole land would have been ours. Well did we know its import. We had encircled it for months, and it was just ripe to fall when the Maid appeared."

"The Maid?" cried Stephen.

"Yea, the maid Joan. Whether she came from heaven or hell I know not, but either God or the devil was with her. Orleans was a miracle that no mortal man could have worked, let alone a woman with a small band. She broke through our lines and reached the city—and ours, mark you, were seasoned men keyed up for victory. From that moment everything changed. She put new life into the starving, beaten French till they came out at us, fighting like men possessed. Never shall I forget the sight. I saw her with my own eyes, clad in white armor, her standard held aloft with JHESUS blazoned on it, leading assault after assault before her."

He paused and wiped his forehead. His face was set in deep furrows. Stephen looked at him in awe. This was what Doggett meant by my lord's bitter day. He wished that my lord would say more about Jargeau.

There was a silence and then Suffolk began again, more quietly.

"Well, we abandoned Orleans and our force divided. My lord Talbot went westward and I moved upriver to Jargeau. There was no need for great dismay. Sir John Fastolf was on his way with a new army of two thousand men. We had but to wait. We marched in good order, banners flying, took possession of Jargeau, closed its gates, and manned its walls. We were there in peace a month."

"You had food inside?"

"Yea, the townsfolk were friendly and we lived well. As for me, with your father as my man I lacked nothing. God forgive me, I grew oversecure, waiting only for Fastolf to join us. Then word came of a great army marching on us—not Fastolf but the French. I ordered a sally through the main gates to meet them. Our men were fresh and at first we scattered them, cheering to see their broken ranks. Then suddenly in the midst of them *she* appeared, standing in her stirrups sword in hand, screaming like a screech owl.

Before God, I never thought to see such a sight. Our Englishmen turned and fled: none could rally them. They ran like cravens, back to the shelter of the walls and slammed the gates."

"And then?" said Stephen breathlessly.

"Night fell and we prepared to face them in the morning. But during darkness they brought up their artillery, and we looked down from the ramparts at bombards and cannons trained upon us, backed by a sea of lances and pikes and maces. The Maid herself, on her white charger, called to us to surrender. I tried to offer terms but they would not talk, so I defied them. Their French trumpets sounded and the assault began.

"They piled faggots beneath the walls to smoke us out, and, half-blinded, as we beat them down, they raised their scaling ladders on the bodies of their own dead, till the pile grew higher and higher and they reached the top of the wall. Then, one splendid moment—a stone from one of our arbusquads struck the Maid on the helmet and laid her flat beneath the ramparts. The English cheer would have felled the walls of Jericho. They thought her dead and the war won. But it was a false hope. In a moment she was on her feet, yelling 'AVANT! AVANT!' and in that moment they knew that they were lost. *She could not die.* They turned and stampeded for the river as the French poured over the top. Though it was the end I, with two knights, stood fast, still hoping for some terms short of massacre. Your father was at my side; day or night he never left me. I heard a yell and saw a Frenchman, battleax raised to fell me. In a flash your father leaped in front, and the ax split him like a butcher's cleaver."

Stephen, deafened by the pounding of his own heart, saw the knuckles white on my lord's clenched hand. He made a sound in his throat and Suffolk turned to look at him.

" 'Tis right that you should know," he said. "War is not glory; it is butchery. I yielded my sword. It was all that I could do. It should have stopped the battle, but it did not. The French had debts to pay. They were hot for blood, and the Loire ran red with it."

Again there was silence. This time it was a long one, so long that the heat of battle faded, the Loire became the Thames again, and Stephen ceased to feel sick. My lord leaned back on his elbow. There was something on Stephen's mind. He wondered if he dared to ask it.

"My lord, the Maid had the name of Jhesus on her banner. Was she a witch?"

"She was burned as a witch—though I thank God on my knees that I had no part in the trial. She had powers outside herself, of that there can be no doubt. No peasant maid could know the art of war or strategy or statecraft, yet she had them all. 'Voices' directed her, so she said. Were they of God or the devil? Ask me not. We English say the devil. She loosed our grip on France. But she was a Frenchwoman and we were France's enemies. It was for her own country that she fought. The French let her fall into the hands of the Burgundians; the Burgundians sold her to the English for ten thousand crowns—a high price when you think that Christ was sold for thirty pieces of silver."

"The English burned her?"

"Yes, we burned her, using the Church to carry the burden for us. We could not have burned her only because she conquered us; no laws of warfare would permit that. But if she was proved a witch the Church could condemn her as the enemy of God and on *that* we could burn her, and burn her we did. I tell you facts, but of this cry of witchcraft I can tell you nothing. The Church defines the laws of God, and the no man's land between God and evil is dangerous ground. She died with the name of Jesus on her lips. It was an English archer who bound two sticks into a cross when she called for one. And an Englishman watching the holocaust cried aloud 'We are all lost; we have burned a saint.' "

The sun had moved around and was now shining in their faces. My lord shaded his eyes with his hand.

"It grows late," he said, the deep note gone from his voice. "The day of Jargeau is nearly over. It is a strange matter that I should have your father's son with me. . . . Think you that you can find the horses? I will come slowly behind you. My foot pains me today."

Stephen went down ahead and stood waiting, full

of thought. The story of his father's death held him fast. He felt inwardly that it was in some way his heritage to serve my lord as his father had done, but not in battle! Pray God not in battle! He watched as Suffolk hobbled, adjusting his foot in the stirrup with a little grimace of pain. He dared to speak out.

"Was it at Jargeau that you got your wound, my lord?"

"My wound? Which wound? I've been stuck as often as a pig at a fair."

"Your leg, my lord. The one that makes you limp."

Suffolk on the tall horse looked down at him and to Stephen's dismay suddenly roared with laughter.

"My *limp!* That's no battle scar. I've suffered it from my youth because I had to wear my brother's armor which was too small for me. I limp from *corns,* boy. You may gape but all my life I've been a martyr. A hair shirt in like measure would be comfort— Now I think of it your father used to cut them for me, as none else could, though, God rest him, often I cursed him roundly. But I've not known such comfort since. Have you inherited his touch, I wonder? One day I might let you try."

Stephen shuddered with dread. He would never dare. But as they rode briskly back to Ewelme he was struggling with a memory of something he had heard. Only as they turned in at the gatehouse did he remember clearly. It was Tom, at the mill, talking at night. "They say that her salve for corns is like none other."

Wormwood
and Mugwort

THE IDEA that had come into Stephen's mind as they
rode in through the gatehouse went on working there
day after day. He had little chance of forgetting it, for
my lord's foot had suddenly become the main interest
of everyone at the Hall. It seemed that the steep
rough climb up Wittenham Clumps had set up new
inflammation. He walked about limping and in pain,
unable to bear anything but an old soft buskin, and
the whole household suffered for it. The barber-sur-
geon from Wallingford was sent for and arrived with
his bag containing knives and scalpels. But yells and
bellowings from my lord's great chamber echoed
through the house, and the barber hurried away more
speedily than he had come.

The following day Master Simon Brayles rode off to
Dorchester to consult the Black Canons, monks of
Dorchester Abbey. One of them, though ancient and
infirm, was reputed to be learned in surgery and med-
icine. No sooner had he gone than Stephen deliberately forsook his books and set off for the hills.

As he climbed he felt his conscience prick him in a new way, for in spite of all she had done, he had deliberately kept away from old Meg ever since Lys went to Goring. But she greeted him without reproach and with no more concern than if she had seen him yesterday. She listened, her old face wreathed in smiles, to his report of Lys's happiness and also to his story of his own change of fortune.

"I knew it would be so," she said simply. "I saw it plainly in the pool. But tell me now what brings you? 'Tis not for nothing, I'll be bound. What is it this time? Squirrel tails?"

He had the grace to feel ashamed as he told her his errand. But she took it good-humoredly and vanished toward the shed at the back, leaving him with Wat who joyfully brought out his latest bit of chipped-out applewood, a little old woman very like his mother. Stephen was turning it over with amazement when Meg herself reappeared. She carried a large dock leaf on which lay a pile of soft pellets, looking like fat grey slugs. Stephen asked with alarm if my lord would have to swallow them.

She broke into a cackle of laughter. "He'd spew them fast enough if he did. They're for his feet, not his belly. They are of wormwood and mugwort compounded with frog-spawn—and other things known only to me. Hark you now: you must bathe the foot with water as hot as he can bear, dry it, and clap a pellet on it to soften. Wrap it in soft linen and let it bide there. Do it day by day till the fire has gone out of it. It works best with a waxing moon—waxing, mark you, not waning. Every humor grows worse when the moon is full."

All the way back to Ewelme he repeated her instructions aloud: hot water, soft linen, a waxing moon. Luckily the moon had not yet reached the first quarter. There was more than a week before it became full. The remaining problem was how to tackle my lord. But he would not allow himself to lose heart. My lord himself had said, "One day I might let you try."

As usual Barnabas was on the lookout for him.

"Dame Alice sent for you," he warned in a hoarse whisper. "My lord is in the solar. They say he is surly as a bear. Dame Alice told him you were good at reading aloud, but when the message came you were not here."

Stephen drew a sharp breath. Here was his chance. Without giving himself time to think he hastened to the solar, dropped on his knees, and humbly asked pardon for his absence. He had been to visit an old woman said to be skilled in curing ills of the feet.

The effect was instantaneous. My lord, stretched on the bed, exclaimed, "How say you?" Dame Alice clapped her hands repeating "Ills of the feet? What does she say?" For answer Stephen nervously opened the dock leaves to show the pellets, carefully repeating old Meg's instructions.

"Well done, boy." Dame Alice did not hesitate.

"Come, let's not delay. Call for hot water from the kitchen. There are basins and towels and linen here in my ewery."

Everyone bustled around, and before he had time for second thoughts Stephen found himself kneeling before my lord and supporting the swollen foot over a steaming bowl. For some reason his fright left him; his whole mind and will was set upon the task of soothing my lord's pain. "As hot as he can bear," was old Meg's order, and though my lord swore like a true soldier, Stephen kept his head. As the pellet softened in the heat he laid strips of linen on it till it melted into a green poultice. It was not long before my lord admitted that the pain was easier, and as the foot was laid back gently on the bed he looked at Stephen with a frown more puzzled than angry.

"'Tis true," he observed, as though speaking to himself, "the boy *has* his father's touch."

"Maybe we will make a surgeon of him," said Dame Alice cheerfully. "But this balm which is so effective how came you by it? An old woman, you say? Who is she? Where does she live?"

This was what Stephen had dreaded. His face was hidden as he gathered up the litter from the floor. With his voice not quite steady he mumbled something about an old woman, known to his mother, who lived not far from Odo's cottage. This vague answer about Odo's cottage was a useful and a convincing one. But his conscience pricked him, for if his mother

knew of old Meg, he doubted if she had ever ex-
changed two words with her. However Dame Alice
seemed satisfied. She said no more except to tell him
that he must without delay attend to my lord's foot
until it was truly cured.

Actually it was only a few days before my lord cast
off his old buskin and called for his riding boot. Stephen was called to ease the foot into it and stood
back, well satisfied, to watch his patient mount.
Everything had gone better than he had dared to
hope. He had come near to filling his father's place,
and old Meg's share in it had not been mentioned
again.

The only person who failed to praise him was Master Simon, who inquired quizzically when he was
going to give his mind to his Latin again. So, rebuked, he worked hard for a couple of weeks until
one day Dame Alice sent for him. He obeyed uneas-
ily, but she received him with a smile.

"Master Simon is riding tomorrow to Oxford to deliver my books for the new library," she said, "and
you are to go with him. He says that it will disturb
your work again, but I hold that the sight of Oxford
may spur you to greater effort. So, boy, see that you
prove me right."

Thus, in spite of Master Simon's doubts, they rode
out the next morning, directly after the morrow mass,
with the precious books in a sheepskin bag strapped
to the back of Master Simon's saddle. The chaplain's

mule was not given to speed, and Stephen's farm pony jogged slowly beside it while Master Simon recited matins under his breath and Stephen, mumbling responses more or less at random, enjoyed the scent of elderflower in the water meadows and the now familiar outline of Wittenham Clumps, misty against the sky.

Master Simon reached the final amen and after a moment's pause began to talk.

"You have never seen Oxford," he said. "You will stand amazed at your first sight of it. From outside its walls it looks like a splendid city pictured in a Book of Hours—my lady has a book with such a picture; maybe you have seen it. Inside it is a teeming anthill, crowded with learned masters who live, dignified, in halls and colleges and poor scholars, many of them half-starved, who issue in their hundreds from every nook and cranny."

"Half-starved?" cried Stephen. "Are they not fed?"

"That depends on their pockets. Mark you, I speak of old times. 'Tis better ordered nowadays. But, remember, a university is not a school; it does not nurture its scholar's bodies. 'Tis more like a market which has learning for its merchandise. Any master qualified to teach may set up his board and lecture to those who can pay his fees. The greater the master the more students he attracts. A teacher famed far and wide will draw students who have tramped half across the world with near-empty pockets to learn of him. But how they live is not *his* business."

"If they are penniless where do they sleep?"

"Where best they can. Maybe on a sheaf of straw in a cellar, at great profit to the landlord. Or they hire some sort of lodging and share a common purse, though often enough the purse-bearer learns how to feather his own nest. But, note, I am speaking of the past. The Masters of Convocation have stepped in to order matters. All halls that shelter students now must be licensed, with a master of arts in charge. But 'tis true all the same that the hunger for knowledge can consume a man so that he will suffer anything to gain it—like the pearl of great price we read of in the gospel. Of course by such knowledge I do not mean only book learning, though book learning is a preparation for it. I am referring to knowledge beyond what has been known before, some fresh truth in the chain of God's creation. Can you grasp my meaning?"

Stephen said, "Yes, sir," though he was far from sure. But the chaplain accepted his word and went on as though talking to himself.

"We know so little and there is so much to be understood. It is a perilous business, like launching a tiny boat onto a boundless sea. The man who ventures after pure knowledge, though his head be crammed with learning, may encounter God—or the devil. That's the crux of it. He must needs tell good from evil or he will betray mankind. Have you heard of Roger Bacon?"

Stephen said, "Yes, sir." He *had* heard the name, though he had no idea who Roger Bacon was. His whole mind was caught up by that same old problem —the one that led, so far as he was concerned, to old Meg: the problem of telling good from evil.

"You'll hear of him often enough at Oxford," said Master Simon, hardly pausing, "though he's been dead for nigh on a century. He was a Franciscan friar who sought to explain the problems of the universe, using mathematics as his handmaid. By mathematics, he believed, man could work out the natural laws. Thus he deduced the measure of the seasons, the ebb and flow of tides, the meaning of the rainbow, and far more than I can tell you here. He had to suffer for it. The learned doctors and masters and his own superiors of the Franciscan order all turned upon him. They accused him of heresy, forbade him to teach, and held him in prison: some even added the charge of witchcraft."

"Witchcraft?" said Stephen sharply.

"Yes, boy, witchcraft, though few believed it. But even masters of learning are not incapable of jealousy, and 'sorcery' is an easy cry for those outstripped in the race."

"Then what happened to him?"

"The Pope intervened and he was at last set free. But be not hasty in your judgment. Outside the bounds of proved knowledge lies the infinity of God but also the cunning of the devil, and who can say with certainty which is which. The man who ventures must move inch by inch, never daring to drop the lifeline of Holy Mother Church."

For a while they rode on in silence. Then Master Simon began again, this time describing the separate colleges sprung up within the university. Each had been founded by a benefactor for some special purpose, and within their walls masters and scholars lived together obeying rules, almost like monks, and working like everyone else to gain their degrees in arts and sciences.

But Stephen was no longer listening. This new idea of exploring *for* knowledge, like exploring new and possibly dangerous country, had gripped his fancy.

Master Simon recalled him from his dreams by pulling up suddenly. He was pointing ahead.

"Look you!" he cried. "Your first glimpse of Oxford."

They stood upon the brink of a gently sloping hill, gazing over a wide sea of treetops veiled in morning mist. As they watched, the mist gradually swirled and rose, giving way to pale golden sunshine. From this veil emerged the towers of a city, seemingly far away, first one tower, then many, amid a background of walls and roofs and chimneys. A single great spire soared above them all, its pinnacles touched with gold. Then a cloud covered the sun and the whole vision faded.

"That was a moment for which you may thank God," murmured Master Simon. "The valley mist plays tricks, and I have never seen it look more lovely. Now—stick your heels into your fat charger. We must hurry. That great spire you saw is St.

Mary's, the heart of the university, which serves all its needs—a church for holy mass and a hall for every ceremony; it also houses the library till a new one is built. That is where we must deliver the books. Wake up, boy; you look half asleep."

Stephen shook himself, and side by side they trotted briskly down the hill until the road flattened out and they joined a stream of people, some mounted, some on foot, but all, like themselves, heading for a bridge over the river. Willows veiled the view, and they were halfway across before Stephen realized that the city walls stood just on the other bank, rising straight up from green meadows, less than a bowshot ahead.

Master Simon led the way to a hostelry beyond the bridge where they tethered their beasts and ate a sound meal. It was the first meal of the day and Stephen found that he was famished. Then with the parcel of books cradled in Master Simon's arms, they joined the string of people passing through the East Gate into Oxford.

They emerged into brilliant sunshine, and Stephen stopped dead, blocking the way till someone thrust him to one side where he remained stock-still, dumfounded by what he saw.

He had expected a town like Wallingford, though twice as big, with narrow streets and jutting roofs. Instead ahead of him was a street almost as wide as the river Thames, sweeping away in a great curve.

But it was the crowd that astonished him most. There were crowds in Wallingford on market day, leisurely gossiping crowds, mostly women clutching babies and baskets, with plenty of time to spare. But here there were hardly any women, only men of all ages, and every one of them bent on some purpose. Here and there elderly masters in square caps and handsome gowns moved with dignity, as way was opened for them. There were monks and friars and grave-faced men in twos and threes discussing as they went. There were boys not much older than himself, pushing their way through as though the devil were after them, and a few lordly young coxcombs fashionably attired with great hats or scalloped liripipes wound around their heads. But by far the greatest number were poor scholars, unmistakable in their faded rags, who called to one another in a tongue of which he could not understand a word.

He gaped so long that for a while he lost sight of Master Simon. But at last, to his relief, he saw the chaplain waiting for him at the corner of a narrow lane.

"Keep close, boy," he rebuked, "or you'll lose yourself in this rabble of clerks. I've set the parcel down on a stone for a while. I promise you I'll be glad to be rid of it."

"Can I take it, sir?"

"You could not carry it. 'Twill do no harm to wait a minute. See you that gray wall with trees, and a small church beyond? That is St. Edmund's Hall, where I lived in my day. 'Tis quiet, away from the turmoil of the High Street, which is like a great artery cut through the body of the town. Now look you the other way, toward St. Mary's Church—with the great spire. See you all that scaffolding? That is the new college of All Souls, still in the course of building. It will be one of the finest in Oxford when it is done. 'Tis the gift of the Archbishop of Canterbury—the present one. He has founded it to offer prayers for Henry the Fifth, his royal brothers, and his lords who died in the French wars; indeed for all who fell in battle."

Stephen felt a sudden upsurge of pride. *His* father had died in the French wars.

"Shall we see it, sir—the new building?"

"We pass close to it. Later we may have time to look at it. The lord archbishop has not spared his purse. His masons and his craftsmen are the finest in the land."

He picked up the parcel again and they pressed on, past the forest of scaffolding that veiled the new building, until they reached St. Mary's, its tower even more impressive than it had looked from afar, and entered through a porch as big as a hall.

"The porch of St. Mary's," observed Master Simon, laying down the books for a final rest. "It's a place of painful memory for everyone who has disputed here, which means in fact every master in Oxford in his day."

"Disputed?" repeated Stephen.

"Yea, disputed. Know you not what it is to dispute? Scholars dispute in argument against each other, here in public, to show how much they know. 'Tis part of the process by which they reach their mastership. How else think you could they be examined and their knowledge put to the test? You may well dispute here in the future."

With his mind on this awe-inspiring prospect, Stephen followed him through the church which was old and dark with round-headed windows and many recesses with side altars. They turned aside into a large chapel and thence up a long flight of stairs. As they mounted, Stephen could see a lofty room above, entirely framed with shelves of books.

In the middle stood two men, pouring over a high desk, their backs toward the stairs. One was tall and broad of shoulder with a head of tow-colored hair. The other was small and so completely bald that his spectacles thrust up out of the way appeared to be resting on an egg. It was the small man who heard them first and turned around. His face, like a piece of wrinkled parchment, lit up with a smile.

"Your pardon, good master; I hope you have not been waiting long? You must be Master Brayles, chaplain to my lady of Suffolk. I had word that you were to bring her splendid gift of books. Let me present to you the principal of St. Andrew's Hall, Master Roger Bolingbroke. Maybe you have met before?"

"A Cup of Wine
with Roger Bolingbroke"

As THE principal of St. Andrew's Hall turned slowly around, Stephen's heart sank like a stone. What a fool he had been not to foresee that he would probably meet Bolingbroke, when, after all, it was through Bolingbroke that Dame Alice had sent her message offering books for the new library. What would happen now? He was angry with himself for being unprepared. There was a double danger—not only about the meeting at old Meg's, but, worse, the danger that Bolingbroke was in possession of Dame Alice's letter.

The two masters, however, were exchanging greetings, both acknowledging that they had not met before. Compliments flowed, and it wasn't until Stephen stepped forward to help with the bag of books that Bolingbroke appeared to notice him.

"Why!" he declared loudly. " 'Tis the young storm cock himself! Master Registrar, you've heard how Duke Humphrey's books were in dire peril at Benson lock. This is the very boy who faced the mad miller single-handed and got them safely through."

"This boy? Unaided?" cried the little bald man. He looked at Master Simon as though for confirmation.

"I was not there but I have been told so," said Master Simon quietly. "Of course he bore an order from Dame Alice but that does not reduce his credit. Truth is that the miller is an old warrior with blood that boils too readily, and Stephen has some skill in calming him."

"A skill we must be thankful for," twittered the registrar. "The boy has earned our gratitude. Does Duke Humphrey know it? He should be told. Come, young man, and I'll show you some of the treasures that you saved."

Much to Stephen's embarrassment he took his stand at the desk beside Master Simon while the registrar, assisted by Bolingbroke, lifted down book after book to show them. Luckily for him Master Simon did all the talking, for he could think of nothing to say. True that the books were wonderful to look at, so beautifully written that the patience of the scribes, copying page after page without a single mistake or a crooked letter, was something to marvel at. But most of them were in Latin, a few in French, but only one or two in English. None had pictures, except for little drawings around the capital letters or tiny patterns down the margin of the page.

At the same time other thoughts were running through his head. "Young storm cock!" That was old Meg's name for him. Why had Bolingbroke used it? To remind him of the secret that they shared?

He was glad when at last Master Simon begged that the good masters would not weary themselves. "Your library is overflowing," he said. "I hear rumor that you are to have a new one."

"Indeed we are," said the registrar triumphantly. "Duke Humphrey has promised to open his purse yet once more. The new Divinity Schools are being erected only a bowshot away, and it is now proposed to build a new library above them. It will bear Duke Humphrey's name. Maybe, sir, you would like to see for yourself?"

"I will be guide," volunteered Bolingbroke, as Master Simon hesitated. "Nay, sir; it is no trouble. I shall be proud to take you."

After polite farewells to the registrar Stephen followed the two masters down the stairs. The whole day, which had in any case seemed like a waking dream, now took on the flavor of a nightmare. Anything might happen.

But Bolingbroke seemed to get on excellently with Master Simon. They left the church by the north door, which opened into a court of small houses with a splendid view of the new All Souls College.

"It is in truth a fine sight," remarked Master Simon as they paused to stare at it. "Who is the master mason? I did hear that the archbishop had commissioned Richard Crevington—or is it Robert Jayne?"

"*Both!*" said Bolingbroke promptly. "Archbishop Chichele grabs all the best men. He has Massingham, the sculptor, into the bargain. But luckily the university has Richard Winchcombe for the Divinity Schools, fresh from work at New College. He is an old man now, but he has built some of the finest churches hereabouts: Addington and Deddington, and I think Bloxham too. The only trouble is that he has worked for the king and rates himself accordingly. Truth to tell, the Masters of Convocation complain that he is emptying their coffers— Come, sir, we will go by Schools Lane."

They threaded their way through a jumble of old buildings into a lane which, though narrow and muddy, did appear to continue straight ahead. There was just room for the two men to walk abreast. Stephen followed at their heels. All this talk about buildings and masons did not interest him, but he was glad to be able to watch Bolingbroke. Gradually his uneas-

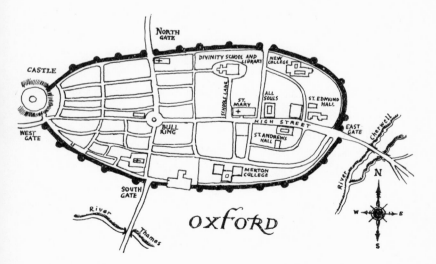

iness died down. The principal of St. Andrew's was in a friendly mood and it was hard to see in him the stranger he had encountered at old Meg's.

"These are the *old* schools on either side of you," Master Simon called over his shoulder to Stephen. "Certainly it is time they were rebuilt. They are more like cattle sheds than halls, but masters hire them to give their lectures in. Even in my day they were rat-ridden, but you, boy, may yet wear out your shoon on these cobbles."

"Indeed he may," said Bolingbroke cheerfully. " 'Twill be years before we have new. But look, sir, *there* lies the future ahead of you."

The narrow lane ended suddenly in a sweep of ground cleared of all buildings. From the middle of it rose a cluster of walls, still little more than shoulder-high, veiled in scaffolding. But compared with Schools Lane it looked like the beginning of a palace, its stones the color of rich cream. Everywhere there was activity. Beneath thatched shelters masons chipped out the curves that were to form arches, laborers with barrows trundled squared blocks of stone, while from within the walls came the ringing of hammer and chisel.

"Look you—there it stands," cried Bolingbroke as though it were his own. "At ground level the Divinity Schools with Duke Humphrey's library built over them —though I fear that is yet many years ahead. But see! There is Master Winchcombe himself—that old man in the red cap. We are in luck; the fellow he is talking to, the one with the riding cloak, is John Massingham, the sculptor of All Souls. If we go forward we may win a word with them."

Master Simon hesitated, but Bolingbroke certainly did not lack boldness. And as he approached the two men it became clear that he was well known. Richard Winchcombe came forward to meet them. He was tall and bent with white hair straggling from under the red cap onto an ancient leather jerkin. On hearing the word Ewelme he held out a scarred and knotty hand.

"Ewelme? A fine foundation. They've made right royal use of brick. Come you, sir, and meet John Massingham, the carver. He is summoned to London, in *this* heat, more fool he. His lord archbishop keeps him shuttling between Oxford and Canterbury as though he were a bobbin. Prelates have no thought for a craftsman's dignity."

Massingham, round-faced and genial, only laughed. "Pay no heed to him, sir. All masons suffer from working at dizzy heights. My dignity comes to no harm and after all one must look to one's patron."

"Then have one worth looking to," retorted Winchcombe. "Duke Humphrey for instance. *There's* a patron for you! Ask Bolingbroke here; he'll tell you—though maybe *his* pull is on the distaff side!" The old man winked and Bolingbroke turned red at this obvious reference to the Duchess Eleanor. But Massingham went on unheeding.

"As it happens 'tis not the archbishop who has summoned me this time. It is the king."

"What does *he* want? Something for his new college at Eton?"

"Nay, nearer to his heart than that. The death-mask of the Earl of Warwick has just arrived from France and his grace would have me make a likeness of the features while the wax is still fresh. You know how he loved his old tutor. Later I am to carve from it a figure for the tomb in the chapel to be built at Warwick. So you see, 'tis a matter in which I cannot make delay."

Among murmurs of sympathy he bowed and walked away. Winchcombe still groaned in mock despair. "Faith, who would give his talents to a task like modeling the dead. A mason's blocks of stone at least do not decay— But now, sirs, what can I do for you? You want to see the new work?"

He led them toward the half-built walls where for the next half hour they all stood first on one foot then another, while the sun blazed down on them from overhead. At first Stephen was filled with wonder how stone arcades as slender as saplings in a wood could be expected to carry the weight of a roof overhead, let alone the weight of a great library, but by the time that Winchcombe had made drawings in the dust to show how he planned to solve the problem, not only Stephen but the chaplain and Bolingbroke too were almost prostrate with the heat.

Once out of sight of the Master Mason, all of them openly sighed with relief.

"Come back with me to St. Andrew's Hall and rest awhile before you ride," cried Bolingbroke, mopping his brow. "A flagon of wine hangs cooling in the well, and it would give me great pleasure to welcome you."

Master Simon immediately accepted the invitation, and Stephen said a silent *Deo gratias*. Not only did he want to see St. Andrew's Hall, but all the strain of the day seemed suddenly to have gone. Bolingbroke and Master Simon were apparently good friends. There was no longer anything to be afraid of. He strolled along behind them, looking around him, pleased that he could already recognize a great deal: All Souls and the scaffolding around it, where Massingham worked; that great spire of St. Mary's, which from this point made him crane his neck; while, ahead of them, he could see crowds scurrying by as the broad High Street cut across the end of Schools Lane.

But his peace was short-lived. Without warning, Master Simon turned inquiringly to Bolingbroke.

"What was your first meeting with Stephen?" he asked. "Dame Alice told me that you knew him already—before the episode of the books?" He spoke pleasantly enough, but the question was deliberate and needed an answer. Stephen was thankful that his face could not be seen, and for a moment even Bolingbroke seemed taken by surprise.

"Why, yes," he said carefully. "Yes, I *had* met the boy before. We met in that great storm some months ago. You may recall it, sir; one of the worst I have ever known. I had completely lost myself on my way to Wallingford. I was thankful to meet him. He guided me on to the right road."

"And then?" The chaplain was strangely persistent.

"I saw him no more till I waited upon my lady of Suffolk to thank her for the safe passage of the books. You may imagine it was a surprise to find the same boy so much the hero of it."

Stephen held his breath. *What* had made Master Simon suddenly ask that question? But Master Simon said no more, and they walked on in silence till they reached the High Street, where they were held up by a stream of noisy jostling students all heading in one direction.

"There must be a baiting at the bull ring at Carfax," said Bolingbroke. "By your leave, sir, wait a minute. They'll soon be gone and we can cross in peace."

Stephen stared after the scurrying mob. There was a bull ring in Wallingford, though he had never been to a baiting; a fellow in Ewelme bred special bull dogs for the sport. But gradually the stream of students poured itself away, and, led by Bolingbroke, they were able to make their way across the High Street and into another network of lanes, this time all sloping downhill.

Master Simon, apparently at his ease again, gripped Stephen by the elbow to point out new landmarks.

"Look, there is the city wall below us and the meadows and river beyond it. That great tower is

Merton College, not even finished *yet*, and that farther one with the short spire is St. Frideswide's Priory —her shrine is there. By rights I should have dispatched you to say a prayer that one day you may come to Oxford as a scholar."

"I will find place for him at St. Andrew's Hall if he should need it," said Bolingbroke promptly. "After his valor with the books I have no doubt that Duke Humphrey would support him."

The chaplain for Ewelme stiffened again. "The boy is in my lord of Suffolk's service," he said coldly. "He will not lack patronage."

Stephen's heart sank. This was getting dangerous. Was there going to be trouble after all? But Bolingbroke gave way.

"Doubtless he would do better in your care," he conceded with the merest touch of sarcasm. "St. Andrew's is not a wealthy hall, it has no merchant's gold behind it. But you shall see for yourself, sir. Here we are."

He led the way along a narrow alley and then down two steps under an ancient timber porch. They found themselves in a hall as bare as a barn, almost pitch dark but pleasantly cool. At their entry birds swept from the rafters and out through tall unshuttered embrasures in the wall. At the far end a patch of sunshine found its way through one large glazed window, lighting a massive table, a single chair, and some benches and stools.

Bolingbroke led the way to the table. "Be seated,

sir," he invited. "There seems to be no one here. I'll wager that they are all at the bull ring, the idle fellows. No matter; I will fetch the wine."

He left them and Stephen stared around him. As his eyes grew accustomed to the dark, he could see a rickety stairway which led up to an open gallery with a pitch-black loft beyond it. The rail of the gallery was festooned with bedding, and in spite of the draft whistling through the smoke louver there was a musty smell of stale food and staler clothing. His eye caught Master Simon's, but before either could speak Bolingbroke returned with a dripping leather bottle.

"This will refresh you," he said cheerfully. "Now for some cups."

Setting the bottle down on the table, he turned to a little aumbry by the window, and unlocking it with a key which he pulled from inside his gown, he brought out two silver goblets, polishing them with his sleeve. In the moment that the aumbry door stood open something inside that glittered caught Stephen's eye. Dangling from a nail was that strange device in copper which Bolingbroke had worn at old Meg's.

Bolingbroke poured wine into the cups and, closing the aumbry door, turned to Stephen.

"Go you to the courtyard, boy, and fetch yourself water from the well. You'll find pitchers on the wall beside it. Half fill one and we'll lace it with wine to give it flavor."

Stephen took his time about drawing water, glad of

the chance to look around. The courtyard, as Master Bolingbroke had called it, was just a piece of waste ground between crumbling walls that apparently belonged to other halls similar to St. Andrew's. On the evidence of trodden paths through the nettles, this well with its ancient bucket and chain served all of them. The whole place was dank as though the sun seldom reached it.

When he got back indoors, Bolingbroke, cup in hand, was standing by the table as though he were lecturing Master Simon.

"But I tell you, sir, it is true," Bolingbroke insisted. "The conference at Gravelines is finished. There is no more talk of peace. 'Twas an ill-seasoned venture from the start, launched by an aged churchman and a stubborn woman—the Cardinal Beaufort and her grace of Burgundy, with none but that captivity-sick dreamer Charles d'Orleans to press our argument with the French. Well, for him it is captivity again. He returns, unransomed, and still a prisoner. The one man who could speak for England was left out of it by these would-be peacemakers. They ignored Duke Humphrey. He stayed kicking his heels with the king, and who will not say he kicked to some purpose. The king has rejected every line of their bargaining.

Master Simon seemed too dazed to interrupt. "But how came such news?" he demanded at last. "Up to the time that I left home this morning, no word had reached my lord of Suffolk."

Bolingbroke looked down at him, the hint of a smile stirring the corners of his mouth.

"News comes swiftly to Oxford, sir. I might also claim that news comes swiftly to *me*. It seems that my lord of Suffolk has seen fit to withdraw from statecraft of late. Maybe he is wise. He has a stumbling block in his most gracious lady. He should really insist that she restrain her pen."

He spoke with such deliberate insolence that Master Simon, white with anger, sprang to his feet. "You are offensive, sir. Were we not churchmen I would hotly call you to account."

Bolingbroke stretched out a soothing hand. "Nay, Master Brayles, be not perturbed. Believe me I yield to none in my admiration for my lady of Suffolk—a most gracious gentlewoman. But here, in Oxford, in a man's world, where women have small place, let us admit it—all women are indiscreet. They bedevil statecraft. They pass on gossip, even in letters, as though it were Holy Writ. Now, about this so-called secret scheme for a French marriage—"

Master Simon banged his fist upon the table. "Be silent, sir, or you may provoke too far. Remember that I have heard it said an hour since and in your presence that *your* authority is from the distaff side. Now by your leave we will be on our way. I must thank you for your hospitality."

Bolingbroke, once more conciliatory, saw them out into the cobbled lane—protesting that he had intended no more than a friendly parley between two masters of the same university. But Master Simon continued as cold as ice. As they parted, Bolingbroke patted Stephen on the shoulder.

"Remember," he said pleasantly, "there is place here for the boy if he should need it."

Master Simon said not a word till he and Stephen had rounded the corner. Then he turned, his face cold and stern.

"I know not how much you understand of all this," he growled. "But of one thing you may rest assured: if you lack Oxford altogether you will never be lodged at St. Andrew's Hall."

Stephen dared not to open his mouth. He plodded along with one thought uppermost. There was no longer room for doubt. Dame Alice's letter had been in Bolingbroke's hands, and it seemed that he had passed it on, presumably to the Duchess Eleanor, but possibly to Duke Humphrey himself. All that had been said about women's gossip and about restraining Dame Alice's pen could mean nothing less, even without the reference to the scheme for a French marriage. He wondered whether even Master Simon himself knew that particular secret. He had not seen the fatal letter. For one moment Stephen thought of telling him the whole truth, here and now. But the harm was done; it might cause more trouble still for Dame Alice, and it would certainly bring Stephen's whole world crashing about his ears.

THE WRITING ON THE HEARTH

They walked on in silence, single file, to the tavern. There they mounted, crossed the bridge, leaving Oxford behind, and began their journey up the long slope in the same order, the chaplain ahead and Stephen a short distance behind.

They had covered some miles before Master Simon waited for Stephen to join him. He was calm by now, but his eyes were watchful.

"Tell me about your meeting with Bolingbroke in the storm," he inquired. "*Where* did you meet him?"

Stephen jabbed the pony with his heel and took a moment to pull back into line.

"I met him in the woods, sir, not far from Odo's cottage." He had made much the same answer to Dame Alice about the balm, and it was no lie. Old Meg's *was* in the woods.

"Who is Odo, and where is his cottage?"

"Odo is my stepfather. He is a plowman and his cottage is on the Old Road, toward Swyncombe. I lived there till I came to the Hall."

"What did he say to you?"

"He said he was going to Wallingford and had lost himself, so I led him to where the ways divide." By this time Stephen's voice was quite steady.

"Did you perchance say that you were in my lord of Suffolk's service?"

"I said my lord had given me place at the school."

"So it could have crossed his mind as useful to have contact near to my lord of Suffolk. Was it *then* that he offered to accept you at St. Andrew's Hall, and did you not think it a great reward for so small a service?"

Stephen nodded. It was not safe to speak. He had in fact known well enough that it was a reward—not for showing the right road, but for keeping his mouth shut about old Meg.

"Humph . . ." said the chaplain quietly, as though he were talking to himself. "That is all very well, but what troubles me is all his hot-foot news. How can he know that the conference is ended, that all hopes of peace are gone? How comes that braggart to have tidings of such importance before my lord of Suffolk has wind of it? 'Tis possible he was drawing a bow at a venture to see what he could get from me." He turned back to Stephen. "And did you never see the fellow again, until he came to call upon Dame Alice?"

Stephen was suddenly inspired. "I *saw* him, sir, but not to speak to, when I worked at Benson Mill. He was in the barge with the Duchess Eleanor as it sped through the lock downstream."

"Ah—*that* is the key to everything. Did you note today how old Winchcombe baited him? He is in *her* service—her whom they call the witch of Gloucester. Clearly he is a most dangerous man."

Stephen's mind was swinging like a pendulum between satisfaction that he had got out of it so well and a sense of guilt that made him want to blurt out the whole truth. They rode on in silence. The heat of the day was over, and the evening was pleasantly cool. Master Simon spoke once more.

"Did you chance to notice a bright object hanging

in the aumbry when Bolingbroke took out the cups?"

Stephen hesitated. "Something that shone like gold?"

"Yes—though more likely copper. Did you note its shape, like a five-pointed star?"

This was perilous ground. He dared no more than nod once more.

"Ah," said Master Simon, "then mine eyes were not mistaken, however speedily he shut the door. What was it? A device of geometry, *a pentacle*. I can tell you no more, save that it is said to be of use in sorcery."

At that moment, to Stephen's utter relief, they reached a narrow bridge across a stream. They were back in the region of water meadows, where they could no longer ride side by side. He was thankful. He did not want to be on the alert any more. He was tired out and desired only to drop onto his bed.

The sun was going down and the mists were rising among the clumps of willows dotted about the marsh. He noticed a couple of horsemen in great riding cloaks moving ahead of them, uncertainly as though unsure of the way. They vanished behind a spinney and then emerged beyond it face to face with the pony and the mule. One of the strangers drew back, but the second came forward and saluted Master Simon.

"Your pardon, sir. These marshes are as confusing as a forest. We seek Ewelme. Have we come too far?"

"Too far or not far enough, sir, according to the way you have come. May I assume that you seek my lord of Suffolk? I am his chaplain."

At these words the second stranger moved forward to join the first. As Stephen stared at him something about his height in the saddle, the long pallid face with dark brooding eyes seemed faintly familiar. To Master Simon they presented no difficulty. He made a sign beckoning Stephen.

"Go you ahead to the Hall," he said quietly. "Tell my lord with all speed that Monseigneur the duc d'Orleans will be with him almost at once."

Stephen's first thought was of Bolingbroke. "The French duke returns unransomed." He was right again.

The fat pony shot off with sheer astonishment as Stephen's heels pounded its flanks. Ewelme in its hollow was quite invisible, but they had come far enough for him to know the way. Soon he joined the road beside the watercress stream. He raced past the gatehouse, tore up the drive, and, leaving the pony untethered in the courtyard, broke without ceremony through the screens passage and into the great hall.

By the light of candles my lord and my lady were supping wine at the end of their evening meal. Stephen did not even wait to drop on one knee.

"My lord," he cried breathlessly, "the French duke is coming. We met him in the meadows. Master Simon is bringing him in."

The
French Duke

*I*T SEEMED like a lifetime before Stephen, aching in every limb, crawled into bed. Barnabas, good fellow, had rolled over to make room for him, but Stephen was too tired to sleep. It was, he imagined, the middle of the night. Though there had been torches to welcome the French duke, with candles and tapers stuck up wherever they would go, there had not been enough light to prevent everyone bumping into each other as they scurried about carrying out Dame Alice's orders. As ill chance would have it, Bylton had, earlier in the day, fallen downstairs and lay with his leg in plaster, though he still tried to direct the flustered servants, who would have been better steward-less. Stephen was called upon from all sides. My lord's own bed in the Great Chamber had to be prepared for the duke, with a truckle for the gentleman beside it, and a meal had to be served for the travelers at the high table without servants to overhear conversation. Stephen himself was privileged to fetch and carry dishes, hindered by Barnabas, but he was never able to catch a word that passed between the five sitting together, talking in low tones—the two guests, my lord and my lady and Master Simon. When the food was on the table, it was Master Simon who whispered to Stephen that he had better go to bed. It was too late to prepare the chapel tonight for the morrow mass. They must bestir themselves early in the morning.

It had certainly been the longest day that he could ever remember, longer even than the day of the thunderstorm, when the roedeer was shot and Lys was lost. But he was too tired to fit the pieces together. Bolingbroke and St. Andrew's Hall seemed like another world, and the journey to Oxford in the morning could have been a year ago.

At long last, just as he was dozing off, a small light shone upon his face, part-shaded by Master Simon's hand.

"Still awake?" whispered the chaplain. "I suppose curiosity keeps you pricking. 'Tis late but I'll tell you this: the fellow Bolingbroke was right; the conference *is* ended, and ended in disaster, thanks to Gloucester's grip upon the king. There will be no peace, though all who took part were ripe for it—English and French and Burgundians. Monseigneur is in despair. He worked as go-between without rest, and now at the end he comes back to prison. From Dover he was being taken to Windsor, but he managed to slip his guard and come here to seek my lord—so certain is he that my lord is the only man still strong enough to work for peace. There, I have told you more than I meant. Get you to sleep now. I will wake you early."

The taper vanished and Stephen, turning on his side, told himself there was no hope of sleep. Then suddenly he felt his shoulder shaken. It was Master Simon still there with a light. But the light was no longer a taper. It was daylight.

He helped prepare the chapel and served mass in a dream, only mistily aware of the French duke wrapped in a furred robe of my lord's, kneeling between my lord and Dame Alice. Not until Barnabas had obligingly poured a pail of water over him in the yard did he really wake up and brace himself for the turmoil ahead.

Monseigneur le duc d'Orleans and my lord spent the morning together closeted over great matters, but Dame Alice, with Mistress Jane at her heels, became six housewives rolled into one. She made no conceal-ment of her determination that if their royal guest should be with them for only one day, it should be a worthy day. Doggett was sent for to unearth the painted cloths, bearing the arms of Orleans, which had hung on the wall behind the duke's seat at the high table during his longer sojourn at Ewelme some years back. The crippled Bylton was praised for his daring in having a swan from the river killed, skinned, and put on the spit to roast before its flesh could cool and grow tough. A swan was royal food forbidden to ordinary folk, but Dame Alice only clapped her hands when she heard what he had done.

"Bravo!" she cried. "Heaven knows whether it belongs to the king or the Vintners Company, or what it will cost us. But let us stir ourselves to good measure or Gloucester will pounce like a tomcat on his mouse before we've had even a whiff of glory."

Every one was allotted a special task. Stephen was sent first to help Doggett with the wall hangings. There were three of them to be unrolled, shaken, and hung. Orleans was in the middle—a fine display showing the lilies of France quartered with a strange device of a serpent swallowing a baby, which Doggett called "the Viper of Milan." The lions' faces of de la Pole hung on the right-hand side and the lion with two tails of Burghersh on the left.

When that job was finished Stephen was given minute instructions for the most important duty of all: to act as deputy for Bylton, who could not put foot to the ground, but who would carve the meals, unseen

CHARLES D'ORLEANS

behind a curtain. Stephen, assisted by pages, was to precede the dishes to the high table and see them offered to the company on bended knee. When everyone was served he was to remain standing behind Dame Alice to take her orders to Bylton if any crisis should arise.

Stephen was overwhelmed by the honor and struggled out of his clerk's gown and into the tight tunic and hose, blue and gold, of my lord's livery, trying to memorize the endless instructions poured upon him from all sides.

It seemed impossible that everything could be ready in time, and yet when the hour was rung from the little belfry the high table was faultlessly draped with its vast white cloth. A great silver salt stood in the center with a fine array of flagons and goblets. A trencher, a knife and a spoon, and a little crisp new loaf were provided for everyone.

Stephen stood in line with my lord's pages, awaiting the entry of the procession. But he had not been warned of the part entrusted to Barnabas, and his dignity was all but wrecked by an outburst of shrill notes on a hautbois, blown windily, upstairs in the gallery. As this shaky fanfare died away, my lord and my lady entered ceremonially through the screens, their guest between them, holding a fingertip of each. Behind them came the French duke's gentleman escorting two excited young mistresses, and the solemn procession was wound up by Dame Eleanor Thorn and Master Simon Brayles.

As soon as the places at the high table were filled, Master Simon intoned a grace, its amen lost in a veritable blast from Barnabas. Another procession was approaching up the hall. Four grooms of the household carried on their shoulders a great dish bearing the swan, still arrayed in its white feathers. As the dish was lowered onto a table, the feathers were ripped off in one piece to reveal the great bird roasted golden brown and already wonderfully scored through into slices. Coached by the steward in exactly what he should do, Stephen stepped forward with a beating heart and, using his fingers and a big knife, detached the slices and laid them on another dish, which the pages then carried to the high table, while he stood back surreptitiously sucking the flavor from his fingertips. When everyone was served, he went as he had been bidden and stood at the back of Dame Alice's seat, watching the pages smother the meat with savory sauces and the grooms fill up the goblets with wine.

The French duke was giving his entire attention to his hostess, gazing at her with melancholy eyes. It was not easy to understand all he said, but it seemed to be principally about the many places where he had been held prisoner during the long years since Agincourt, of which, he claimed, Ewelme and my lord's other domain at Wingfield were by far the most felicitous. The Tower of London was a grim fortress: every day brought fears of death. Windsor was better: at least there was good hunting. The worst was Pomfret in Yorkshire, where they used coal fires and everything was black. As for the English climate and the English beer—he spread his hands in mock despair. Nowhere had he found contentment as with my lord and lady of Suffolk, where a poor exile could enjoy books and music and even versifying with his jailer.

"You must have suffered cruelly, journeying to France, only to be brought back again," Dame Alice said gently.

"Madame, it was the bitterness of death. 'Tis so many years since my lord your husband first planned a meeting at his old house by Lombard Street to which came the Ambassador of Burgundy, and we three discussed a peace meeting with France, where *I* should act as intermediary with my freedom as the reward. These six years my lord has worked and I have hoped, and now it is all wrecked by Gloucester's greed for power."

"He has a wife to prick him on," said Dame Alice in a low voice.

"The Duchess Eleanor? Yea, Madame, you speak truth. I learned that when her father Sir Reginald Cobham was my jailer. I could tell you—" He broke off suddenly and changed the subject as a page approached to pour more wine. "Tell me, my lady, do you still grow those delicious cresses which I relished so much when I was here before—*cresson de fontaine,* how do you say it? Watercresses . . . I remember them always; the only cresses in England to compare with the *cresson* of France."

"We grow them, Monseigneur, or rather they grow themselves. The Ewelme brook is full of them. But the season is wrong. They are old now and tough. Perhaps you may come again in the spring, my lord duke."

Old and tough. Stephen saw in his mind's eye a clump of watercress, young and fresh, which he had noticed without thinking yesterday when he rode out with Master Simon. Its bright green had stood out among the dark leaves of the old plants. It was in the stream that meandered alongside the lane. If he ran quickly across the park the French duke could enjoy it with his wine. He glanced around. All the carving of meat was finished; the pages were serving peaches and pears. On a sudden impulse he slipped away through the little door behind him and was soon plunging knee deep through the long grass toward the stream.

A thick belt of young willows, still unpollarded, grew between the park and the water's edge. He had just begun to break his way through when he heard voices on the far side—men's voices and the jangle of horses' harness. He stopped, well hidden by the undergrowth, and peeped between the branches.

A party of horsemen was halted in the lane. There were at least a dozen of them; all had dismounted to lead their horses to drink. The sun flickered on steel. They were men-at-arms. At the same time his eye caught something else—the badge upon a saddle cloth. It was the chained swan—the badge of Duke

Humphrey. He remembered Dame Alice's words: "Gloucester will pounce like a tomcat on his mouse." His men were about to pounce *now!*

Trusting that the hum of voices and the horses' champing would cover any sound, he extracted himself from the tangle of willows and raced back across the grass. Wet and disheveled he tore into the hall regardless of the company. As it happened everyone had gone except my lord and my lady, the French duke and Master Simon, who lingered at the high table. They all stared as he came to a halt in front of them.

"They are coming, my lord;" he gasped, "a score of them, men-at-arms. They wear the badge of the chained swan. They've halted by the brook to water their horses."

My lord of Suffolk sprang to his feet. "Before heaven this is too much. So they think to seize you, sir, from under my roof. Bar the gates. Call out the guard. We'll teach them manners. Boy, fetch me my harness quickly."

But Charles d'Orleans, also on his feet, laid a hand on Suffolk's arm.

"Nay, my friend. I'll not have you embroiled over me. I expected them and I'll go quietly. There's nothing to fight about. I have not broken my parole, only made a detour on my way to Windsor."

Master Simon broke in with a suggestion. "Good my lord—if I may make bold—if they are halted, there may yet be time for you to sally forth peacefully with Monseigneur, accompanying him on his way. Take the other road and you may be well headed for Windsor before they catch you up. In that way it will be clear that Monseigneur is returning freely, not forced as a captive."

The French duke and Dame Alice agreed instantly, and my lord's wrath abated. Speed was vital, but alarm must be avoided. Everyone hurried to find Monseigneur's gentleman and Monseigneur's cloak and saddlebag and to order horses without causing a stir. Monseigneur kissed Dame Alice, she curtsied to him, and the party set off, riding quietly on grass to the lesser gatehouse which opened onto the Wallingford Road. Dame Alice with Master Simon, and Stephen in the background, watched them go, listening with bated breath for the sound of horses from the opposite direction. But though they fancied that they heard the sound of jangling harness down in the village, nobody appeared, and presently Dame Alice decided that they must all go indoors and behave as though nothing unusual had happened.

The remains of the meal were cleared from the hall and Dame Alice brought her needlework frame, and with Stephen to wait upon her and her chaplain to read to her, she sat down to await developments, presenting a picture of peaceful innocence for any who might come.

Nearly an hour passed before there was a clatter in

the courtyard, and not Gloucester's men but my lord of Suffolk himself stormed loudly through the hall reminding Stephen vividly of that day when Templar had been killed.

He strode up the hall and thumped the high table with his fist.

"Before God, madam, I have finished with all this nonsense—this skulking out of sight, lest Gloucester should do me harm. You've had your way long enough; see where it leads. An honored guest beneath my roof must be hurried out of sight! There will be no more of it. Tomorrow I return to London."

"That must be as my lord wills," said Dame Alice, completely calm. "But tell us what has happened. Did Monseigneur escape or have they taken him? Did they resort to arms?"

"They overtook us with weapons drawn, but there was no fighting. The duke is in truth a royal prince. He turned and met them with courtesy, declaring that he trusted he had caused no inconvenience by deciding to visit a friend. He was now satisfied and presumed that they would escort him. What's more he insisted that I should accompany him in friendship as far as the river. So we rode ahead and they followed, and at the bridge we parted."

"Then there is no harm done," she said soothingly.

At that he blew up like a bombard.

"No harm, when hopes of peace are gone and Gloucester rules the roost? What sort of a lord do you

think you have when a coxcomb can send his underlings to carry off a guest from my very table? Am I to
stomach it? You heard what his grace of Orleans
said. I, William de la Pole, am the one man who may
yet bring peace. Get my gear ready. I sorrow to leave
you, wife, but tomorrow I return to London—to claim
my place. As for Gloucester and his minions, upon my
oath I will see them bite the dust."

After a mass said at cockcrow, my lord of Suffolk
rode away, taking with him pages and grooms and
every man who could swell his train, and leaving behind only sufficient servants to wait upon Dame
Alice.

As the clatter of their going died away in the distance, Stephen turned back to the house not far from
tears, for Master Simon had gone too. Apparently in a
crisis my lord relied upon the wisdom of his wife's
chaplain. But for Stephen it meant no guidance for
his work and no time to do it; no refuge from Bylton,
querulous with pain, or from the endless household
rolls, and no company but Barnabas.

Dame Alice, also turning back, caught sight of his
face and beckoned to him.

"Be of good cheer," she said. "It will not be for
long. We are leaving Ewelme for it to be sweetened,
and the household will move to Donnington—a move
long overdue. Do you remember, you copied lists for
me months ago? But for you it is better still. I am to

join my lord in London, at Pulteney's Inn, our new home, and my lord has decided that you shall be of the party. So make yourself ready for a journey before the week is out."

Stephen followed her back to the house, dazed with excitement. He was to go to London; my lord needed him. It was like a dream come true.

Pulteney's Inn

*B*UT THE harvest was over and the early apples ripe before the party for London gathered in the court-yard in the gray light of a September dawn. Dame Alice was determined that the journey should be accomplished in one day, in spite of a call at Stonor to deposit Miss Jane at the home of her well-loved Mistress Philippa.

For the ride across the perilous Chilterns my lord had insisted upon a mounted escort from Wallingford, each man carrying one of my lady's waiting women riding pillion behind him. Stephen himself carried Barnabas, who clutched him tight around the middle as they plodded up the familiar bridle track that led up into the hills.

At the first news of a move to Pulteney's Inn, Stephen had rushed straight off to tell Doggett. But to his disappointment Doggett had not winked an eyelid.

"I knew all that a week ago," he had said scornfully. "Young Nye brought a bargeload of wine to Wallingford and came on to see his sire, with the tidings that my lord of Suffolk had sealed his bargain with my lord of Huntingdon, and already Londoners were doffing their caps with reverence. Mark you, the de la Pole's old house in Lombard Street was a goodly dwelling built by my lord's great-grandsire, a merchant from Hull who opened his purse to Edward III at the time of Crecy. But Pulteney's Inn is no mere merchant's house; young Nye says it is fit for a prince —the Black Prince himself once lived there. Keep your eyes wide open, boy. If I read the signs aright, Duke Humphrey had best look to himself! My lord of Suffolk is buckling on his mail."

"Buckling on his mail." Stephen's pulses quickened as he remembered Doggett's words. They seemed almost to echo what my lord himself had said as *he* had set off for London. *"As for Gloucester and his gang, I will not rest until I see them bite the dust."*

After the long climb to the top of the ridge, they trotted gently down the other side to Stonor, which lay snugly in a deep valley surrounded by wooded hills, like a castle keep ringed round by curtain walls. The house itself, with its chapel and its cloister of priests, was built of brick like Ewelme; but its quiet dignity was quickly shattered by the cheerful party of boys and girls who came running out to welcome the travelers and to absorb the young mistresses, Jane and Philippa, into their midst.

Dame Alice, however, insisted that there was time for nothing but a stirrup cup—they must press on at once. So young Tom Stonor, grasping at the chance to do honor to the great lady whose father, Thomas Chaucer, had been his guardian, called for his horse to be saddled that he might escort her personally through the confines of his lands.

Once clear of the Chilterns and the courtesies of Tom Stonor, the pace of the party quickened. The sun blazed as though it were July instead of late September. The day seemed endless. Stephen, parched and saddle sore, had never dreamed that London was so far away.

Though it was almost evening when they rode through the arch of Newgate, the heat was still trapped in the narrow streets, and the air reeked heavily of the shambles behind the butchers' market. St. Paul's towered over them like a cliff. They skirted its churchyard and breathed cleaner air, though a faint smell of garbage lingered everywhere. With Paul's left behind them, they strung out single file through a long cobbled street from which a number of narrow lanes ran sharply downhill on their right. Stephen, glancing casually down them, saw the glint of water at the bottom and suddenly realized that it was the Thames, *his* river, which at home flowed between banks of fragrant meadowsweet and thyme.

With a sudden stab of homesickness he moved slowly on until, far ahead, Dame Alice's white coif vanished around a corner and the whole escort followed, turning into a narrow lane where a church tower with a tall steeple rose high beyond a massive gatehouse. One by one the horses passed under the arch and into the wide courtyard of Pulteney's Inn. A flight of stone steps led up to the doorway of the great hall. Light poured out through painted windows. Stephen and Barnabas, at the tail end of the cavalcade, were just in time to see my lord of Suffolk himself lead Dame Alice up the steps and into the grandeur of her new home.

Once arrived Stephen could feel nothing but intense weariness. Somehow he and Barnabas got to the ground. Somebody took the horse, and with utter thankfulness he heard the voice of Master Simon Brayles bidding them come to the buttery. There they shared a dish of cool delicious flummery and were led as usual to a closet outside the chaplain's door. Two fat sacks of straw with pillows and coverlets were set out invitingly on the floor. The journey was over. They were in London.

It seemed no time before sleep was shattered by a clatter of bells, seemingly overhead, against a background of scores of bells farther away. Stephen tried to shut them out by burrowing, but Master Simon appeared to bid them get up at once. That loud bell was St. Laurence Pulteney, just across the way, and they must come quickly to serve his mass.

The sun was already up as they followed him

across a garden surrounded by high walls, except on
one side where it sloped sharply toward the river
with a view that took their breath away. The chaplain, however, drove them on, like sheep, to the
church with the tall steeple; but directly mass was
over they tiptoed out, leaving him to finish his thanks-
giving alone.

"I never dreamed it was like this," cried Stephen,
screwing his eyes against the glint on the rippling
water. " 'Tis ten times as wide as at Wallingford.
Look you, there's the bridge, quite close to us. 'Tis
longer than I thought, you can see the rapids underneath. And all those boats! How do they ply so fast
without colliding?"

But Barnabas was staring straight across the river.

"That must be South Bank opposite," he said. "I
wonder which is the Bear Garden. A fellow in Wallingford told me it was round, with seats on scaffolding to protect the people. There's bullbaiting too—
bulls or bears whichever you will. What say you,
Stephen, shall we go? There are all sorts of japes on
the South Bank."

"That is definitely where you will *not* go," Master
Simon's voice behind them cut in like a knife. "Understand both of you that the South Bank is forbidden. 'Tis a den of infamy—no place for lads like you.
If you want sport you'll find plenty this side of the
river, out on Moorfields for instance, where there are
games all the year round. But for the present you'll

find little time for junketing. The steward will see to that."

Subdued, they found that what he said was only too true. Compared with homely little Ewelme, Pulteney's Inn was a world in itself. The steward, a fine fellow with a forked beard and a sharp tongue, ruled despotically, and everyone did what he was told. The kitchen clerks went daily to market and all their purchases had to be entered in the rolls of the buttery.

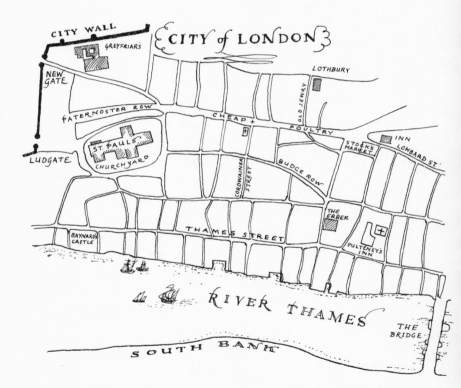

Stephen's secret hopes were shattered by finding that my lord already had his own special clerk, Walter— reputed to be a squire, son of a knight—who gave himself airs and liked to be referred to in the newfangled way as "secretary." Stephen and Barnabas found themselves at the steward's beck and call, with most of their time spent making lists of all the fine furnishings arriving daily from my lord's other seats.

The one relief was to be sent out with Morton, my lord's chief messenger, to learn their way about city streets so that they could become useful for running errands.

Morton was large and friendly and a grandfather.

"Let your first care be to keep out of mischief," he admonished. "A broken head is easily come by in London. Though apprentices thirsting for a fight are not likely to attack *you*, with my lord's badge upon you, there are plenty of others who well may. The great lords are forever snarling at each other, and their underlings are ready enough to back them up. Do you in particular keep yourselves clear of the chained swan, Duke Humphrey's badge, or for that matter of the dun bull of the Nevilles."

"I thought Duke Humphrey lived at Greenwich," said Stephen.

"So he does, but he also lodges at Baynards Castle, his London home. His great gilded barge plies up and down the river any day. Baynards Castle is but a couple of bowshots off; you can see its towers from the garden of Pulteney's Inn. But my lord of Salisbury is at the Erber in Dowgate, too near to be comfortable; so whatever you do avoid the badge of the dun bull. My lord does not favor fisticuffs."

By this time they had reached Cheap, and Morton began to explain his method of finding the way by learning to recognize all the church towers. There were over a hundred within the square mile of the city, so to learn even half of them was enough to provide landmarks everywhere.

"There's Paul's at the end of Cheap; you can't miss that. And note well St. Mary-le-Bow, the church of Bow Bells; there's no other like it. . . ."

But Stephen was deep in thought. The badge of the dun bull: my lord of Salisbury. *"To the most noble Countess of Salisbury at the Erber." "Well beloved daughter—"* Surely he had written those words himself. He ventured to interrupt Morton.

"My lord of Salisbury at the Erber—is his wife not stepdaughter to Dame Alice?"

Morton looked down at him. "Quite right, young prick ears. She is the daughter of Dame Alice's first husband, by a previous marriage. 'Tis through her that the title of Salisbury passed to Neville. But my lord of Salisbury has linked himself to Duke Humphrey. It must have brought sorrow to Dame Alice. Now, both of you, pay attention. I was telling you to note St. Mary-le-Bow."

Stephen had no difficulty memorizing church towers and within a short time found himself trusted with simple errands, such as taking a skillet to a workshop in Ironmongers Lane with the complaint that it burned all the milk heated in it or returning a pair of shoon specially made for my lord by a craftsman in Cordwainer Street that they might be eased across the toes or summoning a furrier from Budge Row to repair the miniver on my lady's mantle, a task which set him wondering if any of the pelts hanging in bunches in the merchant's shop had been prepared by Wat and sold in Wallingford market by old Meg herself.

Barnabas, on the other hand, had no sense of direction. He could not go out alone without completely losing himself. Sent on the simplest message to Cheap, he would wander for half the day and come back empty-handed. It became a joke until, in spite of warnings, he strayed down to the river and actually ended up in the kitchen court of Baynards Castle, where Duke Humphrey's scullions made mock of him, plastered him with mud, and sent him home with the badge of de la Pole torn to shreds. The steward spread his hands in despair.

"What can one do with such a fool? He's fit for nothing but to follow a plow, and even there he'd lose himself between the furrows. From this day on, you dolt head, you'll not venture out without a nursemaid to watch over you."

Everyone giggled, but Barnabas only sulked. When

Stephen offered help he was met by a stony silence; so he shrugged his shoulders and left Barnabas to his own devices. He himself was enjoying London.

One morning Master Simon called him aside. He held a letter sealed with my lord's own seal.

"You are favored," he said in an undertone. "My lord himself entrusts you with a task that needs discretion. You are to take this private letter to Master Robert Large, a mercer, who is the newly elected mayor of the City of London. He lives in old Jewry, north of Cheap. You know it?"

Stephen said eagerly that he could find it.

"See that you make no error. I will tell you *sub sigillum* that it invites the mayor to dine at Pulteney's Inn. 'Tis part of my lord's scheme to woo the citizens of London, but tongues must not clack about it too soon. Master Large's house is an ancient one. You cannot miss it. Once it was a synagogue of the Jews; then a friary; then the inn of the Lord Fitzwalter—his arms are over the door. Here, take the letter. If the mayor is at home present it to him yourself; but above all see that you give it to someone of good standing, not to a mere unlettered porter."

Stephen found the house at once, his eye picking out the Fitzwalter shield above the iron-studded door. The place looked old and grim, and the windows in the stone walls were little more than slits. It took courage to handle the heavy knocker, but as he

STONOR   NEVILLE   FITZWALTER

stretched up to reach it he saw a modern house, tim-
ber-framed, with glass casements, jutting out above
the ancient one.

As he stared the door was opened by a youth, a
head taller than himself, wearing an apprentice's cap
set at a jaunty angle.

"What will you?" the apprentice inquired cheerfully. "I was near the door when you knocked so I
opened it."

Taken aback, Stephen stammered that he came
from the Earl of Suffolk and bore a letter for the
mayor; but he was to give it only to the mayor himself
or to someone of good standing—not to any unlettered porter.

The youth burst out laughing. "Perchance I may
do," he said. "I am *not* a porter and I *am* lettered. I
am William Caxton, the mayor's apprentice—the
third of eight. But the mayor himself is upstairs.
Come you inside and I'll beg leave to take you to
him."

Stephen stepped into a narrow stone passage with a

barrel roof. When the door closed it was as black as a tomb. Caxton gripped his elbow and led him.

"Your eyes will grow used to it. Give me the letter and stand you by this pillar. Don't move or you'll bump your head. I'll not be long."

Caxton's footsteps died away, and Stephen stared into the blackness. Gradually his eyes picked out the shape of heavy vaulted arches like the crypt of a church. A sound of a deep moaning rose and fell, as the wind moans before a storm. Now and again the moaning was lost in a noise like a clatter of gigantic bells, so weird that he braced his back against the pillar, holding his breath. Thankfully he heard Caxton returning down invisible stairs.

"What's that noise?" he demanded. "It sounds like —like a sorcerer's cave."

"Look on the South Bank for sorcerers, not here," said Caxton crisply. "That noise you hear is the roar of Cheap afar off, mixed with the tapping of the coppersmiths in Lothbury just outside. You'd hardly guess that such tiny hammers could swell to so great a din. This old cloister is like a sounding board. But come on. The mayor will see you now."

Stephen fumbled his way up a stone spiral stairway, reassured by Caxton's friendly voice behind him.

"The old part is used for storing merchandise, and Master Large has made a new house above it. Look! There is light at the top."

Sure enough they emerged into a long gallery with

casement windows through which the sunshine poured. Stephen glanced down into a pleasant garden with an embroidery frame lying on a seat and some children's toys abandoned on the grass. At the end of the gallery Caxton tapped on a heavy closed door. A voice cried "Enter," and Stephen found himself in the presence of the mayor.

Master Robert Large was a stout man in a furred gown thrown open to reveal a fine lawn shirt and a massive gold chain. He was seated at a counterboard and writing with a quill pen that squeaked. He looked so imposing that Stephen went down on two knees instead of one.

The mayor glanced up and his plump face relaxed into a smile. "My lord of Suffolk's clerk? Surely a very young clerk! Stand up, boy; there's no need for quite so much ceremony. In fact I need *you* to advise *me*. My lord invites me to dinner at Pulteney's Inn. But there is one point on which I must be clear. Does he invite me as Robert Large a merchant, because his forbears were merchants? Or does he invite me as mayor, complete with mace-bearer and followed by a gaggle of eight apprentices as a bodyguard? There is a world of difference. I am still new to my office and I must not blunder. Can you enlighten me that I may know how to reply?"

Stephen hesistated. He dared not take it upon himself to decide, so he said cautiously that it was Master Simon Brayles, my lord of Suffolk's chaplain, who had entrusted him with the letter. Master Simon might know my lord's mind.

The mayor smacked the counterboard so hard that everything rattled and Caxton came hurrying in.

"By the rood," cried Master Large, "you have your wits about you. You shall go back at once, find the chaplain and beg him of his charity to solve the problem of my lord's intention. Caxton shall go with you and privily bring me word back. Thus I shall know what to reply without discourtesy to my lord. Caxton, go quickly and spruce yourself."

Stephen, watching the mayor's eagerness, felt as though he had hooked a fat roach on the river. Master Large was obviously delighted. "Whence come you, boy?" he inquired. "Your speech shows you are no Londoner—Ewelme, you say? Where's that? I've not heard of it."

Stephen declared that it was my lord of Suffolk's manor near Wallingford, adding that he served my lord as clerk because his father had died to save my lord in the French wars, and if my lord pleased he was to go to Oxford as a scholar.

"A scholar, eh? You should make friends with Will Caxton; he is besotted about books. I've a thought: with my lord's permission he can show you around London. Ah, here he is— Will, hearken! If the chance comes, do you beg leave to show Stephen the sights of the city. 'Twould be good for you both. Now be off with you and lose no time about it."

248

Pushing their way through noisy crowds, they found no opportunity to talk, but Stephen's spirit was rising all the time. To have a friend near his own age who was "besotted about books" was exactly what he wanted.

They trotted side by side down the hill to Pulteney's Inn. As they went Stephen began to worry a little about what he should do if Master Simon were not there. But even in this his good fortune held. They found the chaplain, Book of Hours in hand, pacing the courtyard while he read the prayers of the day. He kept his finger between the pages as he listened to Stephen's story. Then he nodded.

"My lord is within," he said. "I'll take Caxton with me while I see how the land lies. 'Tis all a matter for discretion but I think he is in good humor today. Likely he will enjoy the joke of it."

Feeling like a dog who has dutifully given up his quarry to the huntsman, Stephen mooned about the courtyard until they returned. Caxton, with a mere nod and a grin, sped away immediately, but Master Simon grasped Stephen by the elbow.

"Well done!" he said. "My lord is pleased by the way you handled his business. You have increased your stature. And, by the way, young Caxton pleaded, as from his master, that he might show you the sights of London. The thought commended itself to my lord. I am to let you go whenever you are asked." The chaplain lowered his voice. "I think it suits him nicely that his clerk should be hail fellow with the mayor's apprentice—like a finger on the pulse of the city."

From that moment life opened up for Stephen. Apparently the mayor also saw advantage in the arrangement, for Caxton called nearly every day, and together they explored tirelessly for hours on end.

They began with Paul's, the very heart of London life, not only as a church but as the meeting place of everybody. People dumped their bundles and their babies while they went to market; menservants and maids stood about in the nave waiting to be hired; lawyers, scriveners, and others offered their services to those who needed them; while shut away in the choir and sanctuary, the Church continued its spiritual life without interruption.

From Paul's they wandered out into Paternoster Row, where books were made, and once more Stephen remembered that "Will Caxton was besotted about books." As they moved from shop to shop poring over pages of faultless penmanship and fine binding, Stephen remembered Benson Mill and could not resist the temptation to brag a little about how he had saved the books for Duke Humphrey's new library at Oxford. But Caxton passed over it loftily.

"*Is* there a new library at Oxford? I'd not heard of it. One day I'll take you to see Dick Whittington's library at the Greyfriars. He left it in his will as a gift to London. 'Tis the finest in all England."

For a moment Stephen was disgruntled. He was at the point of asking who was Dick Whittington, but Caxton was already listening to a bookseller's complaint that times were bad. What with the cost of paper and the wages of the scribes, none but the very rich could afford to buy books at all.

Little by little Stephen began to realize what Master Simon had meant by "a finger on the pulse of the city." He was to keep his ears open for what ordinary people were saying and report it to Master Simon. Caxton took him to see the new Guildhall only to find that building was at a standstill for lack of money. It was the same story at the bridge; the old timbers creaked for need of repair. Down by the river laborers stood idle because galleys from Venice and Lombardy, which came to buy English wool, had largely forsaken London in favor of Sandwich or Southampton. There was plague on the South Bank, and the granaries of London were still short of corn after last year's disastrous harvest.

All this was so plain that even a country-bred boy could understand it. The city was ill content. The war in France still rumbled on ominously and every tradesman complained bitterly. In the days of Harry the Fifth money flowed. But now the king was a holy scholar dressed in black; there was no queen to attract a rich court. Duke Humphrey alone spent money freely and so they favored him. But his duchess dared not show her face. At the mere mention of the witch of Gloucester the ordinary Londoner spat into the Thames.

As though to make his cup brim over, Stephen was permitted sometimes to go back with Caxton to old Jewry and add one more to the mayor's huge family of five sons and daughters and eight apprentices, all presided over by Mistress Large, who gathered them around the fire on a winter's evening to talk, tell stories, sing songs, and consume vast quantities of cakes and homemade ale. To Stephen a family was a new experience and a joy he had never known before.

In the meanwhile Barnabas was living a life of his own among the kitchen clerks. He went to market with them, joined their games, and seemed content to be a butt for their contemptuous laughter. Though they still slept in the chaplain's closet, Stephen saw him only when they chanced to go to bed at the same time, which was seldom.

Nevertheless Stephen's conscience occasionally pricked him. At Ewelme they had been good enough friends. They had ridden to London together. But since Stephen had found new interests, he had left Barnabas to fend for himself.

He went so far one day as to unburden himself to Caxton.

"Bring him with you if you like," said Caxton good-humoredly. "I planned to go tomorrow to Whittington's library. He *might* enjoy it. After all he *is* a clerk. He is lettered."

Stephen had his doubts but decided that it was worth trying. Purposely he went early to bed. Barnabas listened open-mouthed.

"Have you lost your wits?" he grumbled. "*A library! Me!* I'll thank you not to make mock of me too. I've no fancy to follow at the heels of the mayor's apprentice. Keep your fine friends. I can do without them."

" 'Tis not like that," said Stephen quickly. "Caxton's a merry fellow, and you'd see all the sights of the city. Just you try it."

But Barnabas only shook his head sulkily.

" 'Tis too late for soft talk. Go your way and I'll go mine. I've got friends too, and I can see all I want. Wait! If it's sights you want, come you with me. I can show you things much more marvelous than any monkish library. You've never seen a bearbaiting; not a bull, mark you: a bear. That's something not to be missed."

Stephen frowned. "Bearbaiting? Who takes you to a bearbaiting? Surely that's on the South Bank?"

Barnabas ignored the last part. "I go with Greg, the scullion with the scarred face. He's son of the flesh-cook so we get out easily, and what's more he *pays.*"

"But you've forgotten; Master Simon strictly forbade the South Bank. And there's plague there, too."

"Master Simon's a priest and priests have queasy stomachs. As for the plague, Greg says you can get it anywhere; Bankside's no worse than any other. Come on, Stephen; it is but sport. There's a juggler who whirls ten knives at a time and a fellow who'll see your fortune in a polished broadsword. A woman lost a purse; he told her where to look, and sure enough she found it, just as he said."

Stephen frowned. This caught him on the raw. A pool or a polished broadsword, what was the difference?

"That's witchcraft," he cried sharply. "Be not such a fool, Barnabas. 'Tis plain that the South Bank is an evil place. Keep away from it. Go there no more."

Barnabas sniggered. "Haven't you lost your milk teeth yet? 'Tis you who are the fool."

Stephen bristled, his temper quickening. At that moment he heard a footstep on the stairs; it was the chaplain coming up to bed. He seized his chance.

"Swear that you'll go there no more," he hissed fiercely. "Swear it *now* or I'll tell Master Simon."

Barnabas held his breath. Then in a voice shaking with rage he muttered, "So you would sneak, you sniveling trickster! So be it! I swear—but I'll be even with you yet." He rolled onto his side and deliberately began to snore.

Long after the chaplain had doused his light, Stephen lay awake, hot with anger. To be called a fool and a milksop by Barnabas of all people! He would dearly love to report him to Master Simon, but it couldn't be done because, however reluctantly, Barnabas *had* sworn. He'd have to find another way of getting even with him and at the same time put a stop to these jaunts to the South Bank.

When he woke in the morning Barnabas had gone, but, still angry, Stephen could not get the business out of his head.

He met Caxton as arranged and followed him to the Greyfriars, a splendid church and cloister, tucked away in an unsuspected sweep of garden and orchard between the houses of Newgate Street and the city wall. With only half his mind he noted that the library, adjoining the west front of the church, seemed to be on a plan very much like the one being built at Oxford—a long galleries with windows on both sides and with bookshelves to form little cells for study on either side of a central passage. On another day he would have reveled in it, but now he was too preoccupied to take in the beauty of the splendid volumes that Caxton, moving reverently, pointed out to him.

Caxton himself had just begun to notice Stephen's gloom when one of the friar custodians, who tolerated boys only because by Whittington's will they had the right to be there, suddenly bustled them to one side and sternly bade them *kneel.* Stephen glanced around, expecting a procession on its way to the church. But the only persons visible were a little party of three approaching slowly along the gallery. Two were elderly friars in their ordinary gray habits. The third, in the middle, was a youth in a plain black gown with a golden circlet holding his hair in place. He was young, in appearance hardly older than Stephen, and his white face was unaccountably sad.

Caxton fiercely prodded Stephen in the ribs. "Doff," he whispered urgently. "Doff, you fool. It is the king!"

Taken aback, Stephen fumbled clumsily with his cap. To his horror it slipped from his fingers, sprang into the air and landed neatly at the king's feet. There was a pause. Crimson with shame Stephen looked up just in time to see the king step deftly over it. The corners of the king's mouth twitched. There was no doubt about it. The sad-faced youth was unmistakably smiling.

When the king and his companions had gone, Caxton pulled Stephen to his feet.

"You made a fool of yourself," he said bluntly. "But at least you'll be able to boast that you're the fellow who made the king laugh."

Stephen's first thought, however, was that he now had the perfect opening for his next meeting with Barnabas. "*Had you come to the library,*" he would say, "*you would have seen the king!*"

Plague!

CHEERED by the thought of the wonderful story with which he could impress Barnabas, Stephen parted from Caxton in Cheap and turned south toward the river. It was cold and foggy, and he was thankful to see light shining through the windows of Pulteney's Inn. He longed for the glow of the fire in the hall, for it was in the evenings that Master Simon found time to keep up Stephen's studies. The two of them would sit at a bench near the hot embers, and Stephen would read in Latin by the light of a special beeswax candle which would not gutter.

But tonight Master Simon sent word that he was busy with my lord. Stephen might either work alone or, if he wished, go early to bed. Secretly thankful, Stephen decided on the second course. It occurred to him that in the coming talk with Barnabas he would be in a stronger position if he was the first upstairs.

He carefully avoided the buttery, where Barnabas was usually to be found, undressed and slipped into bed. There was a moon nearing its first quarter which conveniently shone across Barnabas's pillow. He noted with satisfaction that he would be able to study Barnabas's face while Barnabas would see him only in shadow.

It was comfortable in bed, and while he rehearsed his story about the king he realized that he was tired. He had slept little the night before. He wished that Barnabas would come soon so that he could get it over. Suddenly he glanced up and realized that the strip of moonlight had moved round. He must have been asleep. Barnabas's place was now in shadow, but with eyes accustomed to the dark Stephen could see that it was still unoccupied. Judging by the position of the moonlight, he must have slept for some time. Why was the fool so late? Had he after all ignored his oath and gone to the South Bank? But even so he ought to be home by now.

He lay tense, with his ears pricked, until at last he heard sounds of movement below. The patch of light had by now reached the top of the stairs. Someone was coming up, treading softly. Here he was at last! But as a head and shoulders emerged above the top step he saw that it was not Barnabas but Master Simon, obviously trying not to wake the boys.

Stephen lay tense till the chaplain's door closed and he heard the creak of bed ropes. Then he raised himself on his elbow, straining his ears until they throbbed.

What could have happened to Barnabas? By his own showing he had been many times to the South Bank but never before had he been absent from his bed. Pulteney's Inn was all locked at night. How would he pass the guard, unless indeed the guard was another such scullion as Greg the scullion and his father, the flesh cook? But even so they would be unlikely to stay out all night. Had he been seized by the watch? There was a prison on the South Bank called the Clink, used, he had heard, for the drunk and rowdy. Was that where Barnabas had ended up?

Hours passed before sleep overtook him. He woke to find Master Simon shaking him.

It was broad daylight. He started up dazed. "Barnabas?" he cried. "Where is he?"

"Prepare for a shock, boy," said the chaplain gravely. "You will not see him again. *Barnabas is dead.*"

The world spun around. Barnabas *dead!* His worst fears had stopped short of that. From a dry throat he gasped, "God have mercy; what has happened?"

"He died of the pestilence. It can kill in a few hours." Master Simon's voice was grave but he spoke gently. "It seems that in defiance of orders he had been going repeatedly to the South Bank. How this was possible must be disclosed, but for the present all we know is that Gregory, the scullion, led him only too easily. Gregory came back alive; at least he had the grace not to desert the boy. Last night they planned to see a bullbaiting. Barnabas was feeling queasy but he would not give up. Afterward they went to a tavern near the bullring. There Barnabas all but collapsed, but the taverner, who knew the plague when he saw it, turned them out. The only waterman still on the bank refused to carry them, and Gregory supported the boy along the foreshore toward the bridge till he could go no farther. He laid him in the shelter of an upturned boat and ran to seek help. By now it was dark and he could find none willing to come. At last he met the watch with lanterns. But the foreshore was full of upturned boats, and by the time they reached the right one it was too late. Barnabas lay there dead."

Stephen sat as though turned to stone. The chaplain began again.

"At this moment I'll not stop to question how much you knew of what was going on. I pray God that you knew nothing at all; consult your own conscience and do what it bids you. But there is no time now. By noon my lady's party, including you, will be leaving London."

"*Leaving London?*" Here was another shock.

"Yea. The pestilence gains ground so fast that my lord will not suffer Dame Alice to wait even a single day. He came to that decision last night, before we knew about Barnabas, and now he is impatient of every hour. You are going not to Ewelme but to Donnington. I warn you you will be kept apart because you were bedfellow to Barnabas. 'Tis my lady who insists that you shall not be left behind, so suffer your fate thankfully, if God wills to spare you."

"And you, sir, and my lord?"

"My lord stays and I stay with him. Parliament opens next week at Westminster, and he is determined to be there. Now hasten, boy. I go to say mass for Barnabas that his soul may rest in peace, and it is fitting that you should serve it."

The bells of London were striking noon as they rode out of the city; the twelve solemn strokes sounded like a tolling for the dead. It poured with rain—a fitting contrast to the brilliant sunshine of the day of their arrival. My lord with his own escort rode for some miles beside his wife who traveled in a horse-borne litter. Then, bidding her farewell in a downpour, he turned back toward Newgate.

Stephen rode alone, completely tented in a great riding cloak on which the rain drummed noisily. A slit for his eyes allowed him to see that he was not left too far behind and admitted enough wind and water to prevent him from going to sleep. Whenever the party paused and he dismounted with the rest, he was left standing apart; and when eventually they stopped for the night he was herded, far behind the others, to the remotest end of a long undercroft and given an isolated bed of straw. A monk in a black habit, bearing a bowl of hot broth, was the only person who approached him and told him that this was Reading

Abbey. Donnington was still some twenty miles away.

He slept from sheer exhaustion and woke to find everything shrouded in fog, through which the shapes of large buildings loomed on all sides. Obviously Reading must be a great abbey, as big as anything in London, with the possible exception of Paul's; though it was impossible to compare as the vast frontage of the church was lost in fog.

He was allowed to hear mass from just inside the door, though the interior was like a tall dark cavern supported on huge carved columns. The voices of the monks sounded very far away, and the glimmer of yellow candlelight in the distance did no more than tint the curtain of fog.

The last stage of the journey was in daylight. The fog lifted into a drizzle and the horses squelched through a land of dripping willows. As his numbness, like the fog, dispersed, Stephen miserably faced the truth. Barnabas was dead. No direct blame was his, but he knew that he had let the boy drift. The recent merry life had gone and would not easily come again.

Donnington, a castle of gray stone built on a hillside, had none of the mellow warmth of Ewelme. A gatehouse of two tall towers opened into a chilly courtyard, green with damp moss. The steward, bent with age, emerged at the head of a scanty handful of servants to plead that, owing to the short notice, preparations were barely complete. In spite of his

gloom it occurred to Stephen that he himself had copied orders for the furbishing of Donnington many
months ago.

Dame Alice, however, accepted the old man's ex-
cuses and said that all must take a hand in making the
place habitable. The inside of the castle was as for-
bidding as the outside. The windows of the great hall
were without glass, and the logs in the chimney
would do no more than smolder. Dame Alice and her
women slept in a solar up a long flight of wooden
stairs, while the rest of the household slept around the
smoky hearth—all except Stephen, who lay banished
to a far corner until he should be clear of the risk of
pestilence.

Dame Alice saw to it that this exile did not last
overlong. Since his youth and his skills were called
for by day to help in a dozen different jobs, it was
clearly absurd to set him apart at night. Under Dame
Alice's firm rule everything gradually improved.
Whole holly trees were thrust up the chimney to dis-
lodge birds' nests; green moss was scraped from the
inner walls so that hangings from Ewelme could be
hooked on; bales of dry rushes carpeted the damp
floors; and merchants from Newbury, the nearby
town, brought rolls of buckram to be oiled and
stretched across gaping windows to keep out the
frost.

Almost every day messengers from London brought
letters from my lord and went back with my lady's an-

swers. The pestilence, it seemed, showed no sign of abating, and despite her calmness Stephen could read anxiety in her face. At Pulteney's Inn he had seen her only at a distance; but here, living in her own castle, inherited like Ewelme from her father, she was Dame Alice again. To Stephen she was more gentle than ever. Barnabas's death was not mentioned, but she gave him work to keep his mind occupied or, with a candle of hard beeswax, bade him read aloud in the evenings.

Then suddenly the world changed. It was on a sunny December morning that Stephen's old friend, Morton, my lord's chief messenger, reached Donnington with a letter that brought color to Dame Alice's cheeks. She turned to Stephen, who happened to be standing nearby. Her face was beaming.

"My lord comes two days from now," she cried. "He will be here for Christmas. The plague has grown so vastly that Parliament at Westminster is to be prorogued. The king is going to Windsor and Duke Humphrey to Greenwich. All the lords are leaving London. Parliament will meet again on January 14, and you can guess where? At *Reading Abbey*. Think what that means; within riding distance from here. Pray with all your might that during these last two days my lord will be kept safe."

From that moment no one at Donnington had any rest. What was already clean was cleaned again. With Christmas so near at hand orders went out for food and yet more food. A party of men-at-arms was expected from Wingfield to form an imposing escort for my lord of Suffolk when he rode to Parliament in Reading. Finally young Mistress Jane was expected from Stonor, with the faithful Tom Stonor and his sister Philippa, the governess Dame Eleanor Thorn and yet another escort. Truly the stone walls of Donnington seemed likely to bulge before Christmas was over.

My lord with Master Simon was the first to arrive. Deep within himself Stephen had dreaded the meeting with the chaplain. Would he be faced with questions about Barnabas and the South Bank? But Barnabas's name was not mentioned. My lord took himself off to the marshes with hawks and dogs in search of wild fowl and came back at dusk to set more and more wood crackling up the newly swept chimney. For Stephen the task was the now familiar one of unpacking altar gear, making seemly a neglected chapel, and helping to coach untrained voices in the singing of the mass.

Christmas itself began at midnight in the tiny chapel, bright with the glow of many candles. My lord, like my lady and their party, well wrapped in furs, had ordered that the doors into the Courtyard should be left open so that all outside could see in. The light streamed out over a sea of faces and at the *"Gloria in Excelsis"* a deep-toned hum, like a nest of bumblebees, rolled around the chapel. Stephen, serving at the altar, glanced back and thought suddenly of the faces of shepherds peering in through a stable door.

Stephen had never dreamed of such a Christmas. In the hall, everyone gorged themselves on the same meats as my lord and his family, and everyone drank the same Gascon wine, though many tipped it out as "sour muck" and refilled their mugs with honest English ale. Afterward there were mummers in the courtyard, lit by a blaze which could have burned the castle down. The next day there was dancing in the hall, where the two young mistresses danced with Tom Stonor and the son of a local squire until the party warmed up and they were sent protesting to bed.

The twelve days of Christmas were barely over when preparations began for my lord's imposing progress to Parliament at Reading. Stephen, to his own astonishment, felt no desire at all to be taking part in it. Something had happened to him since those last days in London. Whereas in the past he had longed to be in the thick of things, now he was glad enough to watch from afar. Even when he stood outside the gatehouse on a bright crisp January morning to watch my lord in his furred mantle set out with the caps and breastplates of the escort gleaming like silver and the blue and gold banner held proudly aloft, his only regret was that Doggett was not there to see it.

But in spite of the grandeur of Reading Abbey,

which Stephen had barely glimpsed through the fog on that miserable journey from London, it seemed that Parliament was only half itself away from its proper home. The Chapter House at Reading was magnificent, but it was not the Chapter House at Westminster. My lord returned much sooner than expected, declaring that it had all been a sorry waste of time. All that they had done had been to pass a bill making the French title *visconte* lawful in England and to set yet more curbs upon the activities of foreign merchants trading in English markets.

"They will do no good until they stiffen their courage and get back to Westminster," he declared as he allowed Stephen to pull off his boots before a blazing fire. "There is no point, wife, in remaining here. I shall pack up and be off as soon as may be."

"I beg that you will not go back to London till the plague has truly gone," begged Dame Alice anxiously.

"Nay, not to London yet," he said. "We will go to Wingfield—both of us. There I have duties and you can make that pilgrimage to Walsingham which you have so long desired."

Instantly she smiled at him. "God be praised," she said. "Then, husband, there will be no need for Master Simon at Wingfield. You have your own chaplain there. Would you be content that he should go back to Ewelme? He can speed its sweetening against our next visit. And Stephen can return to his books."

My lord glanced at Stephen, who stood with the riding boots in his hand. "That is a good plan," he said. "The boy has his wits about him. He is worth encouraging."

But it took time for all the household at Donnington to disperse, and the spikes of daffodils were inches high before Master Simon with Stephen, a couple of grooms, and a string of baggage horses set out on their twenty-mile journey across the Berkshire downs. It had been Dame Alice's thought that since they would pass near Goring, Stephen should cross the Thames by ferry, visit his sister, and thence make his own way back to Ewelme, while the slow-moving party went more soberly by Wallingford bridge.

It was the same ferry he had watched with Lys the last time he had been to see her, and now the crossing with his pony seemed to complete the circle. The London adventure was truly over; he was home again in his own country.

The janitor at the Priory gate again recognized him. This time he was led to a small parlor where he waited a few minutes before the cellaress, large and matronly, appeared in the doorway. Almost lost behind her was a young nun in a wimple, with a white veil and a large white apron. It took him a moment to realize that the young nun was Lys.

"She is a good child, and she was so ardent to be a lay sister instead of a mere serving wench that we sent to Ewelme for the consent of her nearest kin,"

PLAGUE!

said the cellaress beaming at him and pushing Lys forward. "You were not there, so Sir John Saynesbury, who had baptized her as a babe, gladly gave his blessing. As a lay sister this is now her home, and you may see for yourself how happy this has made her. I will leave you together for a little while that you may talk of it."

Alone with Lys, Stephen was tongue-tied. He remembered acutely how she had told him about old Meg seeing her mirrored in the water dressed as a nun, and how angry it had made him.

Lys watched him anxiously. "Brother, be glad for me," she pleaded. "Of course I can never be a choir nun; I am unlettered and I have no Latin and no dowry. But I can serve God by waiting on them and being holy in obedience. And I shall pray for you brother."

But he was not to be won so easily. " 'Tis just as old Meg conjured it," he said. "*She* saw you reflected in coif and veil. The devil is in it somewhere. In London there is a fellow who sees things in a polished sword blade, and he's a sorcerer." He shuddered as he remembered that last scene with Barnabas. But Lys was unperturbed.

"Old Meg is no sorceress," she returned serenely. "I know not how she saw it in the water, nor do I know how I did. If it has come true it is by God's will. I only know that old Meg tended me with the kind of love we lost when our precious mother died—God rest her! Such love comes not of the devil. And, though you were so angered at the time, remember, brother, that she saw you too. She saw you gowned as a clerk at Oxford."

He bit his lip, silenced for the moment. Before he could recover Lys changed her tone.

"Brother—I have something that is yours," she cried gaily, and thrust out a closed hand. "You may have three guesses."

He frowned. "This is no time for jesting."

" 'Tis no jest. 'Tis something that you had lost."

She turned her hand and held it out flat, palm upward. On it lay a dirty wedge of folded paper, shaped like the sole of a shoe. It was so black and sodden that it did not look like paper at all. As she pushed it toward him he took it gingerly and saw that on the inside some words were still legible: *"write to you, daughter, begging your help. . . ."* He gasped. The handwriting was his own; it was his copy of Dame Alice's letter. He picked open the thick folds but at his touch the whole thing crumbled and fell to pieces.

Lys was smiling. " 'Tis that lesson you lost, isn't it? Wat must have found it among the rushes before I swept and used it to block the holes in my old shoe. Who would have dreamed it? Now I have sandals. See!"

She thrust out bare toes from under her long habit. Dame Cellaress coming in at that moment reproved her sharply, and Stephen, his head in a whirl, took his leave.

As he rode home he could at first think of nothing but his copy of Dame Alice's letter. It had seemed so certain that it had fallen into Bolingbroke's hands; Bolingbroke's own talk seemed to confirm it. But, by the mercy of God, it was Wat and not Bolingbroke who had picked it up.

Now, as he remembered the gossip he had heard in London, the pieces began to fit together and everything became clear. Dame Alice's stepdaughter was Countess of Salisbury in her own right, and through her the title of Earl of Salisbury had been bestowed upon her husband. He, so it was said, had gone over to Duke Humphrey's side, and she, as a good wife, must have told him all about Dame Alice's letter. It could not possibly have come from Stephen's copy, which had all the time been tucked away safely in Lys's shoe. The truth was just what Doggett had foretold: Dame Alice had been betrayed by her own letter written with her own hand.

As he jogged slowly homeward, Stephen could have shouted for joy. After the long agony of suspense the clouds had rolled away. The troubles that had come to my lord and Dame Alice were in no way of his making. For him the slate was wiped clean.

He was nearing Ewelme before he remembered something else that Lys had said. When old Meg saw in the water a picture of Lys veiled like a nun, she had also seen him—as an Oxford clerk.

The Great
Painted Chair

---

*E*WELME, empty though it might be, was cozy after Donnington, and Stephen was thankful to be home. But the people of the village seemed determined not to allow him to forget his visit to London and the horrors that had ended it. Every time he put his nose out, someone waylaid him, demanding to be told, with grisly detail, exactly how Barnabas had died. After the first week he avoided everyone except Doggett, to whom anything in the way of news was the breath of life.

The old man seemed to have aged during the winter months. Though the bushy brows still bristled and the keen eyes seemed as sharp as ever, he fell asleep over his heraldry and came back always to the same old stories, humming under his breath the *"Song of Agincourt"* in the hope that someone would recognize it, and repeating yet once again the story of the *triumph* when he had marched into London among the warriors of Henry the Fifth, with the young Duke

Charles of Orleans as one of the noble captives. He asked constantly for news of the French duke. Had he yet been set free? And Stephen had to confess that he had heard no word of it. In London no one seemed interested in any but their own affairs.

At the Hall, alone with Master Simon, Stephen quietly devoted himself to work. Never had he felt so much at ease among books. Having left London behind him, his thoughts had returned to Oxford. Not for a moment would he admit to himself that he had been influenced by Lys's story of his reflection in the pool. But the books on the shelf increased in number. Donatus and Cato were joined by Ovid and Livy and Virgil.

There was little news from Wingfield except that my lord was in constant touch with London and Dame Alice was just setting out for her pilgrimage to Walsingham.

"See that you pray that her prayers be answered," said Master Simon earnestly. "'Tis one way you can repay her goodness to you."

Stephen said "Yes, sir," promptly. If Dame Alice had need of *his* prayers, she should have them in full measure. But what was he to pray for?

The chaplain smiled. "I have just told you: pray that her prayers may be answered. Use your wits, boy. Has it not dawned on you that my lord and my lady have been wed these twelve years and yet they have no son?"

273

Stephen suddenly felt more important at being asked to pray in such a cause. He was no longer a schoolboy but a clerk in Dame Alice's own household, with a clear line drawn between now and his former life. Everything had changed: Barnabas was dead; Lys was a nun; Red Jak had moved to a mill farther away and had taken Tom with him. Even Odo had gone to live in his new wife's village.

There still remained Gilles and old Meg and Wat, and he often felt inclined to take the familiar path up into the hills, but he decided against it. Lys had almost convinced him that there was no harm in old Meg. But nevertheless those visions in the water required explaining, and it was wiser to avoid trouble.

At last word came that my lord of Suffolk with his lady had returned to Pulteney's Inn. With the coming of spring the pestilence had almost died out, and matters of state were coming to life again. What was more, my lord's affairs were prospering. He had been appointed Chief Seneschal of the Duchy of Lancaster, a sure sign of royal favor, and now he was made Chief Justice of Wales. He was hand in glove with the lord Cardinal Beaufort, and the two of them were once more working for the release of the French duke in the cause of peace.

"Duke Humphrey is like a peeved child," chuckled Master Simon. "He has addressed a signed complaint to the king against the cardinal and my lord of Suffolk. Rumor has it that he has even accused the cardinal of stealing the crown jewels! Think of it; my lord cardinal! The truth is that during the king's childhood, Duke Humphrey emptied the royal coffers by his extravagance. The cardinal came to the rescue refilling them from his private purse with the crown jewels named as security. Now he is called thief for his pains. This is the sort of business with which my lord has to deal. Methinks we shall see little of him at Ewelme for many a day."

Secretly Stephen was almost relieved. With my lord in residence his books would suffer. Dame Alice arrived just after Easter, but she stayed only long enough to deal with the business of the manor, and as she left she bade him work hard. Master Simon spoke well of him. Soon they must begin to think about Oxford.

At this Stephen redoubled his efforts. Weeks and months slipped by almost without his noticing them. Old Ferry was ailing and Parson Saynesbury arranged that Stephen should help when needed with the clerk's duties, such as reading the lessons in church. For sport he took part in contests at the butts, glad to find that his old skill with the bow had not deserted him. When news arrived from London, he begged leave to carry it to Doggett, who was as greedy for it as ever—especially about the French duke, whose fate hung in the balance all through the summer. In June Duke Humphrey renewed his protest to the king, but by autumn it was known that he had failed.

On November the first, the feast of All Saints, Charles duc d'Orleans agreed at Westminster to pay a vast ransom and swore on the sacrament never again to bear arms against England and if he failed to make peace between England and France, he would faithfully return to captivity. As for Duke Humphrey, he strode out in a rage at the beginning of mass and immediately took boat for Greenwich.

Doggett received this story with a triumphant grin, his forefinger laid against his nose.

"Did I not tell you?" he cried. "Did I not say my lord was buckling on his mail?"

Christmas this year was very different from the Christmas at Donnington. The family kept the feast at Pulteney's Inn, and though Dame Alice gave orders for festivities at Ewelme, it was a homely business, presided over by Bylton, while the chaplain with Stephen assisted at the church. Winter set in with snow, and lasted right through Lent. Reserve stocks of food, salted and stored in barrels, were issued freely from the Hall to those in need of it, and until the snow had melted and the river had ceased to flood there was little news from outside. Even the spring was wet and chill, and it was some weeks after Whitsun before a chance happening roused Stephen from his books.

By this time he was promoted to reading the epistle every Sunday at the parish mass. The Latin by now did not worry him at all. He prided himself on pronouncing it clearly and carefully.

But on this particular Sunday, the eighth after Pentecost, something tripped him up. The words were simple enough—*"in corda vostris clamentem abba pater,"* which meant in English, "In your hearts crying Abba Father." It was the word *abba* which worried him, but he couldn't think why. Not until he was walking from the church to the Hall did the answer come to him: abba was one of those words which read the same from both ends. What did Master Bolingbroke call it? A palindrome.

A picture rose before his eyes of old Meg's cottage and Bolingbroke writing in the ashes. What he had written was 1441, which Stephen had claimed was the date two years ahead and Bolingbroke had described as a palindrome. Now, palindrome or not, 1441 was the date of *this* year, the nineteenth year of the reign of King Henry VI.

He lay thinking of it in bed that night. What had they meant, old Meg and Bolingbroke? He remembered something about the rain on the water: they "would see no more tonight." Was it some foretelling of the future, like seeing Lys reflected as a nun? He shivered beneath the bedclothes. He wished that he could discuss it with Master Simon, but he had concealed it for so long that he dared not reveal it now. He could do nothing but put it out of his mind.

It was barely a month later that some fresh news from London stirred Master Simon to excitement. He actually called Stephen from his work.

"Hark you to this," he cried. "You recall that fellow Bolingbroke, the master of St. Andrew's Hall? *He is in the Tower of London accused of sorcery!* Well may you look startled. Mark you, I was suspicious of him at the time. Do you remember that geegaw hanging in the aumbry where he kept his wine cups? Thank your good angel that his offer to befriend you was not accepted. Heaven knows where you might have stood today."

Stephen, red to the roots of his hair, steadied his voice enough to ask, "What has he done, sir?"

" 'Tis not yet clear to me, but the Duchess Eleanor is involved; also a false priest from the king's own chapel, and Margery Jourdemain, the woman they call the witch of Eye, who brewed the love potions which drove Duke Humphrey into the arms of Eleanor Cobham, as she was then called. The matter must be serious, for when the duchess heard that Bolingbroke was taken, she fled to sanctuary at Westminster. Of course there is no sanctuary for sorcerers and witches—the devil's servants—so she tried to escape by river. But they caught her and now she is to face trial in St. Stephen's Chapel. Bolingbroke will be brought to give evidence. That, so far, is all I know."

Stephen lived in torment, his thoughts circling round and round. *This* was the year 1441. Had Bolingbroke been already conjuring a date for something that he would do? And what was old Meg's part in it? Why had Bolingbroke sought her out? It was easy to think of Bolingbroke as evil. He was a proved sorcerer; but there was no proof that Meg was evil too. He thought again of Lys; it was thanks to old Meg that Lys was now serving God in a nunnery. Surely the devil had no part in that.

The chaplain also was on tenterhooks for more news. When it came he unfolded the letter at once in Stephen's presence.

"Before God this is terrible," he cried. "The plot by that woman and her foul confederates was none other than to kill the king."

Stephen clutched at his bench as the room swam round him. Master Simon looked at him keenly.

"Why, boy, you're as white as a sheet. Have you never heard of murder by witchcraft? 'Tis well known, though praise heaven it is rare. The method varies. They make an image of their victim in wood or in wax and pierce it with bodkins or melt it by the fire, as the case may be, while offering the devil's mass, and gradually the victim sinks and dies. They met at Hornsey near London for their black mass, said by the accursed priest from Westminster over a waxen image of the king, while Bolingbroke, with all his tools and trappings, conjured spells to invoke the powers of evil."

"How was it discovered?" cried Stephen.

"At the duchess's trial. They brought Bolingbroke from the Tower to give evidence, having first tortured him to get the truth."

"What said she in defense?" He wanted to ask, *"What said he?"* but he did not dare.

"She condemned herself by her own words if you examine her meaning. She swore that all she wanted was to know if she would bear a child to Duke Humphrey and—listen to this—to know what rank she might rise to in the future. Now mark, she is already wife to Duke Humphrey, who is heir to the throne; she can rise no higher unless she becomes queen. In other words if the king should die *now*, before he weds, Duke Humphrey would be king."

Stephen sat in silence, trying to take it in, while the chaplain tramped the room, still talking.

"There will be another trial before the bishops. Witchcraft, like heresy, is the Church's business. Till then she is imprisoned at Leeds Castle in Kent. It stands on a lake so there is no escaping. But mark you, Stephen, not a word of all this. There is a commission called and my lord is one of the judges. There must be no tattle from *his* household."

Stephen needed no telling. He had every reason to keep silent. But for a moment it crossed his mind as strange that my lord should be one of the judges when the prisoner was the wife of his worst enemy.

Nevertheless it was not long before the story ran through the village. Every bargeman and every peddler carried it. Doggett of course was the first to question Stephen, but Stephen pleaded that he was too deep in his books to hear anything. Secretly he blessed his angel guardian that he had never mentioned Bolingbroke to Doggett. But he managed to gather any news that was going. The great trial before the bishops had begun, and the duchess was in the dock. There was no sign of Duke Humphrey: apparently he had forsaken her.

And then, quite suddenly, Dame Alice came home. She came alone, with one gentlewoman, and an escort consisting of Stephen's friend Morton, the messenger, and four armed grooms. Master Simon behaved as though he expected her, although he had said no word before. She greeted Stephen with her usual gentle smile.

"You have grown, boy," she said, "but you are white of face. Have you been working too hard?"

Stephen breathed more easily. He waited on her at supper in the hall, sure of hearing the latest news when all had withdrawn except Master Simon. But when the meal was ended she suddenly bade him go to bed. Tomorrow would be a busy day, she said, and though she smiled at him, he made his bow with a beating heart. In spite of my lady's kindness he was once more ill at ease.

In the morning after mass Dame Alice sent for him.

"I have news for you," she said calmly. "Morton returns to London today and you are to go with him. My lord has need of you."

He stared at her. A little while ago those words would have delighted him. Now they filled him with dread. She watched his face and actually patted his arm. "Keep your heart up, Stephen; tell the truth and you have nothing to fear. I pray you may soon be back."

This frightened him still more; but as they started for London, Morton, on a weight-carrying horse from Suffolk, looked down on him friendly as ever.

"You've not been to Pulteney's Inn since the pestilence," he observed. "You'll find some changes in the city. We've a new mayor, just appointed. His name is Clopton; from Warwickshire—a little town called Stratford-upon-Avon. Master Large, whom you remember, has died, God rest him, and his household is dispersed. Your friend, Caxton, has gone to Bruges in Flanders, so I've heard. But of course no one speaks of anything but this business of the witch of Gloucester."

"What is the latest news?" asked Stephen boldly, and held his breath.

"She is found guilty on all charges and the rest of her foul company too; but when I left London the sentence was not yet known. In any case she must publicly abjure her heresies. The arch sorcerer Bolingbroke has already abjured his, in Paul's churchyard for all to see. Never have I witnessed such a display. They put him in the great painted chair on which he always sat to do his acts of magic. It is like a throne with four swords erect at the four corners, each hung with a device in copper that glittered in the sun. The whole churchyard was packed with a howling mob. 'Tis certain that no recanting will ever save him."

Stephen shuddered. The glittering device must be the same that he had seen first around Bolingbroke's neck at old Meg's and later at Oxford in the aumbry.

It was almost dark when they reached Newgate, but nevertheless he paused to speak with the janitor while Stephen waited with the four armed grooms. Stephen glanced up at the spire of Paul's and at the cusped pinnacles of Greyfriars where he had seen the king. But it all felt like part of a dream—a nightmare from which he might still wake up.

Morton rejoined them briskly.

"The sentence is out," he declared. "The witch of Gloucester does not die. She is to perform public penance thrice, on three separate days, though the streets of London clad only in a sheet and bearing a heavy candle. After that she will be imprisoned for the rest of her life."

"And the others?" breathed Stephen.

"The witch of Eye is to burn; the priest will be dealt with by the Church; and Bolingbroke, the blackest of all, is condemned to be hung, drawn, and quartered."

The
Woodpecker Tree

THEY entered Pulteney's Inn just as the November sun was sinking. The courtyard and the hall were both deserted. My lord, it seemed, was still at Westminster. The steward appeared, his forked beard now trimmed to a single point. He chatted with Morton, and after they had been served with a meal in the buttery, he summoned an unknown clerk to conduct Stephen to his lodging.

This was not the familiar closet by the chaplain's door but a small room in the stone tower of a yet more ancient Pulteney's Inn. It contained a truckle bed, a stool, and a bench. The clerk told him pleasantly that if he stood on the bench he would have a good view of the river between the iron bars of a small window. But he did not even trouble to look. As soon as the clerk had left him, he threw himself on his bed, and his misery was complete when he heard the bar slipped across the door at the bottom of the stairs.

When morning came the clatter from all the bells of London reminded him that it was Sunday. He was summoned to attend mass at the familiar church of St. Laurence Pulteney in company with many of the household and then escorted back to the tower to await my lord's summons. But the hours of waiting went on and on right through the night till the following morning. It was barely light when the clerk with a taper came to fetch him. He must come at once, he was told, before my lord started on the day's business.

He was taken not to the hall where my lord usually held court, but to the Great Chamber, a low-ceilinged room with elaborate plaster work and half the floor space taken up by a large curtained bed.

The Earl of Suffolk was pacing up and down, but he dismissed the clerk, sat down at his table and signed to Stephen to stand in front of him where the light would fall on his face.

"You know what has been afoot," he began gravely, "so you can have no doubts why I have sent for you. You are familiar with the prisoner, Bolingbroke. You know that he is condemned for his part in a plot to kill the king by witchcraft. Now do you know that witches, be they male or female, are linked together in covens ruled by the devil? To capture one member and leave others free is useless. To return to Bolingbroke. I am told that he was willing to take you into his hall at Oxford, because in the past you had guided him when he lost his way in a storm."

Stephen said hoarsely, "Yes, my lord," though the beating of his heart all but choked him.

"Surely such a payment was strangely generous for

so small a service? Could it have had other purpose —to keep your mouth shut, for instance? Let us hear more of it. He was going to Wallingford: so much we know. And you met him in the woods, on the top of the hill? Do I guess rightly?"

Again Stephen said, "Yes, my lord." He dared not bandy words.

"The trees are thick up there," said Suffolk calmly, "and doubtless he was mounted. Why should he have ventured with a horse into that wilderness in the thick of a storm—unless of course he was on some errand? Now let us hear what *you* were doing there, where, as you well know, you had no right to be?"

Thankful to be able to speak truthfully, Stephen replied that he had gone hunting for squirrels to make brushes for Doggett's painting. For the first time my lord's face relaxed.

"You must be uncommon active," he said. "But now about the storm. Was it by chance that great storm, two years since, at the time when my lord of Warwick died? I remember it well because my best hound, Templar, was struck down, and the knaves who followed cried 'Witchcraft' and ran away. I chided them at the time but they may well have had cause. Was it in *that* storm that you met Bolingbroke?"

Stephen took refuge in silence. My lord was encircling him and he dared not answer. Suffolk slammed down his fist upon the table.

"I know your stubborn nature. I knew it in your fa-

ther, and it is for his sake that I have patience. Try
me not too far. It would be easy to hand you to those
who would *make* you talk."

Stephen clenched his teeth to stop their chattering,
and my lord began again more gently.

"I'll draw a bow at a venture," he said. "When my
foot was ailing you healed it with a salve which, you
said, came from a crony of your mother's. Master
Simon at my orders has sought out your stepfather at
Brightwell, who says that your mother had no special
crony, but that you were in the habit of visiting some
old hag in the woods, reputed to be a witch. *Now*
what say you? Was it to visit her that you ventured in
that storm, and was it *there* that you encountered
Bolingbroke?"

Stephen's knees turned to jelly. By piecing the fragments together my lord had quickly arrived at the
truth. What could he do or say to save old Meg? It
was impossible to believe that she, with her warm
heart, could have knowingly shared in this long-
drawn-out devilish plot. Then, for a moment, his
mind flew back to the youth in black who had so gently smiled at him that day in the Greyfriars library.
Suppose that by protecting old Meg he should after
all be betraying the king? He looked up in despair
and met the eyes of my lord of Suffolk.

"May I speak, my lord?"

"Say what you will so long as it's the truth. But be
brief about it."

Stephen drew a deep breath and then, not stopping to pick his words, poured out the whole story from the very beginning, where he had fallen out of a tree and old Meg had picked him up. He told about Lys —her flight from Odo into the path of Templar, how old Meg had brought her back to life as tenderly as a mother till now she was safe and happy in a nunnery, how old Meg, if she had powers, had powers only for good. Bolingbroke or no Bolingbroke she was not capable of conjuring ill to anyone.

The only thing in the recital that he concealed was the palindrome. *That*, he was sure, would condemn old Meg completely.

Suffolk listened patiently. At the end he nodded slowly.

"To know good from evil is man's hardest task," he said. " 'Tis the lesson we come into the world to learn. " 'Tis like the matter of the Maid. Whether she was saint or devil we shall never know this side of the grave. But one thing is certain. Your old woman must be questioned; there is no other way. I have told you that witches and sorcerers are linked in covens. If she be one of this same coven with Bolingbroke, the spell might yet be carried out. She *may* be guiltless; God send it so. But we must know the truth. If she be innocent none shall harm her. I pledge you that. Now, here are my orders. You will ride at once with guards to Wallingford, report to the captain of the castle and at first daylight you shall lead them to your old Meg.

You may comfort and reassure her, and they will
bring her to me." He rapped on the table. "See that
you fail me not. You would not thereby help her. A
troop from Wallingford would find her anyway. But
without you she would die of terror, and time, which
is vital, would be lost. You need not return to London. Go you straight back to Ewelme and remain
there."

Stephen left Pulteney's Inn within the hour, accompanied by two burly guards. Suffolk was already holding council in the hall. As Stephen took leave of him
formally, on one knee, my lord held out to him a
sealed letter.

"When your task is done you may deliver this to
my lady," he said. He continued in a lowered voice,
"I trust it to your care to show that I have faith in
you."

With the ice around his heart melted a little Stephen crossed the courtyard. There were no horses
waiting.

"We'll pick them up at Newgate," said the taller of
the two guards, both of whom sounded like men from
Suffolk. "'Tis useless to try and ride the streets this
morning. Hold fast, young fellow. We've orders not to
lose you."

Stephen looked about. Everywhere there were
more people than he'd ever seen before. "What's
afoot?" he asked. "Is it Mayor's Day?"

"Are you asleep?" cried the second guard?" "Have

you not heard that the witch of Gloucester is to walk the streets in a sheet, like any common baggage? Push ahead now. As we're here we may as well see the fun."

The fun. Stephen shuddered. This must be one of the days of the duchess's penance. Morton had told him of it but in his own problems he'd forgotten completely. They pushed on, shoulder to shoulder, through surging crowds, till in a street that he recognized as leading to Paul's they were brought to a complete standstill by a mob, stretching from wall to wall, whose voices rumbled ominously like an approaching storm. The noise grew louder as men of the watch, with pikes lifted on high, cleared a narrow path down the middle of the street.

The yellow flame of a great guttering candle streamed out in the draft. It held the people back from actual contact with a haggard woman with red hair who stumbled along, clutching round herself a sheet spattered with filth and yellow with rotten eggs.

As she passed, the pressure behind him threw Stephen forward, and he found himself face to face with green eyes wide with terror. Surely this had happened before! In a flash he was back at Benson Mill with the water roaring over the weir— Another heave of the crowd and the moment passed. The guttering candle moved on, and the roar became once more not water but an angry mob.

The horses awaited them at the Saracen's Head

outside Newgate. It was a gray November day, heavy with fog, but they mounted and jogged away briskly to the west. At Tyburn they stopped to goggle at a scaffold being prepared. They did not say for whom, but Stephen turned his head the other way to avoid being sick. He felt as though his whole soul was on a seesaw, tossed first one way and then the other. Try as he would, he could not forget the agony of terror in those green eyes. What was the truth? Was this all the work of the devil or was it in part a human conflict? He had heard my lord swear in anger, *"By Heaven I will see them bite the dust,"* and only this morning he had said, *"Whether the Maid was saint or devil we shall never know"*—and yet they burned her, and the charge in both cases was the same: witchcraft.

Did these great men believe in their hearts that they were acting only to defeat the devil or was it in part to triumph over their enemies? Not long ago Duke Humphrey was brought low and my lord rode high. And here was *he* on his way to deliver up old Meg, although he knew beyond all doubt that she was incapable of conjuring a cruel lingering death for anybody. But he had allowed my lord to sway him. He had accepted my lord's word that she would not be harmed. But suppose something happened to reduce my lord's power? Then if she were tortured, or worse, it would be *his* fault.

Suddenly, as though a wave swept over him, he decided that he could not do it. Somehow he must give his guards the slip. Though my lord, as he had said, would send men to scour the woods for her, it would take time. By then he could have got old Meg away. There were hills and valleys far off to which other outlaws had fled since my lord of Suffolk became steward of the Chilterns. Gilles would know all about them. Surely Gilles would help.

Of course it meant that he could not go back to Ewelme; but even that did not matter. If he, in cold blood, betrayed old Meg to torture and death he would never lift his head again.

But how was he to escape from his escort? His horse was on a leading rein and, to make matters worse, they rode on the south side of the river while Ewelme was on the north, and he knew of no bridge until they reached Wallingford. At Reading they changed horses, ate a meal, and drank good ale. Though he snatched a chance to whisper to fellow travelers, "To Ewelme, which way?" they only looked at him blankly and shook their heads.

They emerged from the tavern to find the fog thickening. The road to Wallingford followed the line of the river. For some distance they plodded along with a gray blanket drifting in waves across the water. When the foremost guard almost pitched over the bank, the two men decided that they must lead their horses; it was not safe to ride. Daylight faded; the fog turned from gray to pitch black. It was cold and dank, but how were they to find shelter when they could not see their hands before them?

With every mile Stephen's hopes grew. If only they could get near Wallingford, he would escape into the fog. In his own county he could shake off these Suffolk men. But at the moment he had not the least idea how far they had yet to go.

Suddenly, floating through the mist, came the faint sound of bells. There were only three notes, and *one of them was cracked.*

Stephen's heart leaped. It was like an answer to the prayers that he had hardly dared to breathe.

"Wait!" he cried aloud. "That, I swear, is the bell of Goring priory. My sister is a nun there. We could find lodging."

With fresh courage they pressed on and came to Streatley, across the river from Goring. There they found a tavern where they could lie for the night in the travelers' room. The two men, snoring lustily, shared a bed, while Stephen lay on straw on the floor. This suited him perfectly. He already had a plan in his mind. With the first glimmer of light he would slip out and find the ferry by which he had crossed before, on the way back from Donnington; it was near the priory. He'd drop word with the ferryman that he was going to see his sister and though the two guards, when they heard of it, would curse him for the delay, they'd hardly suspect an escape if he'd left his horse behind.

The plan worked more perfectly than he could have dared to hope. The fog had gone and the first ferry crossed just as dawn broke, carrying laborers to their work. Stephen was careful to mention Lys, but by the time the sun rose he had left the priory far behind and was already approaching Gilles's track through the woods.

With the leaves nearly all gone from the trees it was easier to find his way than he had expected. The path, up and down, swept in a curve across the successive spurs of the hills, and each time he climbed a spur he could actually see Wittenham Clumps lying far away on his left. But even with this landmark to guide him the distance seemed greater than he remembered. He had to slow his pace, and as he did so began to worry lest his guards should reach Wallingford before he reached old Meg. After all they still had their horses. It would take some time for a search party to be manned at the castle, but old Meg had yet to be won over to his plan and Gilles brought into it.

He longed for the first sight of his old landmark, the dead tree. As always when he approached it from an unusual direction he began to fear that he might miss it. But at last to his utter relief he caught a glimpse of it far ahead, its whiteness standing out among the copper of the last autumn leaves. He allowed himself to slacken speed, to get his breath, and to rehearse again what he was going to say to old Meg.

But as he drew nearer a doubt struck him. Something was different. The tree was the same. He could have drawn the pattern of the woodpecker holes. But everything else seemed lighter; though the ground was more tangled, there was far more sky.

He pushed on, suddenly afraid, and then stopped abruptly. The pool was twice as wide, and the dead tree stood not twenty yards back but right on the brink. He stared, bewildered. This must be another pool and another dead tree.

But gradually the truth began to dawn on him. The beech trees opposite were lying uprooted, half under water. In front of him was a crater double the size of the old pool, the water line a foot or more below the bank. The surface was thick and muddy and full of debris, such as spars of wood and lumps of sodden thatch. There was no cottage. It had been swallowed up.

The Lion
with Two Tails

*B*REATHLESS, Stephen leaned against the nearest tree. Where was old Meg? He gathered enough voice to call, and call again, but all that came back was echo. The woods were silent, without even a breath of wind. Steadying himself, he walked right around the crater. At one place a landslide of slippery clay led down into the water. There was no room for doubt; the actual ground on which the cottage had stood had fallen in. He forced himself to face what must be the truth. This was the devil's work. Old Meg *was* a witch; Satan had opened the earth to swallow her.

As he stared at the muddy pond, still cluttered with broken branches, a circle of still water caught his eye. On it floated a small piece of wood. It was smooth and lay face downwards on the surface. He seized a long stick, fished for the wood and drew it toward him. On his knees he shook the slime from it; the thumping of his heart almost choked him. It was one

of Wat's little carved figures, one he had seen before
—the shape of a little old woman, broom in hand,
grinning back over one shoulder. It was in fact old
Meg herself, returned to torment him.

As he turned over the spur of applewood he came
back to life. The cottage was gone but that was no
proof that old Meg was dead. She and Wat might be
alive somewhere in the woods. Suffolk's men might
come and discover her before he could warn her.
There was no time to lose. Clutching the little figure,
he struggled to his feet and crashed his way through
the undergrowth toward Swyncombe where Gilles
lived. As he reached the top of the gully, he shed all
caution and called aloud "Giles! Gilles!" Perhaps Meg
might be *there*. That was the best hope of all. Standing on the brink he saw movement below and reck-
lessly slipped and slithered his way down toward it.
He saw Gilles, face turned upward, and pitched himself forward, landing against a shoulder of rough
sheepskin.

"Is she here?" he cried as he disentangled himself.
"Is old Meg here? In heaven's name tell me where
she is."

"Hold up, hold up." Gilles's voice was deep with
compassion. He looked down at Stephen's hand. "You
found *that* as a testament? Then you've seen what has
happened? 'Twas two nights ago. She and Wat would
have been abed. I woke to hear a rumble as though
the earth had split—as in truth it had. I thought it

but thunder and went to sleep again. But in the morning I went up the hill and found what you have found today. The pool must have opened like a broken bucket and the trees fallen in on top of everything. There was nothing alive and no hope of rescue. Comfort yourself, Stephen. God took them."

Stephen tore himself away. "It was the devil that took them," he cried hoarsely. "She was a witch and the devil dragged her down. This proves it. She and Bolingbroke worked spells with the witch of Gloucester, spells that would kill the king. Bolingbroke is to die for it. They made an image and a black mass and they were caught—"

"Stay your tongue," cried Gilles. "*Who* made an image and had a black mass? I'll stake my chance of heaven it was not old Meg. Come now, steady yourself. You are almost out of your wits. Not another word till you have quietened down."

He led Stephen to a seat on the bole of an old tree and fetched a horn of some home-brewed drink, which steadied him enough for him to tell his story, from his first discovery of the writing on the hearth right down to this very day when he had been sent to fetch old Meg to London.

"My lord vowed that no ill should come to her if she were guiltless," he said as he neared the end. "But on the way I repented of it and broke from my guards to come and warn her. And what do I find but that it is true after all. She *was* the devil's servant and the devil has opened up the earth to swallow her."

"Stop!" cried Gilles. "Stop you and think. Has it not dawned on you that it could be the other way—that Meg is *God's* servant, doing *His* will, and that God wrought a miracle to save her from the fate that *you* would bring upon her?"

Stephen gasped. "You don't understand. It is as plain as a pikestaff. Bolingbroke came here and at her cottage they worked out some spell, connected with the palindrome. And now it is finished. 'Tis the devil who has taken her."

"If the devil himself came and told me so I'd not believe him," declared Gilles stoutly. " *'By their fruits ye shall know them'*—I've said that to you before. If ever I've seen a soul brimming with God's loving mercy it was hers. You have good reason to know it— you and your sister. I have known old Meg most of my life and never have I seen her lack compassion. *I* am unlettered but she had learning. Know you how *that* happened?"

Utterly bewildered, Stephen shook his head. It had always puzzled him that old Meg could read and write.

"Then I'll tell you briefly what she once told me. Her father was a learned man, an apothecary, though I know not where they lived. He was trained in the use of the calculus, and his learning led him to study the stars. He lacked a son and took his daughter as his pupil. But her heart betrayed her into love for a man who was an outlaw, no more than a swineherd. There was a child. Her father cast her off, so she stayed here in the swineherd's cottage for the rest of her days. Even when her man died she did not go back. She grew in wisdom, watching the stars and the water and all around her and calculating what she saw. If *that* be witchcraft maybe she was a witch. There have been others whose learning brought them into trouble."

Stephen nodded thoughtfully. "Master Simon told me of a friar called Roger Bacon. They accused *him* of witchcraft. But old Meg saw things in the water. She saw Lys as a nun, and during that storm she said to Bolingbroke, '*we shall see no more tonight.*' How come she to traffic with him, when there is no doubt of *his* guilt?"

Gilles shook his head. "I cannot answer that. Astrologers use the stars to calculate times that are ripe for some special venture, but there is nothing to show that she knew the nature of his plot. It may be that he used her skill to serve his own wickedness and that she gave to him freely, as she gave to all who needed her, without requiring to know what the end should be. I am an unlettered man. All that I know is that her soul was *white*, not *black*. May she rest in peace, and Wat too, poor simpleton. You would do well to pray for them instead of questioning God's ways."

Stephen looked at him in perplexity. He had taken Gilles for granted without question. He said he was unlettered. How came he to know so much? "You say you had known her all your life?" he asked.

Gilles hesitated. "No one knows my story save Parson Saynesbury and any that he has trusted with it, but if it helps I will tell you. The truth is that I am an outlaw because I am a Frenchman, not English. As a young boy I lived with my parents in a French village beset by the wars. Our homes were burned over our heads. My father and mother, my grandam, and my brothers and sisters all perished. I was given to the monks of Bec in Normandy, and during a short spell of peace I was sent with other boys to the priory of Okeburn in Wiltshire, which belonged to the Norman abbey of Bec. There, as novice, I took my first vows. Okeburn was the mother house of Swyncombe here, which was little more than a farm worked by a handful of brothers. To me it was a haven of the peace I had never known. Then your King Harry closed all the French monasteries in England when he made war again. The monks were sent back to France, but I was determined to stay. I hid in the woods and old Meg befriended me. I have been here ever since, keeping my vows as best I could. If I am known they just call me Gilles the Bowman, an outlaw of the hills; and as France and England are still at war, so I must remain. My bow has kept me in food. From what I take I give to those who need. Now you see how I knew old Meg and how I can say from knowledge that the devil had no part in her. But look: the sun is at its height. You have not eaten since yesterday. Sit you quietly while I get something."

Stephen was ready enough to obey. Until now he had not realized that he was utterly spent. He stretched his cramped legs and so was reminded of the pouch strapped to his belt. In it was my lord's letter to Dame Alice. This brought him back to his own problem.

"What shall I do now?" he cried as Gilles returned with a steaming bowl. "I dare not go back to Ewelme. I have been traitor to my lord. Can I stay with you? Pray you let me stay and live as you do."

Gilles shook his head. "My lord would surely find you, and you are too young to make yourself an outlaw. Better to face your perils openly. Get you back to Ewelme. Dame Alice will surely plead mercy for you, as our Lady pleads mercy for us all."

Doubtfully Stephen held up the letter. "I was to give this to Dame Alice when my task was done. My lord gave it to me to show that he had trust in me."

"Then you have no choice," said Gilles. "Whatever comes of it that letter must be delivered. Remember that though your heart moved you to compassion, it was not *you* who split the earth to let her escape their hands. Maybe they know all about it already. The roar was as loud as any storm."

Stephen's weary legs carried him so slowly that it was almost dark when he reached the Hall. Tired as he was, he felt strangely calm, as though, whichever way it went, this was his last battle.

He was challenged at the gatehouse but was recognized and allowed to pass. There were lights upstairs in my lady's solar, but except for a lantern in the screens passage the rest of the place was in darkness.

While he hesitated, uncertain what to do, the curtain at the top of the solar stairs was drawn back, and light streamed forth as Mistress Jane came pattering down with Mistress Philippa at her heels, each carrying one of the little dogs and both chattering like magpies.

"Mistress Thorn—Dame Eleanor, where are you? Belle has swallowed a chicken bone and is like to choke!" Then both of them caught sight of Stephen and shrieked. "Mercy on us, it's a man!" "Nay, it's *Stephen!* Whence came you, Stephen? Go you up. Master Simon is there. Madam! Madam! It is Stephen."

They continued their flight across the darkened hall. The shadow of Master Simon Brayles filled the doorway.

"Stephen, is it you? Come you up, boy. My lady was expecting you."

With his heart in his throat Stephen climbed the little stairs. Dame Alice was seated at her embroidery frame. Small coals burned in a brazier on the hearth. Cushions were scattered where the children had been sitting. Master Simon returned to his joint stool, an open book in his hand.

Stephen dropped on his knees beside Dame Alice and silently held out my lord's letter. He remained kneeling until she refolded it and laid it on her lap.

"Stand up, Stephen," she said gravely. "There have

been inquiries for you from Wallingford. It seems that you broke faith with my lord's messengers. You were to lead them to the old woman who was a link with Bolingbroke. Where did you go?"

"I went to the hills to warn her, madam. After I had betrayed her I repented of it. Witch or no witch, in my heart I knew that she was not evil. Conjuring spells to kill would have been impossible to her. She was too full of kindness—of gentleness and compassion."

"You are at least honest about your treachery. So you found her and warned her?"

"Nay, madam. She was not there."

"Not there! Then someone else had warned her?"

"Nay, madam. She is dead. She and her son and her dwelling have all gone. The pool beside the cottage has fallen in and they were swallowed up."

So far he had kept his voice steady, but on the last words it broke.

Dame Alice, startled, turned to Master Simon. "Can this be true? Bylton says there is a story going around about an earthquake in the hills. I thought it was another of their whisperings. Has it really happened?"

Master Simon shook his head. "Gossip does not come my way," he said. "But now I think of it I was wakened a night or two ago by a vast rumbling, like thunder where no thunder was. Let us hear more of this—more than a story of an earthquake. Let us have the truth from the beginning. The *truth*, Stephen. We know now that you met Bolingbroke on the day of that great storm. Was it at the cottage of this witch that you met him?"

"Sit you down, boy," said Dame Alice in her gentle voice. "You look worn to death. But let us hear everything now, from the very beginning."

The very beginning was when he fell out of the cherry tree, and this time he held nothing back, starting with his secret visits to old Meg because she was always kind. He told of his doubts, even in those early days—of finding Bolingbroke there in the storm, of the strange patterns on the hearth and of Bolingbroke's offers to befriend him. All this had troubled him, but then came Lys's flight from home and Meg's nursing her back to life as tenderly as any mother and getting her safely to the nunnery. All this proved surely that old Meg could not be servant of the devil. But still he feared to lose favor if he confessed to dealings with a suspected witch. So he had concealed everything. And now had come the terror that he had been wrong and that he *must* betray her. But when it came to the crux of it he could not, and so he had tried to save her and had found— At this his voice broke. Not another word would come.

There was a long silence. Dame Alice broke it.

"Master Simon, I believe the boy. I believe that all this long time he has been struggling to sift good from evil, with a whole world of temptation behind him. 'Tis hard to think that this ancient crone, apparently so full of loving kindness, could have been in truth a black witch. Yet there is the question of Bolingbroke. About him there is no doubt."

Stephen raised his head. He found Gilles's words on his lips, as though they were his own. "Could it not be, madam, that she gave freely of what powers she had without knowing to what end he would use them—just as she gave of her best to everyone?"

Dame Alice stared at him. "I think she has taught you a measure of understanding," she said, "a compassion beyond your years. Master Simon, I have a mind to do something singular. I am going to read aloud the letter that Stephen has brought from my lord. I think he has need of comfort and it may help to restore him."

She unfolded the letter again and began:

> I send this by the hand of Stephen who goes to uncover the old witch visited by Bolingbroke. She may well be another in this devil's coven. It was she who furnished the balm that eased my foot; the boy believed in her and was loath to disclose her. I am persuaded that he himself is innocent. I beg you hold him safely in Ewelme. He is soft of heart and could in the end fail in his duty. It matters not. There are men enough at Wallingford to find her and bring her here, even if it costs a little time. The boy is not of soldier stuff, like his father, but maybe he would make a scholar. Do with him as you and Master Brayles think best and use my purse to defray the cost.

She paused to look at Stephen as he kneeled, his face buried in his hands. "I have read you that letter," she said, "to prove that this horror is no longer for you to judge. Get you to bed. Tomorrow we will speak of Oxford."

Oxford! Stephen raised his head. He looked first at Dame Alice and then at Master Brayles.

"What good can I do there?" he cried. "Even now I cannot understand. If old Meg was evil how could she do good? If she was good how came she to have powers of evil? Shall I ever know?"

"You can set yourself to *learn*," said the chaplain gravely. "That is as much as any of us can do. We can give our lives to the search for knowledge. We can stretch ever upward, but in humility, each man to his uppermost, willing that the next man may build on him. Only thus can our knowledge of God's Creation grow. But beware that in your search you do not mistake knowledge for God Himself. Do you remember what I told you of Friar Roger Bacon? He dared to probe, to test, to explore in what he called '*domina omnium scientiarum*'—about experimenting in science. He suffered for it, as all true seekers must suffer, but—"

Dame Alice interrupted. "Good master Simon—the boy has had as much as he can bear. Tell him in simple words what is planned for him. Nay, I will tell him. Stephen, you will go as soon as may be to Master Brayles's own hall, St. Edmund's Hall, till you have gained your Mastership. After that I have begged a place for you at St. Mary's College by St. Mary's Church—from its great window they call it Oriel College. They will take none who are not already masters of arts, and even then it is a privilege to be accepted. They have granted me this favor—if you earn it—because the great Bishop Burghersh, a kinsman of my family, was one of their founders. You remember that I bear the arms of Burghersh?"

Stephen, worn out though he was, yet managed to smile.

"Yes, madam, I remember: *The lion with two tails.*"

*B*EFORE I begin the usual postscript at the end of the story to tell you what is historically true and what is just made up, I would like to defend myself from a charge which somebody might very likely bring against me. The charge concerns the disaster which disposed of old Meg and her cottage so conveniently at the climax of the book. It is quite possible that some reader will say, "What nonsense! As if the earth could open up like that. Of course it's just a silly invention."

Then listen to this:

In January 1953 only a mile from where this book was written (which is, itself, only some twelve miles from Ewelme) some local men were enjoying their midday pint at the bar of a small country pub. Suddenly they were startled by a great rumbling noise, which seemed to come from the wood across the road. They rushed out just in time to see a group of four fine oak trees, eighty feet tall, sink slowly, upright, into the ground, with as much dignity as though they had gone down in an elevator. They vanished so completely that when measurements were taken a few days later, down a hole as neat as an elevator shaft, the tips of the topmost branches were found to be forty feet below the surface of the ground —making a drop of one hundred twenty feet in all.

The oaks had stood close to the edge of a big pool (similar to the pool described in the book) surrounded by great trees. Before the rumbling of the oak trees ceased, there came another sound, a roaring and a crashing as, apparently, the bottom of the pool fell in, the water rushed through, and trees along the edge toppled and collapsed in all directions.

This episode caused a great sensation at the time. Geological experts from London and Reading University explored, tested, measured, and finally gave their opinion. The Chilterns are chalk hills permeated by underground streams that flow through cracks in the chalk to form caverns. These caverns occasionally break down, and the ground above them falls in, forming a basin on the surface which fills up with water. The numerous pools and ponds on the *top* of the hills prove that the process has gone on for centuries. In the miles of uninhabited beech woods the ground is constantly changing. Pools appear where no pool was before. Some endure, but others vanish in a night, leaving craters, large or small, full of dead leaves.

So old Meg's fate is *not* impossible. The collapse of

1953 (known locally as "The Hole") is already almost forgotten. It remains as a great cavity, half-filled with water and tangled with fallen trees—with a notice board to warn the curious about the danger of subsidence.

From what happened in 1953 let us go back a little over five hundred years to the date of the present story. Though nowadays the mention of witches and witchcraft seems to suggest broomsticks and fairy tales or the strange doings of eccentrics in ancient churchyards, witchcraft was in its time taken very seriously indeed both as a problem of evil and as a political weapon used by one party against another.

The trial of Eleanor Cobham, Duchess of Gloucester, condemned for plotting to kill the young King Henry VI by sorcery is true; her punishment in the streets of London is true; so is the part played by Roger Bolingbroke, a sorcerer, master of St. Andrew's Hall, Oxford, who was hung, drawn, and quartered for his share in the plot. The Duchess Eleanor herself was not executed but, after the penance described, dragged out the rest of her life in various prisons, abandoned by Duke Humphrey, who apparently washed his hands of her. The two political parties fighting for power were, as described, Gloucester's party on the one side and that of Suffolk (under Cardinal Beaufort) on the other. From their bitterness grew, in the next generation, the terrible strife of the Wars of the Roses.

William de la Pole, fourth Earl of Suffolk, and Alice

his wife (granddaughter of the poet Chaucer) are drawn from life as accurately as I could devise. So is their Oxfordshire home, Ewelme, where the alms-houses and the school which they founded as "God's House" in 1437 still flourish in all their beauty, still doing the work for which they were erected. Dame Alice is buried in the church under a tomb that is one of the finest of its kind in England. Carved in alabas-ter, she lies on the top, a portrait full of the character of a very remarkable woman. Parson John Saynesbury is also buried at Ewelme, and there is a stone to the memory of Master Simon Brayles, who went on to be parish priest of a church in Somerset.

Among many other true characters is the French duke, Charles duc d'Orleans, prisoner in England for the twenty-five years after Agincourt. During the time that William de la Pole was his jailer, a real friendship grew up between them. They both enjoyed the arts and wrote poetry in competition one against the other, and it was de la Pole who brought the French duke into the plans for making peace with France.

Another little group of real people are the Oxford craftsmen: old Richard Winchcombe, the master mason (architect) responsible for much of New College as well as the Divinity School; Crevington and Jayne, partners at All Souls, and John Massingham the carpen-ter, summoned by the king to carve the portrait of Richard Beauchamp, Earl of Warwick, whose death caused a stir at the beginning of the book.

This little scene demonstrates how the tombs of great people are often true portraits. A wax mask of the face was made soon after death. From this mask an artist carved a copy in wood which could later be cast in bronze or sculptured in stone. It was Massingham who carved the likeness of Richard Beauchamp for the superb bronze tomb at Warwick. The face appears alive—head slightly raised, eyes wide open, staring as it were at the vision of Almighty God pictured in the great east window.

If you have happened to read *The Load of Unicorn* you will know what Bendy, thirty years later, suddenly understood when he found himself gazing at this very tomb.

On the other hand I will confess that I invented Dame Alice's letter to her stepdaughter, the Countess of Salisbury, though a number of Dame Alice's letters survive in the Stonor Collection. For Mistress Jane did in fact marry "young Tom Stonor" and become the ancestress of the subsequent Stonors, who still live at Stonor Park, with its chapel built, like Ewelme, of bricks from the kiln at Crockers end near Nettlebed.

A further detail which I will, in honesty, point out is the use of the figures *1441* written on the hearth and explained away by Bolingbroke as a palindrome. In actual fact Stephen would not have instantly recognized these figures as "the year after next" because probably he would have learned the old method of Roman numerals for writing the date. But, after all, as

313

the dates themselves are accurate, no great harm is done by this small concession to give a good jumping-off point for the story.

Ewelme itself, still almost hidden between its enfolding hills, is basically little changed. The almshouses are now allotted to pensioners of both sexes, and the roofs are tiled instead of thatched. The school, though it has been adapted inside to meet modern needs, is extremely conscious of being the same school. Even the watercress beds have survived the centuries.

The Hall alone (now a private house to which the public is not admitted) is altered beyond recognition, though traces of its skeleton remain, both inside and out. But if Parson John Saynesbury, shocked and astonished, could once find his way through Benson airfield and the desert of red brick which goes with it (both, mercifully, invisible from Ewelme village), he would have little difficulty in recognizing the heart of his parish.

The Old Road is indeed old—far older than Ewelme. You may find it marked on ordnance maps, sometimes as a mere footpath, sometimes as the Icknield Way, running across half England; and it is quite reasonable that local people, not knowing why, should refer to it simply as the Old Road.

There are so many real people in the story that it is almost easier to list the imaginary than to list the true. Stephen and his family are, of course, invented; also

Doggett, old Ferry and the unhappy Barnabas, Red Jak and Tom. So are old Meg, Gilles the Bowman and Wat. Though Gilles the Bowman is imaginary, the little monastery of French monks at Swyncombe really existed. They were sent packing by Henry V.

But if Stephen and his story are fiction, his problem is a basic one, as valid today as ever it was—the problem of sifting good from evil. To him it came in the guise of witchcraft—an unlikely one in this day and age. We have outgrown such nonsense—or so we tell ourselves. But in essentials the world does not change very much, although it has moved on a great deal since Roger Bacon solved the riddles of the rainbow and the rise and fall of tides. We are still seeking. It is our vocation to stretch our minds wider and wider in search of knowledge—but at the same time to maintain a true balance in our understanding.

Before we finally part with William de la Pole, fourth Earl (and later first Duke) of Suffolk, husband of Dame Alice, friend of Charles duc d'Orleans, and father of young Mistress Jane, I would like to tell you a little of his subsequent history. He did succeed in arranging a French marriage for the king and consequently of making peace with France. But the princess concerned, Margaret d'Anjou, was a turbulent young woman who brought trouble to everybody.

It was largely thanks to the unpopularity of the marriage that Suffolk was eventually tried, banished, and murdered by pirates on his way to France.

Shakespeare in *Henry VI* depicts him as a villain, but
Shakespeare was not above tinting historical characters with the color that best suited the politics of his
own day.

For a true picture of William de la Pole I would
rather trust a very personal letter which he wrote just
before he left England as a friendless exile in 1450. It
is a letter to his little son, born in 1442, therefore just
eight years old. (You may remember that in this story
Dame Alice went on pilgrimage to Walsingham to
pray that she might bear a son.) I am quoting this letter in full; you can skip it if you wish. But if you do
read it I think you will agree that it throws a very
human light upon the character of Stephen's lord and
master.

> My dear and only well beloved son, I beseech our
> Lord in Heaven, the Maker of all the world, to bless
> you and send you ever grace to love Him, and to
> dread Him; to the which, as far as a father may
> charge his child, I both charge you and pray you to
> set all spirits and wits to do, and to know His holy
> laws and commandments, by which ye shall with His
> great mercy pass all the great tempests and troubles
> of this wretched world. And that also, wittingly, ye
> do nothing for love nor dread of any earthly creature
> that should displease Him. And there as any frailty
> maketh you to fall, beseech His mercy soon to call
> you to Him again with repentance, satisfaction and
> contrition of your heart, never more in will to offend
> Him.

Secondly, next Him, above all earthly thing, to be the liege man in heart, in will, in thought, in deed unto the King, our elder most high and dread sovereign Lord, to whom both you and I bee so much bound to; charging you, as father can and may, rather to die than to be the contrary, or to know anything that were against the welfare or prosperity of his most royal person, but that as far as your body and life may stretch, ye live and die to defend it, and to let his Highness have knowledge thereof in all the haste ye can.

Thirdly, in the same wise, I charge you, my dear son, always, as ye are bounden by the commandment of God to do, to love, to worship your lady and mother, and also that ye obey alway her commandments and to believe her counsels and advices in all your works, the which dreadeth not, but shall be best and truest to you. And if any other body would stir you to the contrary, to flee the counsel in any wise, for ye shall find it naught and evil.

Furthermore, as far as father can and may, I charge you in any wise, to flee the company and counsel of proud men, of covetous men, and of flattering men, the more especially and mightily to withstand them, and not to draw [nor] to meddle with them, with all your might and power. And to draw to you and to your company good and virtuous men, and such as been of good conversation, and of truth, and by them shall ye never been deceived, nor repent you of. Moreover never follow your own wit in no wise, but in all your works, of such folks as I write of above, asketh your advice and counsel; and doing thus, with the mercy of God, you shall do right well and live in right much mercy worship and great heart's rest and ease. And I will be to you as good lord as my heart can think.

And, last of all, as heartily and as lovingly as ever father blessed his child in earth, I give you the blessing of our Lord and of me, which of His infinite mercy increase you in all virtue and good living. And that your blood may by His grace from kindred to kindred multiply in this earth to His service, in such wise as after the departing fro this wretched world here, ye and they may glorify Him eternally amongst His angels in Heaven.

Written of mine hand,
The day of my departing from this land,
Your true and loving father

SUFFOLK

About the Author

CYNTHIA HARNETT studied art when she was young and collaborated with her cousin, the artist Vernon Stokes, on many successful picture books. She was the winner of the first Carnegie Medal awarded in England for *Nicholas and the Wool-Pack* and is the author of several widely acclaimed books re-creating important aspects of life in the decisive history of fifteenth-century England.

Miss Harnett lives in a medieval thatched cottage in Henley-on-Thames, some twelve miles from Ewelme, where much of *The Writing on the Hearth* takes place.